Rob Palk has previously published work in *Litro* magazine ███████████████████ s his first novel, wr████████████████ndy and Haifa. The autho████████ Leicester with several other writers and a cat.

ANIMAL LOVERS

Rob Palk

SANDSTONEPRESS
HIGHLAND | SCOTLAND

First published in Great Britain by
Sandstone Press Ltd
Dochcarty Road
Dingwall
Ross-shire
IV15 9UG
Scotland

www.sandstonepress.com

Badger sketch on p278 by Elee Kirk, by kind permission of
Will Buckingham.

The publisher acknowledges subsidy from
Creative Scotland towards publication of this volume.

ISBN: 978-1-912240-03-6
ISBNe: 978-1-912240-04-3

Cover design by Two Associates
Typeset by Iolaire Typography Ltd, Newtonmore
Printed and bound by Totem, Poland

For Sarah McInnes

One

Let's start with her leaving, with Marie, my wife of four months and girlfriend of four years, dashing round our little flat shoving her clothes in a case. She had a look of regretful but necessary purpose, as though she were packing for a lengthy stay in hospital, scooping up armfuls of clothes, letting stray items fall upon the floor.

I was lying on the double bed, shifting occasionally to check my phone, pretending to read a book. It was difficult. I didn't want to seem aloof, unconcerned, glad for her to go. But if I plunged into the business of bargaining, of pleas, I'd have dignified something I'd much rather not take seriously. She was leaving, she said, for the badgers. She was off to the woods to protest against the badger cull.

'You're being ridiculous,' I said.

This didn't seem quite the right tone. She was struggling with an especially recalcitrant blue dress and when she stopped to look at me, it was like she had a new face, a face I didn't know. There was no love in this face. Fondness, true, and the sort of camaraderie you might find among hostages, but nothing close to love.

'You're obviously not going to leave. You love me. We only got married a few months ago, remember? We had cake. All your friends came. Why don't you go and have a run, come back and we can talk?' I could hear myself sounding pompous, stiff, Gladstone addressing the Queen. A run though, a run would set her all straight. The wind in her hair, the marshes under her feet, the wonders of nature in her bones, and all this talk about badgers would be done and she'd come back, sweaty and exhausted, and be Marie again.

I didn't resent the badgers. I liked her having found something she loved. I just didn't see why it meant she had to stop loving me.

'I'm sorry,' she said. Her voice didn't sound like her own. It was metallic, unnatural, steel-lined, as though she were speaking down into a thermos. 'It's, I don't know, it's a calling. I need to feel I'm doing something. I can't stand by and watch this cull just happen.'

'You've stood by enough other stuff. We both have. We've both stood by and watched Syria or homelessness or the ...' I tried hard to think of something weighty. 'Listen. I need you. To look after me. I'm still not out of the woods.'

'Oh, you're well on your way,' she said, in her old, friendly voice. There was a smile there too. Panic started to form in me, at how I would miss that smile.

'I'm not in the clear yet. Look. Don't go.'

'I'm going.'

I followed her through to the front room. 'For badgers. Badgers! They don't need you like I do. They aren't even fucking sentient, Marie.'

'They are,' she said, softly. 'Sentient has a dictionary definition. They just are. Sentient. Factually.'

'Jumped up fucking weasels is what they are. Please don't go.'

'There's no point getting angry,' she said. As though I were standing selfish in the path of the inevitable. 'Goodbye Stu.' She was going then. This was really it.

2

Four months of marriage and I'd been displaced by another species. I wished I hadn't told her to choose between me and the badgers. I couldn't even challenge one to a fight. Instead, I had to make her realise that the cull was unimportant. That what really mattered was me.

Not me. Us. The essential unit, us. 'Do you want to go back to bed?'

She ignored this, stepped across the floor and kissed my cheek, whispered 'be well' like a faith healer, knelt to ruffle the cat, flicked a few stray hairs behind her ears, and vanished from the room. She didn't even slam the door.

'Don't go,' I said again, but she wasn't there to hear it. There were fierce winds outside and I didn't know what to do next. I went into the front room, which was far too full of plants, and I sat down on the sofa to wait for her return.

Two

That night, our flat, with no concern for subtlety, fell apart. A storm sent chunks of our building's roof flying into the street and left five cold streams of rainwater gushing into the front room; I only had four plastic basins to catch them with. Chunks of plaster lay across our wooden floorboards like snowflakes turning to slush. Mould bruised over the cracked and sagging ceiling, yellow and black and green. Our cat, Malkin, sat in a corner, shivering reproachfully. Whenever there was a noise from outside, he would run to the front door and scratch it in anticipation. This struck me as manipulative.

It's hard to know what to do when someone leaves you. For the first week I called in sick to my job at the animal charity, the job I'd been putting up with while I tried to write a book. (Marie, when I'd first met her, had been excited I worked for this organisation and her face had clouded when I told her it was only to pay the bills. I'd said I liked animals well enough but they were hardly a major concern. She'd said it was attractive in a man, if he got on well with animals. I'd told her that my job was mainly administrative. That animals were rarely, if ever, seen in the office.) My line manager listened to me explain that my wife had gone to save the badgers and begrudgingly gave me the week off.

On these free and lonely days, I looked over my

manuscript, but somehow there was nothing I could do with it. It seemed, already, to be the work of some other person, a person with a talent for needless words.

I thought a lot about what it would mean to be single. This was something I'd thought about before, only from my previous vantage point it had seemed kind of attractive. Single life, from the protection of being married, looked an awful lot like freedom. I'd pictured warehouse parties, an absence of responsibility, hospitable but undemanding girlfriends. Instead there was shabbiness and time. You develop a smell, an untouched smell. You smell like whatever love doesn't. You turn over at night and it doesn't feel like freedom. It feels cold. You've lost a section of you. The section that keeps you happy. The section that keeps you good.

On Wednesday my boiler decided to stop working. I got shingles, pinkish rings, like crop circles on my torso, echoing the mould marks on the wall. The plants Marie had bought began to die. They were all over the place, withering, their leaves becoming yellow.

On Thursday she came back and took what was left of her stuff. She waited till I was out. I don't know how she knew. I got home to find the things I'd bought her left behind, the books and pictures and bric-a-brac. Most of what had come with her was gone. Half the dishes, half the pans. Half the cutlery, half the bed sheets. Self-pity became tempting. But this would mean admitting she had left me and I wasn't prepared to do that. She was away for a while, I told myself, and would soon be back again. I called her and got no response.

After that, I started pouncing at people on Facebook, waiting for the green dots that showed they were online and waylaying them with the news, sticking to the script that she had gone but should be back before long.

Her friends first. Some of them knew already, others were surprised. All were sympathetic, without exactly offering to help. I tried my own friends, but most of them were married now themselves. They had wives and kids and jobs that sounded important. They played football on a Saturday morning and listened to music made by men in cagoules. They didn't want chaos erupting into their lives. One wife gone and others would surely follow. I tried getting in touch with girls I remembered from before, but they were women now and reluctant to pretend the last four years hadn't happened.

I finally got through to my old friend Alistair, from university. Alistair was one of those very posh English people who tell everyone they are Scottish. His own marriage had floundered and I felt he'd be sympathetic. The next day he came over, looked at me and shook his head as if I'd disappointed him. I told him Marie had gone to protest about the badger cull. He seemed shocked for a second before risking a smile. 'Was she into badgers before?' he said. 'I know she's been into them recently, but were they always her thing?'

'She always cared about animals,' I said. 'But never as much as this. Only since the wedding.' I shrugged.

'No setts before marriage,' he said and then laughed for a very long time.

'Haha,' I said. 'Haha.'

'It gets better,' he said. 'Look at me.' Alistair's wife, Lucy, had left him some months before. She'd come round ours in fact, not that Alistair knew. She'd drunk a lot of our whisky and said unflattering things about him. Marie and I had laughed about it, in a condescending way. The mistakes that others made. I'd sometimes lusted, vaguely, over Lucy. Since then I'd only seen her in a series of exotic

6

locations on Facebook. She had lost a lot of weight and started using a lot of hashtags.

'One day you'll look at this as the best thing that ever happened to you,' Alistair said.

I told him that I doubted this. 'I am lonely. I am cold. I am stuck in a flooded room with an angry cat. It has to get better than this because this is like being in the Life of fucking Pi.'

'Trust me,' he said. He didn't look very trustworthy. He had reacted to being jilted by purchasing a variety of floppy hats and growing a hypnotist's beard. He'd told everyone he was going to live life how he'd always wanted. Aside from all the hats, I was unsure what this involved. Still, he did look happy. 'For a start you'll get more time for writing. More room in the bed. You don't have any ...'

'Kids, yes, I'd already thought of that one.'

'The main thing is to accept it. Accept that it's all over. Accept that you are now a single man. You shouldn't be scared of the future. I was, at first, but now, and I really mean this, I can honestly say that I'm happier than I've ever been.' He got up and started making a cup of tea. This act of kindness was small on the scale of things, but it very nearly made me cry. 'Oh, and there's a room going at mine if you like. Don't suppose you'll want to stay here.' I nodded and took a gulp. I was grateful for his offer and for what he said. But I wasn't going to accept things, just like that.

When Alistair left I took a bin bag and went round getting rid of the dead plants. Malkin had bitten the heads off half of them anyway. The rest hadn't survived my neglect. Over by the little window near the sofa, a lone basil plant looked to be coping. It must have got some of the rainwater, just enough to keep it alive, not so much as to drown. I brushed a speck of dust off the leaves and moved it through to the bedroom.

I was thirty-three years old. I was partially blind. Or partially sighted, as an optimist might say. Since my illness my employers had moved me into an undemanding job taking calls, despite my protestations that I was ready for harder, better remunerated tasks. I didn't think this marital development would persuade them. My manuscript was, it dawned on me, unfinishable, let alone publishable. And I seriously doubted I could find another wife. Not a wife like this one, a wife of such *possibility*. She was a fluke, my Marie, a never to be repeated stroke of luck. All that was needed was for her to stop caring about badgers – or at least, to stop caring about badgers quite so much – and to start caring about me again. What was needed was for me to win her back. I was going to do that, I knew. I was going to do it in no time.

Three

I would make sure, this being my goal, that I stayed who I truly was. I would not become embittered. Bad look on a man, embitterment. Alistair, say, was not exactly embittered, but you wouldn't be surprised to hear him talk about 'females' or how things had 'gone too far the other way'.

Alistair was wrong. There were to be no generalisations. Marie was Marie, and I loved her in all her uniqueness. (Christ, how I loved her! Christ, how I wanted her back!) She was typical and representative of nobody but herself. Nor would I make any claims on her. A man is nobody's keeper. She was free to go if she wished. She would always have my support. In this, at least, I would be a good loser. If I could show myself a good loser then I might not lose at all.

I was going to get her back. I wouldn't even risk becoming embittered because there'd be nothing to be embittered about. I would be patient, I'd be supportive, I would try to understand. I was going to win.

In the meantime, it was Friday, it was Halloween, and Alistair had invited me to a party up the road. I got off the mildewing sofa, filled a glass with water, poured it into the basil pot and went downstairs to the shop.

I shaved, carefully, as you have to when some of your sight isn't there. I daubed my hair with viscous globs of gel and put on the dark suit I had worn on the day of my wedding. I had purchased, earlier, a cape. I reckoned I could pass for Dracula. I'd forgotten to get the teeth, but I was sure there'd be plenty of blood doing the rounds at the party.

The thought of a party scared me. It had been a long time since I'd been to one on my own. What happens now, at parties? Small talk, I imagined. *Dancing*. I hadn't been much of a dancer in the days when I could see. I couldn't imagine I'd got better at it since. The bathroom mirror showed not Dracula, but a ruined version of myself, a chamber of horrors waxwork that had been left against a radiator.

Marie's old unguents and lotions sat on the side, collecting dust. I could still smell the waft of her in here, the one room that hadn't succumbed to the stink of the damp elsewhere. I wondered if I could somehow will another stroke. Get myself out of this mess. A few minutes' grimacing proved I couldn't. I set off to the pub to meet Alistair.

He was in the far corner, in a cream suit, under a shelf full of 1980s board games. He had the look of an unusually secure mediaeval monarch, one whose enemies have long since all been vanquished, leaving plenty of time for wassailing and tiresome fol-de-rol. He was talking to a squashed-looking man, with a face like a disappointed knee. This man wore a headless Scooby Doo costume, the severed head on the floor next to them.

'Stuart,' carolled Alistair. He waggled a glass of Brooklyn lager in the air as though it were a flagon of mead. I made my way towards them, trying not to trip. My eyesight kept reminding me it wasn't what it was.

'Block,' Alistair said. 'You met your new flatmate? Raoul, this is Stuart Block. We went to college together.

Known him since I was, what, eighteen? We used to, Raoul, we used to go walking along the Greenwich foot tunnel at night. We'd look out over London, do you remember, and we'd say one day we're going to take on this city? Do you remember we'd do that, Stu?'

I said I did and it was funny what you thought when you were young. Alistair told me he still felt like that. We had, he said, plenty of time.

'Stuart, this is Raoul. Raoul is an American. He's a Liberation Theologian.' I told him this was an interesting thing to be and that I quite liked the new pope.

'Oh, everyone likes the new pope. Gotta love the funky new pope. It's like when your team does well and you suddenly get all these supporters. Where were you when we had the shit pope? I liked that pope. He just didn't look as much like a pope. This new guy's kinda like the Pope-Obama, says all the same shit, just looks more handsome saying it.' Raoul had an unexpectedly mellifluous, womanly voice, a voice you could relax in. It offset his look of disappointment, made amends.

'Stuart's wife just left him,' said Alistair.

'Sorry to hear that man,' said Raoul.

'Not your fault,' I said. 'It's mostly over badgers. And anyway, I'm going to get her back.'

'You need to stop thinking like that,' said Alistair.

I started asking Raoul about his Catholicism. He had not been raised in the church.

'I was an atheist since I was twelve. My mom's one of those, I don't know if you have them here, she's a womanist. And that can be kind of hard headed but also involve a lot of goddesses and healing. So I turned pretty strong against that and then, I dunno, I hit thirty and I started to want something real.' There was a lot of it about, this thirst for reality, for truth. I wondered why I

11

didn't want it. It explained the beauty in his voice though. We had none of us yet lost hope.

'I'm a total atheist, aren't I, Stu?' said Alistair. 'No, that's wrong. I'm not, you know, full on. I'm more of a pagan. I hate organised religion.' He licked his lips, a delighted self-listener. Disorganised religion, cack-handed religion, was evidently okay. 'I always say, if you hear me praying, it's to the sun. Or, I don't know, Odin. He's a good one.'

The two of them started arguing about theology, a conversation hampered by Alistair's not listening to anything Raoul said. I wondered if they were nerds. I wondered if *I* was a nerd. Only a few months ago I'd been going to the theatre and galleries with my beautiful wife, like I was Bernard Henri-Levy or someone. Now I was here instead. Although there'd been so many times that Marie and I had wandered down here for a closing time pint on a summer night, so that the place was ... although thinking about it we hadn't done that very much. A couple of times at the most.

I wished we had done it more. There'd always been time spread before us.

'All I'm saying,' said Alistair, 'is I don't see why I should compromise my beliefs. Or lack of them.'

'She's your mother. And she's asking you to go to midnight mass like once a year. Just go, sing a few carols, keep her happy. You're in your thirties, man.'

'I'm not a prostitute,' said Alistair.

We sloped from streetlight to streetlight in the cold, hands in pockets, attempting a good time. A party! There would be women dressed as rabbits or witches. There would be the chance for awkward small-talk. Alistair had put on an even bigger hat with an enormous rim, making him look like a tall and voluble table. Raoul and I slouched.

12

Perhaps this was all a chance to live out my twenties again, only with hindsight and wisdom and fatigue and much less eyesight. No. I was going to win Marie back. This life, this exile in immaturity, it was unthinkable.

'Stuart, you're slouching,' said Alistair. 'You have to walk proud again. Remember when I met you? What happened to that guy? You need to learn to walk again. Walk like you have a bottom. Say *I have a nice bottom.*'

'No.'

'Say it.'

'I have a nice bottom.'

'You're still slouching.' He had the look of a man charged with turning a tone-deaf wallflower into the toast of Broadway. Frustrated with the difficulty but excited with the challenge. I tried to straighten my back.

The party was at Keris and Leila's house in Clapton. I didn't know Alistair was still friends with the two of them but he told me he had been in the same book club as Keris, before leaving in high dudgeon after the organiser disputed his more controversial views. I felt he wanted me to ask him what these views were but I maintained a judicious silence. I had known Keris since third year university when she had been the first out lesbian I ever met. She seemed very sophisticated then, in her Oxfam Weimar get-up, reading books of theory and seducing straight girls. Leila was one such, an Egyptian actress who took the lead in all of Keris's plays. I had seen one of these a few years back. There had been an awful lot of shouting and rolling on the stage.

'You don't look very scary,' Keris said at the door. 'What have you come as, Alistair? Colonel Saunders? Mark Twain?'

'I'm not wearing a costume,' said Alistair, with dignity. Raoul put his Scooby Doo head on. You could still see

13

his face through the mouth. I explained to Keris that I was Dracula, but also that Marie had left me and this was almost a costume in itself. She nodded and yanked me into a hug which I realised was the first I'd had since Marie had left. Human contact again. Maybe I could offer free hugs on street corners and kid people I was doing them a favour.

'I'm sure someone here will look after you. There are white witches doing laughing gas in one of the upstairs bedrooms. But are you okay? You must tell me what happened.'

'Well.' It would be good to tell her. She batted me on the wrist.

'Not now. I'm off my tits. But definitely sometime soon.' She drifted into the house as though being led by her cigarette holder.

Alistair looked as though he were planning to start talking about 'finest foaming ale'. Divorce either made one bitter or made one hearty, I supposed. He seemed to take immense pleasure from the world and from himself. Before I knew where I was he had dashed to a crowd of strangers and was telling them he had been offered a safe seat by both of the major political parties but was considering letting them stew. This was the first I'd heard of that. He seemed to have got more confident with the years, they had hardly chipped his surface. I thought about going over and apologising to the crowd but they seemed to be attentive, rapt. This was how conversation was made: you had to be masterful, yank their interest towards you. One of them said something mocking but Alistair threw his head back and roared with laughter. He was able to access a joy I couldn't imagine.

Raoul and I went into the backyard. 'It gets better,' he said. 'Look at Alistair.'

'What gets better?'

'You know. Life. After a divorce.'

'Have you had a divorce?' I said.

'No.'

'So how can you say it gets better? I mean, people kill themselves, don't they? After divorce.'

'I dunno then. Maybe it doesn't get better. It just seemed the right thing to say.'

'At least the rain has stopped,' I said. Raoul nodded with the appearance of relief. 'Look at all these people, milling. Congregating. Alistair would just wander up to them and talk, wouldn't he? And they'd listen and like it too, wouldn't they?'

'They would listen. That much is sure.'

'Should we do the same?'

'Maybe in a bit.' We stood in silence and drank our beer.

There was a group taking up most of the patio: a zombie, a bride in a tattered dress, who I tried hard not to stare at, a brace of witches, someone who might have been a warlock, a female serial killer and some kind of bondage rabbit. They looked like a fun-run as arranged by Goya. I both yearned for and feared them, as was right for the season. Quite a lot of my confidence had come from having Marie by my side. Raoul didn't really cut it. I couldn't see him starting a conversation. I would have to do it myself.

There was an uncomfortable-looking space on the wall at the edge of the group and we set off there, making apologetic greeting sounds. We sat ourselves down on the brick. One of the witches glanced at me and I made a friendly sort of yelp. Two sets of false eyelashes rose and fell in disdain and she turned back to her friends. They were talking about a film director. The warlock kept calling him by his first name as though they were brothers or friends. I felt I had not much to offer. The men all seemed very certain of where they stood, on the man and on his work. The women seemed to be doing a good job of looking interested. The warlock was talking about cinematography, I think. Jump cuts, he was saying. The texture of the film. The emotional weight of celluloid. Reminiscent of Malick.

I kept quiet. What was there to say? I quite liked the one film by this director that I'd seen. Did quite liking something count as an opinion nowadays? I was older than them all, a failed age. My opinions were uncertain, shy of being slated. I began to drink faster but that wasn't any help.

Raoul had somehow managed to get into a conversation about science fiction with a man in a cracked leather jacket, a man who was both balding and long haired. This social success was beyond me.

'You all right?' said a witch by my side. I was unsure whether to claim the status of all right or admit my not all right-ness. Would she sympathise, this witch? Would she tell me things would get better, as though this were guaranteed? I would believe it, coming from her.

She had black lipstick and silvery eyelids, glittering like fish scales. I told her my wife had left me. I told her because of badgers. I told her I had almost died. I told her I had glimpsed something inexpressible during the months of my recovery and now it was lost forever.

'Fuck,' she said. 'It's like talking to Syria. That's some bad luck you've had.'

'I feel a bit like Job,' I said. She stared at me. 'Never mind,' I said. Raoul would have known who Job was. He was talking about *The Silmarillion* now, as though this were acceptable.

16

'Pete,' she said, 'Pete. Listen to what happened to this guy.'

I told the warlock some of my story. He stopped talking for the duration.

'A van ran over my foot last year,' he said.

'Oh god,' said the witch.

'I once got hit in the face by a frisbee,' said the serial killer, 'and it knocked me out altogether.'

'It's funny,' said the witch, 'but nothing bad has ever happened to me. Like, never. I've never been dumped, I've never been ill. I've never even lost a job. Someone was talking about headaches and I was like, mate, what's that?'

'My sister once got bitten by a lamprey,' said one of the witches.

'I just got back from Berlin,' said a corpse bride. 'There was this guy I met online and I got him to tie me up for a week and spank me with a brick.'

'My marriage might be ending,' I said.

'There's more to love than marriage,' said the corpse bride.

I decided to remain silent. There was nothing useful to say. My role would be to collar people at parties and recite my woes to them, while they made sideways glances. I would hang around weddings, hassling the guests and unnerving them with my beard and glittering eyes. I stood up. My drink was done and the night was cold and there was nobody here to talk to.

In the front room someone who looked like, and may have been, a cabinet minister was playing ten-year-old R&B records. Alistair was doing a dance that looked like a man in skis climbing upstairs. Keris and Leila were slow dancing to fast music. Discarded silver silos jewelled the carpet. I was not about to dance so I went into the kitchen. A man in Devil horns was explaining his job to a murder victim. I explored the fridge until I found a can of lager shoved behind some pickles and a jar of pesto.

'Got any vod?' said a voice behind me. It might have been my conscience. I looked around to see another witch, green-skinned, in a bustier and a conical hat. She didn't look like my conscience. She looked like quite the opposite. 'I'm trying to find some vod,' she said.

This quest had my sympathy. I told her there was none in the fridge but that we should hunt for some elsewhere. She gave this idea an exuberant response and slipped a sweaty hand into mine. Was this what an adventure felt like? She led me across the kitchen and started opening cupboards with more force than was needed. She was soon successful, discovering a three-quarter-full bottle of Lidl own-brand vodka and, from the next cupboard, two water-scratched plastic cups. A grin of victory upon her leaf-green lips. Next, she ransacked the fridge, gleefully extricating a bottle of near-flat Coke. She was now a happy witch. She flicked a cavolo nero-coloured curl from her emerald forehead and led me to one of the bedrooms. We climbed onto the bed, propped pillows up on the headboard and sat next to each other, swigging the vod.

'I split from my boyfriend,' she said. 'This afternoon. Over costumes. He said he wasn't going to bother.' I hoped my own near be-civvied state didn't bring back painful memories. 'I said, I've spent hours on this. Least you can do is dab on a little blood. He said what was the point? Then he looks up from his Mac and he says I look like a cabbage. All day painting myself green and he says I look like a cabbage.' I shook my head in sorrow. She did look a bit like a cabbage. 'I spent ages. Did the under-soles of my feet. Dyed my hair. All of it. Spent tons on non-toxic paint. I'm fed up.' A tear crossed the verdant arc of her cheek.

I tried not to imagine hunting her naked body for any remaining patches of pink. 'My wife left me a few days ago. I'm going to win her back.'

'That's a shame,' said the green witch, sagely. I agreed that it was, wondering which bit she meant. 'Good luck with your persuading,' the witch offered. I thanked her. 'I think you're really nice,' she added. She was definitely a witch of unusual wisdom and judgement.

We were lying on the single bed, limbs scissored, her head on my shoulder. Our talk became muted, as though we were scared of distracting ourselves. We had entered a space in which kissing was possible. I wasn't at all sure I wanted to be in it. Retreat could still be managed.

'It's odd walking around married,' I said. 'And even odder when it stops.' She nodded, as though she understood me well.

'A cabbage,' she said.

'Nothing at all like a cabbage. Sort of undulant. Full to bursting.' Shut up, I thought, shut up.

'Have some vod,' she said. I slurped it down. I could hear the garden revellers outside, still loud in praise or dismissal of artists, filmmakers, politicians and bands. I couldn't hear Raoul. All these people – all these men – with such certainty in their opinions. Copernican selves, the world turning around them. And here I was, off-kilter. And oh dear, had we to kiss now? Her lips were a darker green. When they pressed against mine I could taste the lipstick, then a plump tongue swabbing my own. She tasted of not-Marie, of difference.

'That was nice,' said the witch. We kissed some more. One of her breasts had spilled from her witchy bustier and the nipple was dyed a blackish green, a miniature

19

cabbage. Our kisses became frantic, directional. Both of us wanting to get things over with.

The door opened and a young man with a blond buzz-cut and lips that looked like they'd been slammed in a door, came in and began fishing through the wardrobe. I jerked up, galvanised, and started telling the intruder off, my speech slowing to a trickle as I guessed I was in his bed.

'I honestly don't mind,' he said. He opened a desk drawer, gave a happy whoop of discovery and pulled out an airport box of cigarettes, slotting one between his lips. 'You two carry on.'

'Thanks. Only it's difficult when you're here.' Thinking, thank you, stranger, for saving me in time. Thank you for keeping me faithful.

'Justin,' said the witch. 'This is Stuart. His wife left him and he's exploring the underbelly.'

'Tits,' said Justin in a stage whisper, clutching his own imaginary pair. The witch covered herself. 'Look you two, I'm not being nosey? Only I had to get out, cos all these Nazis showed up, pissing everyone off.'

'Nazis?'

'We thought it was a costume? Cos, you know, Halloween, so we were all live and let live, come in Nazis, have some booze and a dance. Share our lager, cavort with our women. But then it turns out they were really *into* being Nazis. They started separating people into groups and punching them and shouting.'

'Bit much,' said the witch.

'It's fucking harsh. I mean it takes all sorts but then if one of those sorts doesn't like all the others?' He stopped before he could continue his detour into political philosophy.

'We should go out and fight,' said the witch. 'There's more of us than there are of them.'

'I went on a badger thing a while back,' I said. 'I'm kind of an activist now.'

'I was thinking just wait here until they leave. Like Anne Frank or whoever.'

'It didn't work for her, did it? We should go out and fight.'

'There's no back way out of here, is there?' I listened for sounds of shouts or screams, but the party sounded amiable as ever. What would happen to Alistair and Raoul? Although I could imagine Alistair thriving.

The witch had bundled herself out of the bed and was swigging down the vodka in a combative fashion. 'We need weapons,' she said.

'I'm worried this is taking it too far,' I said. She gave me a familiar look of disappointment. This look scared me so much that I was about to feign courage, face a thumping, do anything to take the look away, when the noise of the sirens came.

Four

Alistair was in charge. He had a knack for it, boarding school born. Pacing around the quiet street, leading the constabulary through their jobs. 'There's really no need for you to be here, officer.' He put his arm around the policewoman's shoulder and looked surprised, even a little hurt, when she shook it off.

On the pavement across from Keris's house was a line-up of skew-whiff zombies, half-dressed beldames, unclad ghouls, shivering vampires. My witch and the blond boy had wandered off somewhere. I was alarmed to see that one of the Nazis in full beetle-black SS gear was marching with the police.

'Don't listen to him officer,' said one of the ghouls. 'He's a Nazi.'

'Thing is,' said the Nazi. 'I'm not a Nazi. I'm Irish, I don't think we can even *be* Nazis. It's cos of Halloween.'

The ghoul sighed, as if the Nazi had disappointed her. Alistair started critiquing Irish neutrality during the war.

'It wasn't me doing all the hitting and shouting,' the Nazi continued. 'It could have been Derren, my mate. I don't know where he's got to. He's not a Nazi either. I mean, he can a bit right wing. He would, at a push, vote Tory. But he's not a fucking Nazi.'

'We had a report saying someone got punched.'

One of the zombies started a chorus of 'why are we

waiting?' Keris floated from the house, doing a good impression of someone disturbed from years of slumber. 'Is everything all right?' she said. 'There seems a lot of fuss.'

'We had a report that Nazis were hitting people,' said the policewoman. She looked rather jealous of the Nazis.

'I'm really not a Nazi,' said the Nazi. 'I go on climate marches. My girlfriend is one-eighth Caribbean. I'm a great one for *Curb Your Enthusiasm*. Listen, there was this one guy, we met him on the bus. He might have been a Nazi. We let him come with us cos he had the gear.'

'There you go,' said Keris.

'More I think of it, the more he seems a Nazi. Like he was out on his own on a Friday night, in full Nazi uniform. That has to be a giveaway. And he kept talking about Nietzsche and whatsisname, Gobineau. Now I personally quite like Nietzsche but you got to admit that's suspect. And when we got here he was—' he scratched his head '—measuring people's skulls. With some special kind of skull-measuring equipment he had in his bag. And he kept asking to go to the living room. Living room, we must have living room, he said. It was him who did all of the hitting.'

'Plausible,' said Alistair. 'You should be after him.'

The police went over to their car and held a whispered discussion. I didn't think they could go much longer without arresting someone. The Nazi was asking Keris for a fag while the line-up of ghouls was starting to loosen. I couldn't see my witch anywhere.

'Alistair,' I said. 'I kissed a witch.'

He smiled at me in a fatherly way and patted me on the head. 'That's good. You're moving on.'

'I'm not moving on,' I said. 'I don't want to move on. I wish I hadn't done it.'

There was my witch coming back to us, wobbling on her architectural heels, bag swinging as though she were

23

about to start demolishing property. On arriving, she kissed me wetly on the mouth. She did the same with Alistair, which cheered me up a bit. Probably everyone kissed each other now, and were Nazis, and did horrible things in Berlin.

I told them I would be a few minutes and started off back home.

First there was happiness. From being in bed on a Sunday, with work a day away. Next up came memory, at a cell level, of alcohol, the check to see that I was still alive, the guilt of having drunk when I really shouldn't. Then other memories, tumbling downhill and into my consciousness. Marie had gone. Marie had gone because she saw an anger that wasn't in me. Marie had gone because the badger cull had taken over her thoughts. I had been drunk. I had kissed a witch and might have done even more, if it wasn't for the Nazis. Three cheers for the Nazis, I thought.

I had called Marie. No, that was okay, she hadn't answered. Except then I had texted her dad. I had texted Frank Lansdowne on my way back home. And I had no idea what I'd said.

The texts started off okay: I told him I was looking for Marie. I told him I was worried about her. This was fine, this was true. I told him, I told him ...

I had told Frank that I thought Marie had a drink problem. I didn't actually think this and I wasn't at all sure why I'd said it. 'We have to help her,' I'd said. 'I'm going to need both of you to help me get through to her.' Which must have been why I'd said it. 'She really has a lot of problems I need to sort out.' Frank hadn't pshawed this. There was nothing that could be construed as a pshaw. He had asked me to come round the next day. Which meant, I realised, today.

24

Five

'Stuart?' Frank Lansdowne stood at the door wearing the plush white type of dressing gown they give you at a health spa. It was late in the day to be sleeping but it was possible he'd had a bad night. I stood at the door and feigned wellness. 'Bit early for trick or treating, isn't it? Or late I suppose now. Come in, Stuart, come in.' He stepped back, rummaging in his dressing gown pocket for Marlborough Lights. He didn't usually smoke in the house, the fags being reserved for when people could see him. Marie, he said, had gone out.

So, I was back at the Lansdownes's. I'd only been there a fortnight before but it felt a good deal longer. The old familiar house again, the posters of art deco cats, the photographs of Judy from a 1986 *Observer* magazine, and most of all the pictures of Marie. Marie as an impish toddler clutching a cat, Marie blowing out birthday candles at age eighteen, Marie in a beret and a stripy top, smiling so hard that her cheekbones bracketed her eyes. Marie's features on endless repetition around the walls and she looked different in every shot.

'I don't mind admitting this business has taken its toll,' Frank was saying. 'Judy is scared to leave the house in case she's asked about it. Thank heavens for Ocado, I say.' He did his usual grin, that of a schoolboy caught skiving, willing you into complicity. 'How are you Stuart?

You look ...' My appearance seemed to exhaust even his gift for simile. I followed him through to the front room to find Judy on the sofa, lost under a heap of rugs and cushions. She looked, I thought, diminished.

Now, I liked the Lansdownes. I'd known about the two of them before I knew their daughter. She'd mentioned them on the first date, used to the men she'd been with vaguely recognising their names but not actually being excited about it. Whereas I was not a fan, exactly, but I owned a few of his novels and two collections of essays (while steering clear, as most people did, of the poems). His last, bulky volume, *Memory, My Mother*, was one of the books I read on the toilet when slightly drunk: erudite, clever and weightless musings on literature, history and life. His avian face on the cover. And I had read enough autobiographies of the heroic old *Granta* generation to know about his youth in Manchester, the grammar-school-aided clamber up to Oxford, the early promise of greatness he never quite fulfilled. The friend-ships with Salman, Tom and Milan, the stories of having bedded two Booker winners and an editor of *Spare Rib*. The masterpiece that never seemed to appear.

Marie had been slightly embarrassed to tell me about her folks. 'It's overwhelming. All through my life you'd have to watch what you say around him in case it turned up in one of his books. And they've both become grand old things now but when I was younger they were, well, they were sort of cool. I'd see them mentioned in the papers, say. Having to connect the person telling me to finish my dinner with, you know, the *enfant terrible*. Or comments about mum's legs on *The Late Show*.' I remembered her mother's legs. She was American, and somehow, as part of a generation's easy ascent, wound up on British television and in the broadsheets, wryly expounding on books. I'd seen her in the nineties on BBC2, her blonde prettiness unsuccessfully obscured behind outsize glasses as a concession towards seriousness, explaining Proust to insomniacs.

I *knew* about these people. These people were *it*. They were where the art was. They were garden parties and memories of the sixties, they were films and they were prizes and stories about the Prague Spring. I'd even borrowed her father's tone in my work from time to time, fallen by accident into his seen-it-all-before style, his hand-sweeping cadences. All those grand garden parties at their house near Regent's Park, all those luminaries guzzling Prosecco. I'd arrived right there, smack bang in the literary world and I hadn't even started my book yet. I'd got there by falling in love. And I *liked* falling in love. Only now she had gone.

'Stuart, Stuart,' cried Judy Lansdowne, from somewhere among the chintz. 'Marie is out at some meeting. With *that man*.'

'That man?' There was a man, then. There was always going to be a man. I put my hand on the back of the nearest chair.

'She's brought him here. This *badger man*.' She looked around in case anyone was listening, although clearly no one could be. 'We don't really know what to do. We can't turf her out. But he's enormous. And he *smells*.' I held onto the back of the chair. My face did a good impression of a dinghy having its air let out. Marie had gone for Henry then.

Judy went on, 'And as for the other one!'

'The other one?' My wife seemed to have formed a badger seraglio.

'I still say we turf him out,' said Frank. 'Although as to how we do that. We could always get some bailiffs.' He lapsed into one of the 'ard man voices he liked to use in his fiction. ''Ire some muscle.'

'Love, you know that's impossible. If he goes she goes. It's not as though we *like* him. He's so *big*, isn't he? You can't take a man like that seriously. So what are you going to do Stuart? Are we talking divorce? Do you have any idea how much we spent on that fucking wedding? That's half her inheritance, you know, gone on a bunch of napkins.'

'I don't actually want a divorce,' I said. 'I want Marie to come back.'

'The problem is *she* seems to want one, you see. And what's all this about her drinking?'

Frank put his hand on my arm. 'Come with me, Stuart,' he said. 'Come with me.'

We went through to the kitchen. I had spent so many days in this place, pulling Pinot from the fridge, break-fasting in the conservatory. This house was a haven for me. It was the civilisation I yearned for. It was books and peace and my marvellous bloody wife. I wasn't giving her up in a hurry. I wasn't giving any of it up.

'Frank,' I said. 'About the texts.' Even in here, of course, the photographs of Marie. Holidays and outings and, oh spare me this, our wedding. Did she know even then that she was going to leave? She didn't look unhappy. How do unhappy people look? I don't picture them looking so pretty.

'Stuart. Stuart. Stuart.' Frank looked different, sitting at the kitchen table. Shrunk, somehow, and unprotected, as if an unkind word could smite him.

'I might have maybe given, not the wrong impression, but not entirely the ...' He looked rueful. He looked frail and very tired and ready for bed. 'Frank,' I said, deciding to risk it. 'I might have—'

A feathery cloud of fag-smoke. 'We've tried, you know, Stuart,' he said. 'Our one and only child and she came late. I know I haven't always been perfect.' His eyes glazed as he thought of his many imperfections. 'But I never wanted her to get so *lost*. A home like this,' he waved his hand through the smoke. 'It's a centre isn't? And she doesn't seem to have a centre. It's here, it's supposed to be here.'

'I mean, she does drink, a bit, who doesn't, but I might have given—'

Except now the old man was sobbing. That head from which had come all those novels, those essays, those hundreds of ignored poems, was rocking with every sob. 'What did we do?' he said. 'It's been awful since this happened. I just keep asking myself, what did we do?' He was actually whimpering now. Hopefully the real-life situation was making him cry. Hopefully my texts hadn't done this.

'We can get her back Frank,' I said. 'I love her so much, you know. But you have to help me. You, and Judy too. Do whatever it is you can.'

He nodded, but kept on crying. It was starting to make me uncomfortable. Was I supposed to hug him? Supposed to somehow *comfort* him? He was a regular guest on *Front Row*. He should fucking well hug himself.

I should tell him, firmly, that the drinking wasn't real. That would be a start.

The door opened and a young man in pyjamas stood before us. He had a look halfway between a cherub and a rat, thick deposits of sleep in the corner of each eye and duckling-coloured hair sprouting at angles. I knew him from somewhere. It was . . . it was George, the mumbling boy from the badger camp, the one who followed Henry around.

29

'Guys,' he said, talking as though he had his fist in his mouth. 'Could you keep the noise down? Trying to get some sleep.' He yawned and his whole body stretched a few more feet before concertina-ing into a slump. Having exerted himself that far, he set off back upstairs.

I muttered goodbye to my still teary father-in-law and darted after the boy. He must have seen me coming and hoofed it four at a time up there, but I was quick enough to nab him before he got to Marie's room. I had stayed in this room countless times and now it seemed it was his turn. 'George,' I said, 'George.' He looked at me in a confused sort of way, as though he had stubbed his toe on something and it had turned out to know his name. 'What are you doing here?'

'Stuart,' he said with what passed for a smile. I agreed that this was definitely who I was. We sat on the bed, the bed I'd first seen on my second night with Marie. The room was the same, the same pictures on the wall, the same dusty crowd of old books. It was different though now, because now I had no stake in it. It was a room I no longer belonged in, that was all. George sat cross-legged on the bed, his shins showing, pink and hairless. He tugged at a string of beads around his skinny wrist. There was a sleeping bag on the floor and I realised I was now sitting on Marie and Henry's bed, that the two of them had been sleeping here with George at their feet, like a dog. I was glad he was there to stop them having sex.

I assumed that his being there stopped them.

'*She* said I could,' he said. He pronounced the word 'she' like he was pronouncing a sentence. He did not have much love for my wife, it seemed. 'They've gone out. To a meeting. I stayed in cos I wanted to sleep but you were making a row.' He stuck his forefinger between each toe consecutively and rubbed hard for grease. 'Not seen you at camp for a bit.'

'I've been busy.'

'You should come and get her back. We're all going back there tomorrow. Get her back and then she won't be around all the time. Henry,' he said, 'he's not right when she's around. Not *practical*. That's what's great about him, he's practical. When she's around he's just looking after her. Waste of everyone's time.'

I had the feeling I'd found an ally. Not the sort of ally I'd like, but you take your luck how you find it. I lay down on the bed, where I had lain so many times, and put my hands behind my neck. George, having finished cleaning his toes, started on his ears, digging for gold.

'I'll tell you what I think,' he said. 'Everyone's got a purpose. Everyone has a function. And his was the camp. Yours is, probably, complaining. Hers is listening to you complaining and telling you you'll be all right. And now she's joined him it's making everyone else go off too. It's got me here and you talking to me when you'd rather be with her and I'd rather be with the badgers, *and* him not paying attention to the badgers cos he's looking after her. She's messed everything up.' This speech seemed to exhaust him. He started ruffling his hair at startling speed, as if trying to perm it by hand.

'For an anarchist you don't seem to like change very much.'

He looked at me for the first time. His eyes were a pale grey, as if they had run out of colour halfway through making them. 'I *said*. It's about everyone finding out where they're supposed to be and then staying there. Not messing things up. If you mess things up, you just end up building things and bulldozing things and jetting around

31

the world. Will you try?' he said. 'I think she'd listen. I think she would come back. I'll tell you something.'

'I'm not taking relationship advice from a kid,' I said. We sat in silence a while. 'Go on though, you might as well.'

'They aren't, you know, *doing it*.' He screwed up his face at the thought. 'She says that it's too soon. That she needs to be sure or something. Henry's really cross at that. He says he isn't but I can tell.'

'Well,' I said. This news had some restorative effect. 'We'll just have to try and get things back to normal then.'

When I got downstairs, Frank and Judy were in the front room, deep in a whispered conference. I looked at them from the doorway, not the public duo but a couple locked in privacy, knowing all there was of one another. I set off for the door.

You know what? I felt sort of satisfied. I felt sort of all right. There were things that could be done. At least, I thought, as I headed for the station, I was making a bit of effort.

Six

My dad pressed down the car boot, sealing the last of my possessions inside. It had been hard for my parents, this year. They had only just got used to my nearly dying when I'd gone and got married on them. Now I was separated and moving house. It must have been like watching one of those speeded up films of plants growing and dying, except with the narrative spliced. My mum had cried in the flat as we piled up my books into boxes. My dad kept up an act of sympathetic stoicism that just about made things worse.

'You know you can always come home,' they said. I considered this. It wasn't unambiguously awful, was the worst thing. Imperial Leather and clean carpets. The heating a little too high. All my meals made for me, nights in front of the telly. Catch up with old school friends. The ones who'd stayed and had kids as soon as they could, the ones who'd been cool in their day. The kids would be almost twenty now. I could feasibly marry one of my old friend's kids.

Still, it would mean defeat. Back with his folks in his thirties. Shambling round the shops behind his mum. My Stuart back from London. Slowly accepting them buying all my clothes. Dinner for the three of us. Masturbating in bed while keeping my whole body still for fear of the mattress and thin walls.

'I'll pass,' I said. 'But thanks.'

'I still don't understand why she's done this,' said my mum. I told her it was temporary, it wouldn't last, that I was moving out to save rent but we'd soon be together again.

My parents looked at me and around the flat and neither of them spoke.

The days leading up to the move hadn't been so bad. I imagine if I hadn't known I was going to get Marie back then they might have been pretty awful. But I was confident I was doing all I could. I'd be lying if I said there weren't moments, of course. I heard from Frank that she was back in Gloucester at the camp. Packing our things wasn't fun, the letters and the photographs and the goods bought for the future.

Then, one cold morning, I broke. I'd spent most of the evening looking at Facebook, her profile and the badger guy, Henry Ralph his full name was, my head full of unwanted pictures. I called, not caring where she was.

'Hello.' Her voice had that morning softness to it. Unguarded, ungirded.

'Just wanted to say hello.' I don't think my voice was nearly as soft. I tried my best to change it.

'It's early,' she said. 'I nearly asked you if it's early where you are too. Like we're in different countries.'

'Feels as though we are.'

'How are you?'

'I'm awful. I want you back.'

'Look, I still care about you a lot. I just know that I have to do this.'

'I know.' I felt that being understanding was the smartest move to make. If I kept on being supportive she would eventually start doing things I could support.

'I thought about you, you know. In the middle of the

night. I'm staying at Irene's. You remember Irene? I went downstairs about one, to get water. And in her garden there were these two baby foxes. Completely still, with eyes like lamps. Just looking through the window until somebody came. And, I don't know, I thought about me and you.'

'Come back. It is important that you come back.'

'I can't come back.'

'It is ridiculous that you are not in bed with me right now.'

'It does feel ridiculous. When I wake I expect you to be there. Farting or snoring. Or Malkin knocking your book pile off the shelf. How is Malkin?'

'He prospers. Except he misses you. We both miss you. Come back.'

'I can't.'

'Did I ever tell you I dreamt about you? The night before my op? The big op?'

'You didn't.'

'I was in the ward. I mean really and in the dream. And you came to me. You were wearing, you know, your fake leather jacket. Which I assume is okay because fake. Although if someone sees it and likes it they might go and buy a real one. Anyway that was it, you hadn't anything else on and you had shaved your, you know. I guess as some kind of a treat. Or maybe my unconscious is just porn, I don't know. But you had. I mean, I'm not someone who is fussy about that. It's not *necessary*. But it was the thought of it, I think, and you were standing by the bed. And I remember thinking, Christ, I want to live. I want to live so much. Because of you.'

'Because of my vagina?'

'I know that doesn't sound great, or maybe it does now,

35

I don't know. Should we just not have got married? Was getting married the mistake? Was moving in the mistake? You aren't really a wife. Who wants a wife? You could be my girlfriend. I could come over once or twice a week, at night or on unexpected afternoons, and we could kiss and then fuck on the floor. That's what we should do. That's really all I want.'

There was a long time without speaking, just the sound of her breath down the line.

'That isn't what I *wanted*,' she said. 'I wanted to be a wife. I wanted to be a mum. But you want this *girlfriend* now.'

'It's the same fucking person.'

'And now there's the cull to fight. I can't be all the people you want me to be and sort out the cull as well. I've found where I need to be now. This suffering, I can't stand it. I have to try and help.'

'Where does Henry fit into all this?'

'He's been very supportive. He knows a lot about animals. He's making me read Peter Singer. I'm learning from him. I'm interested in animal rights and he encourages that. You want this girlfriend. And I'm not that any more. I'm not sure I ever was. I'm interested in badgers now. Animals. You'd get bored of me, as a badger wife, rather than this cool actress girlfriend you've invented. I'm not that. I never was that.'

'I want you back no matter what you do.' Now that I'd said this she might come back and start acting again, doing it a bit better this time before it got too late for her, and the badgers would soon be extinct.

'Henry, we talk about badgers, but he asks things about me. And not what did I think of the book he lent me or whether I like the thing he wrote himself. He asks me about my day.'

36

'What you had on your sandwiches.'

'Yes. I like that. It's nice. It's how people are supposed to talk.'

'What did you have on your sandwiches?'

'I had hummus.'

'Did you like me asking you that?' Come back and I will ask you about sandwiches all day. Come back and I might even listen, the first few times.

'I did. But, Stuart, it's really too late.'

'Is this, I read your play, your play thing. Is this because of that? The thing with the chair?'

'The play, the play. I don't know. Maybe that was a metaphor. It did scare me, that day.'

'Because I haven't got this anger you describe. I am not an angry person. I am, maybe, angry if I stub my toe. But I don't stomp through life being angry. I am peaceable. I am known for my amiable nature.'

'You are mostly very nice. It wasn't the chair. I just, oh god, I just have to.'

'I felt it was a little overwritten. Promising but it needed serious work. You've gone quiet.' In her silence, I told her the basil plant was doing well. It was now twice the size it had been and when I pulled a few leaves off to sprinkle on my food there were always new ones the next day.

She seemed to appreciate this.

'Ahoy!' roared Alistair. He had wandered down to the forecourt, arms outstretched to greet us, although not to help with any bags. 'Welcome aboard.'

My mum and dad liked Alistair. I think they would have liked anyone who seemed to want to look after me. As for Alistair, he seemed near ecstatic. His beard exploded out around his smile. My parents helped me lug boxes up the stairs, and managed not to notice the general mess. Mess was something they liked to notice but my troubles had led to a slackening of standards. Alistair made a fuss of them, offering cups of tea until it turned out he had no milk and not enough clean cups and only one teabag. They seemed to appreciate the offer. Once I was in they set off to a Travelodge and left me 'to settle'. I said this might take a while.

'We're going to have the *best* time,' said Alistair, as soon as they were gone; 'We're going to live how we always should have. Do you still write?'

'Not much. I've been distracted.'

'Mate, look at this.' From behind a sofa he pulled out a vintage typewriter with a ribbon wrapped around it and smiled and nodded a lot. 'A present,' he said. 'For your writing. I've got one myself.'

'Two lots of keyboards hammering all night,' said Raoul, who was darting round with a cloth, trying to find and polish surfaces.

Alistair took his hat off revealing a red-rim, a tonsure, of indented skin below.

'Ignore Raoul,' he said. 'He doesn't really get it. There's a sensuousness to a typewriter, isn't there? You feel, how can I put it, connected to the page. Oh, never mind. This move will do you good, Stu. Productive.'

'I am curious about your kitchen.'

'What makes you curious about it?'

'I am curious as to how neither of you are dead. There are things in it. Baleful things.' Food furring on piles of broken plates, carrier bags lining surfaces, each one a makeshift bin. The sink half full of slushy yellow rice. The salad trays in the fridge were flooded with a rusty and nacreous ooze.

'When Lucy left me, Stu, I made a vow to myself. Do you want to hear the vow?'

'You'd stop washing up? You would never go hungry again?'

'I'd live how I wanted to live.'

'Is this how you want to live?'

'It is. Come on. We're going to have a great time.' He certainly seemed to be happy enough. I had never seen a man so blissful and content in proportion to the facts of his life.

Raoul shrugged, muttered something about always having to be the adult and shuffled into the kitchen where he began a brave attempt at cleaning it all up. There were crashes and a silence that sounded as if it wanted to be filled with swearing.

'Should we help him?' I asked.

Alistair winked at me and started assembling a spliff. I had the strong impression it wasn't his first of the day. 'Don't worry about Raoul. He likes doing good things. It's part of his whole Christian thing, he gets to butter up his god.' My cat, who had been padding nervily around the carpet, glanced at Alistair, hissed in a way that left no room for ambiguity and hid behind the sofa.

'She'll come round,' said Alistair.

'He,' I said.

'Hey man,' shouted Raoul. 'Did you know we have a dishwasher?'

I spent the afternoon listening to Alistair. It was hard to do anything else. Doing exactly what he liked seemed to involve a great deal of self-assertion. He existed in a happy world of anticipatory success. I think he was mostly living off rent contributions, his parents having bought him the flat some years before. Aside from this he was writing a hundred things at once and had publishers interested in all of them. A novel 'about twenty-first century urban living', a play in which an everyman figure is put on trial by a jury of banshees for reasons I didn't quite follow, 'at least one really good aphorism', the libretto for 'an actual space opera, I mean, an opera set in space' and, he concluded, 'an epic poem'.

'Tell me about the epic poem,' I said. I had to say something. And it was all good practice, this listening. We were stood out on the balcony, the wind rustling my hair and the space where his had been. From this vantage point, we looked out over the neighbouring flats, the back of a waterworks and a patch of grass obscured by abandoned furniture.

'It's all about masculinity,' he said.

'Of course it is.'

'Masculinity in crisis. Partly inspired by the end of my marriage.'

'Crisis, eh?'

'Oh, I say it all in the poem. I think I've just about sorted masculinity.'

'A strangely neglected topic.'

'Yes! Some people, you know, they act like it's all been said, but you, I knew you'd get it. Do you want to know what it's called?' He had a beam on his face like he'd just invented orgasms and remembered to sort out the patent.

'Tell me.'

'Rage!' He stood as though he were demonstrating republican virtue in a history painting. 'With an exclamation mark, you know.'

'You should,' I said. 'You should call it R-Age. With a hyphen. Works as a double meaning that way, you see. Our Age.'

His beam, already fulsome, grew bigger. 'No,' he said. 'No, I don't think that works. This is why you need to get back on it, Stu. Remember those nights in Greenwich.

When we thought we'd own this place? We still can,' he said. 'We still can.'

I wasn't so sure about that. I remembered those nights. We'd leave our student halls in Deptford and stroll through the echoing foot tunnel, embarking on a walk through the empty streets. Standing by the cold black Thames across from the empty Dome. The things we planned to do. I was studying English and Art History combined and was hungry for culture, swallowing novels and racing to exhibitions as though I'd been starving all my life. Alistair was always confident that we'd both of us make an impact. He'd grown up knowing this stuff, I thought, and it was only later I came to suspect he didn't know it so well.

When I met Marie I'd remembered it, my early thirst for culture. Sitting in her Regent's Park house, with all those pictures and books. I'd finally got where the art was and I wanted so much to stay there.

It would be fun living with Alistair and Raoul, if it was only to be temporary. They both seemed pleased to have me.

That night Alistair announced he was cooking a meal. A welcoming meal, he said. I thought of the state of their kitchen but tried hard to overlook it. I spent the afternoon arranging my little box room, putting up pictures and books. I put a photograph of Marie next to my bed.

There was a knock on the door. 'You eaten?'

It was Raoul. He stood in my doorway, like a Transylvanian inn keeper who feels he ought to put in a word of warning.

'Alistair's cooking.'

'Eat,' said Raoul. 'Eat something first. Say you forgot, I dunno.'

41

'Does he not cook much?' I said. Raoul glanced to the chest of drawers. I put the picture of Marie face down before he could see it.

'No, he cooks a lot. But the food is ... It isn't ... I don't want to say anything bad.'

'I'm vegetarian,' I said.

'No,' said Raoul. 'That won't work. He's vegetarian too. You'll need something better than that.'

'I actually am vegetarian,' I said.

The chickpeas sat on the plate, sullen and grey. There were breadcrumb-covered orbs next to them, from a box. A sad scrap of lettuce sat wetly on the side.

'I actually ate in my room,' I said. There was a moment when disappointment clouded his face. The beard seemed to droop. The dome of his forehead rumpled. But a smile dispelled it all.

'Just means more for me,' he said, his fork pronging an orb.

Back upstairs, I thought about Marie. There was no way I'd be staying here for long. And the way back had to be badgers. They were my main rivals, counting Henry as a sort of honorary badger.

I began to think of tactics. Now you don't get rid of rivals, amorous rivals, by making them look bad. I wasn't at all sure I could make a badger look bad anyway. I had to borrow some of their brightness. Marie loved badgers? I would love them more.

The next day I went down to Kirkdale Books and bought a second copy of *Badgerlands*, Marie having taken her copy in the move. I read up on the animals and tried my best to like them. It wasn't as hard as all that. They were impressive, resilient beasts. They were known to bury their dead and hold strange badger funerals. They were unappetising to eat. They had inspired a really good poem by John Clare. It was more than I'd ever done.

Rupa, my colleague and best friend at the office, insisted on coming back with me from work that week. I'd tried not to tell anyone there about all this, but she had somehow guessed, stomping over to my desk to ask me what was up. I tried hard on the phrasing. I told her I was fine, that I was going to sort things out. Now she was here in my new home.

'This place is very—' she shook her head '—manly.'

'I'm not going to stay here for long,' I said. 'I just need to sort things out with Marie.'

'And what happens if you don't? What happens, Stuart, if chasing after Marie is a really bad idea? Look, I like Marie. She's very *nice*. But you were married four months and she left.'

I smiled. It was hard for me to ignore how into me Rupa was.

'Then you'll be stuck here in this dirty place. Weird men in their thirties pretending to be students. Only students without the conversation, without the appetite for learning new things. Jaded students. Tired students.'

She had walked out on her own marriage back home when she moved here. Her ex was understanding, available for late night Skyping, Spotify swaps. It had done him no good at all. She was living in Bethnal Green. There was a philoprogenitive librarian who kept rubbing his hopeful fingers on the maternity dresses in shops, but she was keeping him at arm's length.

We went out on the balcony, so I could watch her smoke. She said, 'The problem is, there's this whole weight of being told you're selfish. Why haven't you had kids yet, how can you walk out on such a nice man, do you really mean you'd rather read books than watch telly – cos that's the main difference between being alone or with someone isn't it, you read instead of sit in front of a screen? How can you be so selfish? Me doing what I want is selfish. Them telling me what I want, that isn't selfish at all.'

I asked her what she wanted.

'I don't know, do I? I know I'm not going to find out unless I try. Your Marie, she spent years making you happy. Even now she's left she's trying to save the planet.'

'And what are you doing?'

'I'm working Stuart. Not just showing up like you. I'm living a life. I read a lot. Sometimes I think about ditching the librarian. There's these nice dopey boys at the Buddhist Centre who are very well behaved. They won't be fussing at me to move in with them and make little versions of themselves.' She pulled a white cigarette out from a silver case and let it roll between long fingers, without bothering to light it. 'Trying to give up,' she said. 'The second one, I just hold. Listen, you and Marie, you were great. First time round yours I called Saleem, you know, I said I've finally found a couple who got it right. I was excited, I thought, these two have cracked it. I'm glad somebody has. But you hadn't. You hadn't cracked it at all.'

I smiled, tried to agree. I didn't tell her I was booked to go down to Gloucester that weekend.

Seven

The thing about my Marie – aside from all the other things, the nerviness, the acting hopes, the feeling she had of not having quite got started, the literary parents and the urge, never satisfied, to create a family of misfits around her, friends who had no other invites, a cat that bit everyone's ankles, even, I suppose, a husband who might not live the rest of the year – the *other* thing about Marie was this: she had only saved my life. It seemed unfair of her to leave me, after that. Wasn't there an obligation to stick around, after you'd rescued someone? A debt owed by the rescuer?

I'll zip back a bit. Our flat a year or so earlier, minus all the plants. A few less books perhaps. It was just coming up to Christmas. Marie and I had been living together two years. It had been going well, I thought. We'd taken on a cat, which always implies permanence. The odd disagreement, yes, the occasional bit of bickering, but for the most part we were okay. Everyone seemed to think so and I tended to concur.

The night before it happened we'd gone to see a play with her parents. Frank was friends with the playwright, obviously, and Judy had been in the play, or inspired the play, or had the original idea for the play, back in the seventies. Maybe it was written about her. If there had ever been any tensions about this they were all forgotten now.

After the show, Frank had warm congratulations for the playwright. Marie and I had stood there, smiling, trying to look promising. The playwright had asked how her acting was going, without seeming too interested. We had gone on to a Turkish restaurant where I had filled up my glass once too often. There'd been an actress in the play who had very red hair and very pale skin. I thought about this actress in my sleep.

Morning came and I had the slightest of slight headaches. I could smell coffee bubbling on the hob and hear the faint sound of aquatic mammals and panpipes accompanying Marie's yoga. I enjoyed these morning rituals. I stumbled through to the front room and smiled upon the scene, the table pushed towards the corner of the wall, panels of winter sunlight on the floor and Marie, curling, stretching, on the unfurled purple mat. It was good to wake up to these things. I let her finish, kissed her and poured myself a bowl of cereal while she got ready for work. We said goodbye and I hopped in the warm and slippery bathtub for a shower. While I showered, I thought, in a more demonstrative way, about the actress from the night before. I hopped out, dabbed at myself with a towel and decided I needed to piss.

The moment that I started, a black wave of pain passed over my sight. It travelled from right to left, shooting, inky, across my vision. As slowly as I could, I lowered myself to the floor and vomited into the bowl. There was a lot more vomit than I'd ever seen before. There was wave after bitter wave of it. When I was finally done, I closed my eyes and lay down on the cold floor. I could hear myself gasping, fast and painful gasps. I think, for a time, I slept.

When I woke my head was hurting and I needed to be sick again. Halfway through doing this, other bodily functions started clamouring for my attention, all at once. I hauled up onto the seat and emptied myself while roaring through my legs. My sweat was all leaving me and hurting in the process, needles threading my pores. When I strained great jolts of soreness knocked through my head, until I fell off the seat and back onto the floor. Everything – the light in the bathroom, the smell of my fast-departing fluids, the traffic rumbles from the road outside, the faint scent of ammonia from the litter tray in the hall – was a source of nausea and pain. I was allergic to existing. I was scared.

I'm not sure how but I managed to scrape myself across our flat and climb up into the bed. I must have left a trail of waste behind me, like a giant, ailing slug. I lay pressed against the mattress, panting and gasping for air. My body felt robbed of liquid.

Somehow I found the energy to call work and tell them I'd be in late. I don't know if I made sense. I remember they sounded annoyed. Once I'd done with explaining I put my phone on the bedside table and blacked out.

Eight

'Stuart.' And again. 'Stuart.' I was in a paddy field, whatever that was, scything whatever you scythed there. I was
a Chinese peasant in a lightshade hat. Tinkly music was
playing, imitation Nyman. I was an Arab drinking coffee
in a sandy backstreet bar. I was a montage of swarming
humanity in a 1980s film. I was home in bed and it was
dark outside and I was slick with sweat all over.

Marie reached down and touched my face. This made
me scream some more. Oxygen, human contact, the feel
of the sheets on my skin – everything was poisonous. I
was wrenched out of my element.

'There is sick in the hall,' Marie said. 'Are you okay?'
I told her I didn't know how it got there. I could hear her
cleaning it up. I lay shivering, poleaxed. 'I don't think you
are well,' she said. 'You were saying you were Chinese.'

'Was I speaking Chinese?' I said. I was hopeful.

'You were not speaking real Chinese. You were
speaking a racist, Walt Disney version of what a Chinese
person sounds like.'

'I have a cold,' I managed to say. 'A bad one.' When
she switched on the light I screamed and covered my eyes.

'I'm not sure this is a cold,' said Marie. 'I think this is
something worse.'

Nine

A word or two about sight. I hadn't been especially *sighted* since I was eight. Or at least that's when my sightlessness was spotted. I was in the back of the car on the way to Chester Zoo, excited, as only a child can be, by the proximity of animals, and I'd cried out at the vision of a field of grazing pandas.

I'd had my eyes checked and it was discovered I needed glasses. It had bothered me sometimes, myopia. Writers are supposed to be *noticers* aren't they? Alert to texture and colour, beadily in search of detail. I was never going to be like that.

When the blackness had leaked across my eyes that morning, my glasses had dropped to the floor. Two days had taken place in a salad of vision, a blur. What sight I had seemed intent on hurting me. Light and colour had turned offensive, gone hostile. I kept my eyes closed as much as I could. I rolled and I moaned and I sweated and around about every hour I would stagger to the bathroom to be sick.

On Wednesday afternoon, Marie came back early from work and said she was calling an ambulance. I rebelled at this. We lived, after all, just five minutes' walk from a hospital. Marie pondered, said she wasn't sure I could get there but she was happy to give it a go. She reached out and touched my brow, flinching only slightly at the-now-familiar screams.

'You'll have to put some clothes on,' she said. 'Give me a shout if you need a hand.' I told her I would be fine.

Forty-five minutes later I had managed to get a sock on. I had lost the argument and so I grunted and passed out.

When I woke, blurred men and women were all around me, and there was an atmosphere of emergency, made worse by the softness of their voices. 'I feel much better,' I said.

'He does not feel better,' said Marie. Her voice was strained. 'I mean, look at him.'

They all looked at me. I'd been asleep, all over the place. I'd been a pearl diver, a Bedouin, a bored girl on the checkout counter at Boots. My identity swimming into others, escaping its sore little shell.

'Have you been drinking liquids?' asked one of the ambulance people, as though I might have been drinking anything else. I tried to answer but my voice was a croak. Marie said that when I drank anything it came straight out again. I started to feel scared. How many fingers were they holding up? Had anything like this ever happened to me before? Had I taken anything I shouldn't? Marie's hand squeezed mine and this time her touch didn't make me shrink or scream. This time her touch felt necessary. It felt a link with life.

I found myself unfussily arranged and lifted from the bed, positioned onto a stretcher and carried across the room. I could just about enjoy it, this helplessness, this happy relinquishing. I was weak and I was cared for. At the same time, I was able to feel important. I was being carried out of the flat, like an emperor in a sedan. People might see me and wonder who I was and what was wrong. They carried me smoothly, without bumps.

Marie was out of sight but kept on saying she loved me, that I would be okay. I smiled to show her I was fine, but also that I was brave. She told me I looked frightening.

'Stuart,' another voice said. I was out in the cold, feeling the crunch of the winter air on my skin. I wondered if people on the street were watching us, concerned. Maybe I ought to be concerned as well. Maybe this was serious. Panic, belated, started to take over. 'Can you tell me if this was sudden or if it came on gradually?' I told the voice it was sudden, gripping Marie's hand. The clunk of an opening ambulance door and I was carried back into warmth. The cold seemed to have infiltrated my skin. I lay there and I shivered as the ambulance drove the two minutes to the hospital.

Ten

The accident and emergency ward in our local hospital was like a theatre in the round. The doctors and nurses had an office set up in the middle of the room with curtained beds surrounding it. The staff yelled and dashed and slammed things down as if to keep their audience entertained. The light bore into me, the noise attacked my skull.

I was still scared. We were in hospital and this was serious. Patients yelled at one another from bed to bed.

'Stuart,' said Marie. 'That bed has a police guard.'

I tried to say it was all right for some, but it came out as a croak. I tried thrashing about and moaning but it didn't seem to help. I tried putting on my glasses for the first time since the blackness came, but they were heavy and thick-framed, like everyone's glasses in my part of London, and they weighed down on my head. I worried that, even with them on, I couldn't see as well as I used to. Marie offered to read aloud from the book I was reading, *Herzog* I think it was, but the sound of a few paragraphs made it worse.

'My vision isn't right,' I managed to say. A large part of the world had been cordoned off. As though I were watching a play and the curtain on my right side hadn't been fully drawn, the stage lights not quite turned up. I took the glasses off. Crashes and thuds of activity all around. A nurse came over and handed me a tiny hexagonal cardboard gourd with a Paracetamol inside. I gobbled down the pill with a sip of water and was surprised how much better I felt. I was still sweating though, alternately hot and cold. Every so often I would blink or shake my head and this sent pain echoes sounding through me. Another nurse arrived and asked if I knew who I was, or the name of the prime minister. I answered with a groan, which she accepted as close enough. She asked me to press on her upturned hands then quizzed me on how many fingers she had held up. I obeyed, uncomprehending. All around me patients kept up a chorus of complaints.

Dave, right, my Dave he got chucked out didn't he? Only he doesn't listen does he, he comes straight back with a blade? Only these guys, these guys, they've got fucking *hardware*, like they're properly *kitted out* and all Dave's doing is waving his little blade around like a fucking *sparkler*. They've got *crowbars* and shit. Fucking *hammers*. Take him round the back and they dislocate everything, like there's nothing left to lo-cate.

Dalek. Dalek. I hear you. I hear your suffering, dalek and I'd love to soothe away your cares. I'm an old man dalek but I still got it in me. I can melt away your frustrations, worse comes to the worse.

I don't want your consolation. I want my Dave to get well again.

He's dead you daft cunt.

You can't say that. You cannot. fucking. say. that.

I put my glasses back on. An orthodox Jewish family walked through the ward with careful, birdy steps, blinking in curious disbelief. The bed across from mine had nine or ten visitors around it, all wearing sports gear and eating pizza. The man in the bed had a bandaged torso with a maroon stain showing through. He had a satisfied look on his face.

If someone shows you the blade, his friend said, then

53

you ain't getting proper shanked. It show-shanking is that. Not *serious*.

'Doesn't seem much point in trying to read,' said Marie. I could tell she was uncomfortable. She was receptive to the pain of others, she caught it off them. Closed her eyes at the violent parts of films. We lived across from a patch of grass near to this hospital and she'd sometimes stare through the window at the people sat on the benches. She said she was wondering what bad news they'd had, to make them want to sit there on their own, with dazed faces, ignoring the cold. I'd said they were probably addicts. She'd sit at the window gazing at the loners nodding out, feeling a sorrow towards them they couldn't feel themselves. I sometimes used to worry that she'd one day invite them all in.

The doctor, when he turned up, was a flushed young man who looked as if he'd just jumped off a horse. The look of a duellist contemplating his felled opponent. 'So then, Stuart. Block, is it? What's the matter with you then?'

Marie leant forward and told him what was wrong. The doctor nodded at her several times as though memorising directions to a country pub, before getting a nurse to check my pulse rate. He bent his face close to mine until I could smell toothpaste and coffee. 'We're going to get some fluids into you. You're very dehydrated. After that we'll take another look.'

There was a moan from a neighbouring bed. Marie scratched at her knees. She'd been doing that a lot lately, scratching parts of herself, pulling at her fringe. Sometimes there were red patches on her arms, from all her scratching. I warmed to them, the blisters empathy gave her. 'This place,' she said, closing her eyes. The doctor brandished a hypodermic and took hold of my arm.

Not long after the needle entered my vein, my body started to tremor. My teeth chattered, until I shook the bed. Marie stood and ran for help. *He's dying, somebody come.* They told her my reaction was normal. 'If it's normal, why did no one say? If it's normal why didn't you warn us?' Even shaking, I could savour it, that wonderful *us*. We were a team, Marie and I.

My convulsions slowed down to a hardly discernible twitch. My panting began to subside. My headache mellowed into a dulled throb, like the sound of distant reggae. I was starting to feel like a person again. But my eyes still didn't seem right.

'S'flu,' said the doctor when he returned. He stood with his hands behind his back and his legs apart, as though warming himself by a fire. 'Nothing but flu. You can go home.'

I felt, through the sickness, the thrill of triumph. 'Told you I was okay,' I said to Marie. I leaned on her in my dressing gown, walking back home in the dark. I was relieved. The worst was over. I was going to be okay.

But I was not okay. As the rest of the week went on it became harder to ignore that some of my eyesight was missing. Areas of vision were denied me, only noticeable when, say, Marie would pad over and tap me on the arm and it would shock me like an ambush. It was as if my world were being slowly hemmed in by sightlessness. Fear, that I'd managed to ignore when the pain was at its worst, nudged at my consciousness, waking me up at night. I told myself the sight problem was a temporary thing, a side effect of the flu. Flu can do that, can't it, cause some temporary blindness? And they are temporary, aren't they; the visual scars that flu leaves you? So in a few short days I'd be healthy and vigorous, healthy and vigorous and seeing?

Eleven

On the first Monday after I'd collapsed, I set off to work. I said goodbye to Marie and stood outside our building, adjusting to the wintry air. It was five minutes' walk to the station.

Except I hadn't accounted for the tiredness in my bones. I hadn't accounted for my sight. I had to walk forward very slowly, one arm half outstretched like a bashful fascist. I sloped, one step at a time, along the more characterful end of our neighbourhood. Kids on bicycles and old ladies walking dogs would appear out of the dark at me, as though I were riding a social-realist ghost train. 'Mind where you're fucking going,' they said. It was easier to stand still. So long as I stayed rooted in the middle of the pavement no one bumped into me at all. That said, it wasn't much help in getting to work. Carefully I let myself budge forward, my arm a little more outstretched. I kept on going until I got to the end of the street. Here was a road. It was the sort of road where they speed up when they see you coming and it had been hard enough crossing it back when I could see.

What would it mean, to go blind? I hadn't really thought about that. I'd be poorer, chances were. I would cut myself while shaving. I would have to listen to a lot of audio-books and the unabridged versions would be hard to get and expensive. I might, I thought, go under. People did.

The area where I lived was home to a thriving community of the unwell. They circled the hospital for knocked-off painkillers, they sat out, alone or in messy congregations, spitting, staring at the air. One woman wore a home-made radiation-proof hat. The old man who stumbled in his dressing gown, blue-shinned, gesticulating. They all of them started off somewhere. I'd be the man who keeps bumping into things as he nervously goosesteps to the station. You could go under these days, the net was being cut. The jaws of the world could open underneath you.

While I'd been worrying about this, the traffic hadn't slowed. The cars seemed jammed and speeding both at once. There was a fresh white bicycle tied to a lamppost by the road, a bleached memorial to someone careless or unlucky. Not having a bike, I would have to make do with a wreath.

I waited and I waited. Eventually I decided there was nothing for it but to put my fate to the gods. It had worked so far, more or less. I closed my eyes, crossed my fingers and stepped out, reaching the other side with a renewed headache and a pounding heart. Evidently this approach was unsustainable.

My options felt foreshortened. Maybe if I kept up this lurching and arm-waving, someone would photograph me for an art project on blind people and I wouldn't even see it, because I was blind.

I carried on, slowly pacing, down towards the station. Everyone around me seemed speeded up and zooming. Hectic nurses galloped to the hospital, packs of children charged at breakneck speed for school. I trudged along the pavement, unsure if they knew I was there. Two trains whizzed over the bridge in the time it took to get to the station. I spent a few minutes finding my Oyster card and I set off up the ramp to the platform. Normally I climbed

57

the stairs, but today was not a normal day. It might not be a normal life. A train came when I was halfway up the ramp. I managed to get on the next one, clinging to the rubber handhold, feeling weak. It was already 9.30 and I had another train to catch.

The next train wasn't too crowded. It got to my stop around quarter past ten. Once I'd got this far, I only had to make it down a few streets until I was safe at my desk. I had a few short breaks but I made it in twenty minutes or so.

I reached my office, triumphant and sat down. I was a couple of hours late. I switched on my computer and found I was squinting at the screen.

Twelve

'I think you need to get a second opinion.' Marie dropped the coffee-browned script she was reading, jumped off our salmon-coloured sofa and ran to fuss over my hand. 'I don't think you can put off doing that.'

I had been trying to make us both a cup of tea and had misjudged the distance from kettle to cup. The boiling hot water had gone straight over my wrist. I was shocked enough to think she had a point. I held my arm under the cold tap till it numbed, and pink soreness rose from the white.

'Isn't this sort of thing common? Going a bit blind after the flu? This sounds like something that happens, frequently.'

'I don't think it is common. I don't think it is flu.' She held my hand up, looked at it, frowned and stood back. 'You're going to have to get this looked at. It isn't normal to lose this much vision. It isn't normal to spend two days screaming and howling like that. You need to talk to someone else.'

'I'll go at the end of the week. I'll go to the opticians.'

'Go tomorrow.' She folded her arms. This was the first time I had seen her be determined. It was something I would get to know well.

'I'll go at the end of the week.'

'Tomorrow. You need to do this.'

'I'll go tomorrow.' And, not knowing she had saved my life, Marie refilled and flicked on the kettle, poured us both a fresh cup of tea and went back to the sofa with her script.

Thirteen

After I was out of the woods and past the worst of it, I went back to my GP. I told him I'd been through a period of intense and wondrous joy and now this joy had gone I found I missed it. He scribbled away on his pad.

'It isn't the lack of eyesight,' I said. 'I think I've got used to that. It isn't even having this illness hanging over me. It's more, I can't get excited over the things that everyone else does. Stuff like jobs. Children, having children. A really cool restaurant they went to. Something on the news. I feel like I had something bigger than that, something that was more real and now I've lost it.'

'Do you think that you love life now, would you say?' I told him I thought I did. 'But a version of life in which useful employment, procreation, eating and current affairs are of minimal importance. This is a lot of life to turn your back on. These are what life consists of, some would say.'

'I mean, I know I'm lucky. I was reading, what's his name, Oliver Sacks. There was a guy who had what I had, you know with the visual cortex. He couldn't see at all. Not only that, he couldn't remember *having had seen*. And my sight, it's not so bad now. I'm kind of used to it. So I feel bad for feeling bad.' My GP wedged his glasses further up his nose, showing the deep trench-lines where they pressed into his skin. 'Is there anything I can do?'

'No. No, I don't think so. It sounds like you are a mystic. Not a good thing to be in this day and age. You just have to hope you snap out of it. And make sure you eat plenty of eggs. Vitamin D, it's terribly important.'

About this time, I was trying to write a novel. I'd started off fine, the words seeping from my fingers, liquid, full of grace and then, one day, a month or so in, I found I couldn't write. I was stumbling. My brain felt strapped in, bound by limitations. I couldn't find the words. Marie came back that day and found me weeping over an adjective. 'Have some time out,' she kept saying. 'Wait. There's plenty of time.' I was scared my brain wasn't what it had been. I pressed my face into the pillow. My fainting became more regular. We were to marry at the end of the month.

'Marie,' I said. It was two days before the wedding. 'I think I'm starting to be okay again.'

She was writing something, probably wedding related. No, it was a play, a play she was writing. This was her new project. She was bored with just acting, needed to try something new. She was always trying new things. Before the acting there had been a period of learning to dance. Before that, a spell trying to paint. She'd take on a passion, build a life in it, get unsatisfied and move on. She looked up at me.

'I'm glad you're feeling better,' she said.

'I know I've possibly been difficult. Something eating at me and I'm not sure what it is.'

'You've seemed cross with me. Angry, almost.'

'I know. I'm not angry. I think I know what it was.'

She lowered her screen and scratched herself. I wasn't sure if she'd been doing that much of late. She had certainly lost weight. A wedding thing, I thought.

'I've wondered what was up.'

'I've got it. Nothing was up. What it was, was ... well, it's obvious. My brain. It's a physical thing. My feeling strange, my acting strange. It's a response to that. Just a physical response.'

'I'm not sure that's how it works,' she said. 'You're you, a person. Not just a set of synapses.'

'There's nothing else wrong,' I said. 'It was obviously just that. And this means that now I know that, I can go back to feeling fine.'

'That's good,' she said and went back to writing, the concentration making her frown.

Fourteen

The morning of the wedding arrived. It felt like being stretchered. Other forces were in control; all I had to do was place myself, soldier-like, in the correct and pre-ordained flow and things would happen for me. I didn't feel fretful or scared. Somehow that feeling had passed. I examined myself carefully, and yes, it was all gone. I was coming through, it seemed. Physically, I felt stronger. I only noticed the eyesight at times of stress, the new glasses had made a difference. Although I knew I was at risk of a second bleed, I knew this risk was small and I wasn't walking around in fear of my life.

I was happy, I decided. It wasn't euphoria but then, not everything was. I was happy and in love and sometimes this was enough. God knows, I couldn't lose her. God knows, being alone was unthinkable.

That day, after we'd recited our self-scripted vows, after we'd said hello to Marie's beautiful Regent's Park friends and my more ungainly university ones, after my mum had cried and Frank had pretended to flirt with her, after he'd stood up to deliver a rambling, vaguely obscene speech, replete with quotes from the classics, after I'd made my own speech, which was simpler and less obscene, after we'd eaten vegetarian food and I'd allowed myself a couple of glasses of champagne, the time came for the first dance.

I hadn't really danced since I'd been ill. We'd practiced in our front room, shifting the table, standing on each other's feet.

We swayed in front of the crowd, trying to pretend we were alone. She was looking past me, at the wall. We jerked and bobbed, we shimmied.

As the dance continued, it became a race, a gallop. The song ended and she kissed me and ran straight off the stage.

The next song began. I could see her at the back of the crowd, laughing with some friends. I stayed at the front, bopping on my own, grin soldered to my face.

Fifteen

I am trying to remember the moment the badgers crawled into our lives. Our wedding was in 2013 and earlier in the year the government had announced a cull. I think I tried to be funny about it. First they came for the badgers but I did not complain because I was not a badger.

The cull was to deal with TB, the line went. The badgers were supposed to have been spreading the disease to cows. I remember Marie reading the paper, saying she didn't think a cull would work, but she didn't seem too exercised. After our wedding, they were back in the news again. I was at work answering the phone to people with lost cats, neighbours troubled by unhappy barks, and more and more I'd get calls about the cull.

It was good though, being married. Sometimes I'd think about the first dance but not for very long. I had carried on trying to write. Marie had been working on her script in her spare time. One day she said she was stuck with it, that she couldn't give it shape. And then it was badgers, just badgers.

'I've been thinking about the badger cull,' she said. 'I think we should do something about it.'

'Like what?' Go on a march, I expected. I couldn't see it happening. Marie was far too cleanly, far too *kempt* for marching. A couple of years before this there'd been Occupy. I'd let myself get excited, to my surprise. Every now and again I lapse into politics before invariably losing faith. Still, I was enthused. Marie had shrugged. I should be finishing my book. We'd argued. History had started again, I said. It was easy for her, with her Regent's Park parents and her *nice hair*, while out on the streets of London, battles were being fought.

I went down to the protest camp on my own. It smelt slightly of soup. I came home and forgot about it.

'I've been in touch with the anti-cull people,' she said. This was a surprise. I didn't even know there were such people already. 'The whole thing's up and running. They're looking for volunteers.'

I muttered something about my health. I didn't fancy patrolling the woods at night but Marie had always cared about animals. It was she who had chosen the cat.

The acting seemed to have been forgotten for a while. It always puzzled me how she never got far with that. She was beautiful, after all, but she never could quite lift off. Maybe she wasn't good at it. She'd been doing a lot of temping, wearing a trouser suit like a suit of armour. She told me she'd considered giving up acting altogether, that she was sick of the unreality, the unnaturalness of it. She needed, she said, something new in life, something authentic and real. She had started filling our little rooms with plants. Herbs and rubber plants, flowers, a bonsai tree. I liked them. They were calming, but I felt they were excessive. I was forever bumping into them.

The other thing: since my illness she'd been reading J. M. Coetzee. 'John can be a bit funny on some issues,' Frank had warned. 'Takes things a bit far.' But she fell for him, his ascetic complexity, the clearness of his gaze. She had cried over *Disgrace*. There was something *in there*, she said. Something odd and inexpressible, something around power and sex and truth and it was all mixed up in the way we handle animals. She reminded me of our day out at the zoo. I couldn't really follow her. She said the book chimed with her thoughts. There was something growing in her, something transforming. And now this obsession with badgers.

'Okay then,' I said. 'I suppose we can lend a hand.' I didn't know when I said it how much she'd resolved to do.

Sixteen

When I was a kid, visiting London, I would usually insist upon a trip to Paddington because of the glamour added by the eponymous bear. With adulthood the gold-leaf glow of ursine fame had passed and I knew that Paddington was pretty far from anywhere and hadn't got that much going for it. I don't think I'd ever been back. But on the first weekend in October, there I was again, this time with Marie, dashing, married, from the tube and into the station with fifteen minutes to spare before our train. We were never usually this early for anything but then, this was important. We were off to do something for the badgers.

'Oh look, there's photos,' I said. We were on the train, paper spread out on the table, water bottles and crisp packets nearby. 'Look. Badgers. In the magazine.' Two-tone faces with inquisitive button eyes, wide black noses sniffing for danger. Appealing beasts, I thought. You wouldn't want to kill them. Marie snatched the magazine from me and gazed at the photos, a rapturous look on her face. A look I hadn't seen for a while. Not since the honeymoon, I thought.

'Gorgeous, aren't they?' she said. I made an appropriate grunt. I didn't want to sound too enthusiastic. They were, after all, only badgers. I didn't dislike them – I wasn't a farmer or a psychopath – but I wasn't going to give them a round of applause. Marie furrowed her brow for a second, but obviously decided her energies should go elsewhere. She pulled out her phone and started firing off texts, making sure the hard-core badger crowd knew that we were coming.

It had been something to see, her transforming fervour for this cause. It was as though, she said, she'd accessed an intensity she'd never had before. She said she felt like Nietzsche on seeing that horse. She'd almost felt reluctance at the responsibilities ahead. But also this vast enthusiasm, the joy that comes from knowing your purpose is clear. She had realised, she said, that all of her previous passions were just hobbies, just means of filling the time. Animal rights was a revelation, an all-consuming goal. There was now a photograph of a badger above our bed. I bought her a stuffed badger toy. There were books about badgers on our shelves. She'd beleaguered the members of her extended family who'd had the temerity to vote Conservative. She had even started listening to the music of Queen, as their guitarist was against the cull. I was scared, to tell the truth. Something bigger than me had come along.

'I hope I don't lose my glasses,' I said. 'I mean, it's not like I can see brilliantly at the best of times. And it'll be dark. Take away the glasses and I'm not going to be much use.' I had adapted to my lack of eyesight, but not enough that new situations didn't bother me.

Marie sighed. I expect she felt I was subtracting from the dignity of the cause.

'It's true,' I said, as though she were suggesting it wasn't. 'I'm still not entirely well.'

'Okay,' she said, 'I suppose that makes it all the braver of you to come.' Satisfied with this formulation she pulled out a book, about badgers, and read with a transfixed smile. She had spent weeks liaising with a hodgepodge, sprawling collective of the animal-loving aggrieved. Environmentalists, post-scarcity-anarchists, sentimental shires-women and vegan townies. I couldn't get enthused. Still, at least I was dressed for our adventure. I wore a pork pie hat and a holey cardigan I thought made me look like an anarchist. I hoped anyone seeing me would assume I cared deeply about animal rights. I looked like a shambling bucolic scallywag, the sort of person who tries to sell you a boat in the local pub. It occurred to me that a really successful anarchist would probably not dress like an anarchist. But then, I wasn't really an anarchist.

I hoped we didn't get arrested. I really didn't want to get arrested.

We reached Newent at noon. There was an unseasonably bright, caressing sun, the summer of our wedding still clinging. It seemed a long time ago now, three months down the line. The first thing we saw when we'd ambled from the station was the sort of gift shop that normally gets called quaint. In the window were figurines of woodland creatures, a fox, a mole, a weasel and a beaver.

'A beaver,' said Marie. 'A fucking beaver. I've a good mind to go in.'

'Please do not go in.'

'They've definitely hidden the badger,' she said. 'When was the last time you saw a beaver in the woods? And weasels? Badgers are more popular than weasels. Nobody likes weasels.' She checked herself. '*I* like weasels. But I am committed to animal rights. Your average gift shop buyer isn't looking to buy a statue of a weasel. There is an agenda here.'

'We should probably head to the bed and breakfast, get some sleep.'

'I'm not going to complain,' she said. 'But that is because you are here.'

71

A police van cruised down the narrow street, followed by two more. The last one especially slowly, with the driver winding down the window to assess us, in case we'd been thinking of smashing up the shop. Which wasn't that far from the truth, I supposed. Still, it felt a bit much. This was West Gloucestershire not the West Bank. Maybe we were outlaws now. I really hoped we didn't get arrested.

'Should we tell the bed and breakfast why we're here?' We strolled down to the war memorial while Marie called us a cab. The number had been given to her by the badger folk and was guaranteed reliable.

'I don't know,' she said. 'Let's wait till we get there and suss out the vibe.' Suss out the vibe? She didn't normally say things like 'suss out the vibe'. This must be how anarchists talk. 'The driver's safe though.' I wished it wasn't too late for me to start smoking again.

I paced around the memorial while Marie read her book. The sky was incredibly blue for the time of year, a picture-book spotless blue. I worried, dutifully, about climate change. If only she'd been passionate about *that*. That was the sort of issue you could take seriously. My wife? She's an actress. My wife? Oh, she's the Lansdowne's daughter. My wife campaigns about climate change. You could tell people at parties that your wife cared about climate change and they wouldn't smirk at all. There was dignity in it. There was no dignity in badgers.

A 4x4 chugged close, a cab sign over the windscreen. Marie skipped over, smiling widely, ready to take charge. I remembered that, when I was a teenager in Lancashire, listening to Britpop in my room, she had been out in Essex, attending actual illegal raves. She was streetwise in the way that only very posh people can be. I sat in the front next to the driver while she sprawled in the back with our bags.

72

'Down for the weekend?' said the driver. He had burnt toast stubble and leaky tattoos and an air of some faint decay on him. Through the window there were curvy green fields with farmhouses dotted at the backs of them, as though they'd been dropped from the sky.

'We're here for the protest,' said Marie, in her crispest, North London-est voice. 'We're part of the Badger Patrol.'

'Ah,' said the driver, non-committal, thick wrists on the wheel. As long as he got his money it didn't matter what his cargo thought about badgers. 'Gets people riled up that one does.'

I glanced round at Marie and gave what I hoped was an encouraging smile. She was scratching the fingers of one hand with the other and I worried if this was one of her nervous tics, but her face didn't show any tension. Instead it showed fixity, calmness.

'Have you had a lot of people down?' she said. 'For the protests?'

'A few,' he said, 'from London. Couple of us locals involved too. Course I'm not really a local. Originally from Kent. Been driving these all over. Berlin, I was, for a while. Florida for a few years. Cardiff. I've seen the world. In the end, don't ask me why, but I felt myself missing England. I said, Mike, you better go home. Get yourself in the country, find a wife.'

'And did you?' said Marie. She had the knack of sounding interested in these people, like the Queen.

'Not yet,' said Mike. 'Not so many single women in the sticks. Lot of the lads round here, they go for those Thai girls. Second wives. Save their cash all year then go and find a bride. All the pubs round here have Thai curry now. You see all these kids with old dads and Thai mothers. I'd do it myself but I couldn't stand the lemongrass. No, I've got a woman in the village. She's got these cold hands, though, I always say to her, you need to get some gloves. Even in summer the cold. You two married then?' I smiled and told him we were. It was interesting, being married. It felt sexier, more adult, than I'd expected. Sexy like a seventies colour supplement. My wife will have the salad. Thank you, my wife won't require a wake-up call. No, my wife does not take sugar in her coffee.

I never did this. I never ordered her stuff.

'Good on you,' said Mike. 'A lot of the young folk don't, do they? Well, apart from the gay lads. Keeping it all going. You do right, marrying young. Horrible, missing your time.' We rode on, feeling married, feeling that all these adventures were worth their while. That's how I was feeling. My wife will have the dessert. I'm afraid my wife was rather disappointed with the quality of the napkins. Oh, there was a power in it. Tradition and ownership and other things I didn't believe in.

The cab turned into a gravelled driveway with a thatched and gabled guesthouse at the end. A sign on the lawn read 'The Grange'. There didn't seem to be a main entrance. Going down a path to the right we found a side door which led us into a shadowy bar-cum-slouching space, empty apart from a dozing and lumpy black cat and two collie retrievers, both of whom recognised Marie as a Friend to the Animal World and pounced on her in a joyous wriggling scrum. She jumped onto a leather sofa, laughing as the two dogs rolled and writhed all over her. I smiled at this, her capacity for love. Even a dog could recognise it. Neither of them glanced at me.

I sat on a stiff-backed wing chair and leafed through the magazine. It fell open upon the badgers. I wondered if we'd see any. I hoped that if we did they wouldn't be dying or dead. Actually, I thought it would be nice just to spend the weekend here. They had at least one decent ale. Probably okay food. It would be romantic, sort of, another honeymoon. Of course, getting shot at by Tories was pretty romantic too.

A middle-aged woman, with skin as brown and polished as the table-tops, strolled through and said hello. Marie shook off the collies and went over and within minutes they were happily chatting. About, of course, the animals. People warmed to Marie. Some quality she had. I hoped she wouldn't mention the badgers. I was happy to get through this weekend without upsetting anyone. Marie took the keys and marched back to me, a smile upon her face.

Our room was high-ceilinged and draughty and for some reason we had been given two single beds. I hooked my shoes off and stared in the mirror. Twin satchels under each eye, my lips starting to chap with approaching autumn. A married man. 'You look nice,' Marie said. 'You look actually sort of rustic.'

'I'm wearing Gap jeans,' I said. 'Will the anarchists object?'

'I don't think we'll meet any anarchists.' She lay on one of the beds, hands under her head, face tilted to the roof. 'We're not going to run into any of the hard-core sabs.'

Hard-core sabs. Now what would they be like? I hoped that she was right. I already felt like the most timid and vacillating liberal. They'd detect my urge for compromise. Still, at least sabs didn't have guns. I was going to spend the whole night getting in the way of men with guns. I hoped that the badgers appreciated it. I wasn't sure they would. One set of noisy lumberers would aggrieve them as much as another, I felt, regardless of intentions.

'Come to bed,' I said, patting the duvet. It had been, how long, more than a week since we'd had sex. She was busy with the badgers and I hadn't always been well. Now seemed a good time to make up for this. I patted the duvet again and undid my trouser button in a way I hoped was seductive. It might have looked more like I'd just finished a hefty meal. She looked at me as though I'd suggested playing leapfrog.

'Not now Stuart. Not with all this. It feels indecent. When this is going on. I'm maybe too caught up in it.'

'It's supposed to feel indecent,' I said. 'And it's been a while, you know. Badgers do it, don't they? Nature and all that. I bet they have a right old time.'

'They're too scared to do anything,' she said. 'That's the problem. I told you this. All those hunters marching around. They'll be too scared to mate.'

'It doesn't mean we shouldn't.'

'Get some sleep,' she said. 'There's a long night ahead of us. Please, can you do that for me, try and get some sleep?'

I closed my eyes and dribbled and dreamt about badgers and guns.

By the time we got the cab back down to Newent, the mood and the day had darkened. I felt as though everyone knew exactly why we were there. Teenagers, acne bumps on close-shaved necks, gobbed outside corner shops cider-less, resentful of the interlopers who had brought the police to the village. Patrol cars parked on every street, with watchful officers scoffing sandwiches. Troupes of shirt-sleeved boozers muttered as we passed. We ducked into a DIY shop and bought two heavy black torches.

'You could kill a badger with these things,' I said.

'Please don't talk about killing them,' said Marie. Her body gave one large twitch, as though she'd just had a mild electric shock.

76

'Would you do it, if you had to, though? You know, if it was ill? Or if it came down to you or the badger?'

'Please shut up.'

'I reckon I could do it. If it was injured, I mean. I hope that I don't have to.'

'You almost certainly won't. You're supposed to call a vet, not ... Just stop. Please.'

I put my hands in my pockets.

We went into a pub, the Rose and Crown. Honeysuckle on the walls, a swinging hand-painted sign, an A4 poster in multiple ugly fonts, advertising Dave 'Elvis' Fenton's upcoming gig. I was nervous, I admit. I thought the place would be full of farmhands, drunk on the blood of mammals, ready to show practical opposition to any drippy, squeamish urbanites they saw. It wasn't quite that bad. They seemed ruddier variants on your typical pub-dwelling Bloke. I sensed hostility all the same. The barmaid was a teenage girl, who I thought would be sensibly unconcerned with rural politics, but might, for all I knew, be courting some badger-slaying lunk.

'Glass of Pinot ... Glass of the house white and a pint of the—' I pointed at the beer, certain that I would not be able to convincingly say its name.

'Pint of Licky Miller,' she said. 'Any food for you?'

'Scampi and chips,' I said, 'and ...?' Marie was frowning in a new way she had developed. It was a frown, I felt, of conscience.

'They haven't anything veggie.'

'There's scampi. They've got fish and chips.'

'Fish aren't some kind of moving underwater lettuce, you know. Cod isn't an aquatic cabbage.'

'They're not really animals. They haven't any fur.'

'I think I should go vegan.'

'We'll come back to order food.' Picking up the drinks

I lolloped across the pub to an empty table, praying no one had heard. We sat down, Marie glancing distastefully at the menu, her blue eyes showing the saintly spiritual fervour they seemed to have gained of late. Martyr's peepers, sorrowful yet patient. Princess Di on Panorama.

'Veganism now? When did this happen?'

'It's something I've been thinking of a lot. I mean, the dairy industry is pretty much sponsoring this cull.'

'It's ethically consistent. It is. But I like cooking for us. I like cooking for you. And I like cooking with cheese. Sometimes milk. Cream, there is. Butter too. Eggs. Eggs are important.'

'All those calves they have to slaughter.'

'Don't talk so loud about that.'

'Why shouldn't I? Do you think the civil rights movement were scared of upsetting people? Anyway no one cares. I wish they did.'

'They probably care about their sick cows.' An unhappy silence came over us. I felt she sensed I didn't care. Well I did care. I just cared more about her.

'Are you really thinking of going,' I mouthed the word, 'vegan?'

'I really think I have to.'

'Okay,' I said. 'Okay. I'm going to say something that might irritate you now.'

'You could just not. You could just not say it.'

'I am going to say something.'

'Really, I think you might want to consider not saying anything.'

'I am going to.'

'I probably know what it is. Anyway.'

'In which case you will be able to temper your annoyance. And prepare yourself.'

78

'If what you say is what I think it is then I will still be annoyed.'

'I am going to say it all the same.'

'Okay.'

'Do you think this might be an eating disorder? Only you maybe have lost weight.'

'That is what I thought you would say.'

'Are you annoyed?'

'I am very annoyed.'

'Am I possibly right?'

'You are not right. You are saying that a choice, a choice I have thought about, is actually a sign I'm not well. You are like those doctors in the Soviet Union who said dissenters were all mad.'

'I don't think I am exactly like that.'

'You are saying my rational choice is an illness. You are saying the decision to eat ethically must be because I am psychologically unwell.'

'I like cooking for us. This will make it harder and harder to do that.'

'So your concern is that this will impact on you? That is what you are worried about.'

'No. No. That's not what I meant at all.'

'It's actually controlling, this side of you. Wanting to cook everything, wanting to make sure I eat what you want. It's a very controlling side of you.'

'I don't think I am in control of anything, least of all you. I'm going to the loo. Buy some crisps or something, come on.'

'You're doing it again.'

'Sorry.'

'Because without the nutritional value of a packet of fucking Wotsits I might starve?'

'I'm going to the bathroom now.' I made my way

through the crowded pub, wishing I'd dressed a bit less like an anarchist. Eyes trailed my clumsy zigzag across the room. I wondered why we kept arguing so much. There'd been a time we never had. Badgers were causing a rupture. In the narrow urinal I tried my best to go, expecting, at any moment, to be coshed. There were two posters on the wall. One advertised condoms and showed a surprised looking young woman holding a piece of fruit. The other said that the local primary school were soon to perform the *Joe Meek Story*.

I stepped from the bathroom and straight into an oncoming local. He bounced back, wobbling on his heels and for a second there was a moment when, united in fascination, we watched the lager rise over the rim of his glass, arc, glinting, through the air and land down the front of his shirt.

'I can't see,' I said quickly. To illustrate this I pointed at my right eye. It was crucial I get this key fact across before he hit me, like a politician doing a hostile interview. 'I'm partially ... I'm blind. In one eye.' A necessary exaggeration. His arm, which had been raised ready to strike me, dropped to his side. He seemed disappointed, robbed of a chance for aggro.

'You going to buy me another?' He said this as if I might try and weasel out of it in the same way I'd dodged a beating, perhaps pulling out a certificate to say that spending money made me ill. I told him of course I would, asked him what he had been drinking, apologised about seven times and turned to the bar.

'I haven't got any cash,' I said. The drenched local and the barmaid looked at me with something short of pity. 'If you hold on I can ask my wife.'

'You knock over my drink then you go crawling to your wife to pay for it,' said the local. His tee shirt, which was mostly cream-coloured, now had a central island of yellow between the nipples.

'I'm not crawling,' I said. I made sure I stood up straight.

'Just leave it,' said the local. 'It's fine.'

'I really am par ... I really am blind. On the right side. And it's kind of the pub's fault they don't take cards. If they took cards I could have got you one by now.'

'You blaming me now?' said the barmaid. Various drinkers looked up, foggy eyes snapping into murderous clarity. I explained that I blamed no one but myself.

'What was all that about?' said Marie. The anger had gone from her voice, replaced by a strived-for patience.

'Nothing. You know, your drink probably has rennet in it. It actually probably has.'

The scampi was already going cold, shrivelling, dead on the plate. In half an hour we were due to meet the Badger Patrol. Marie held onto her wine, not looking at me. I thought about reminding her of the time she had saved my life, sent me to the opticians, but I didn't see any point. She had other lives now to save.

Seventeen

'Right so, what you do,' the optician said, 'is when I turn the lights down you should see these little red dots crossing the screen. Just these little red dots. And when you see one of these little red dots what you do is you press the buzzer. Simple as that.' He seemed to enjoy saying 'little red dots'.

It was the day after Marie had told me to get a second opinion, so I had gone down the road to do that. I sat with my chin on a plastic rest and my face enclosed by a hollow half-oval device, the creamy beige colour of vintage computer equipment. The optician turned a dial and the view before me dimmed. Everything was black until across the sky a red dot zoomed, a pinpoint crimson will-o'-the-wisp. I pressed the buzzer and the red dot disappeared. This was easy. I would shoot down as many of these dots as I could manage. I was a guard, a sentinel, standing lonely watch across a galaxy. I was protecting my universe from attack. Buzz. Buzz. Buzz.

'Don't buzz unless you see one though,' said the optician. I told him I thought I had seen one. The game went on for a further ten minutes. My neck began to ache. The plastic rest began to irritate my chin. I zapped as many of the red dots as I could. The optician told me I could stop buzzing and went to examine my score. It began to feel very important I pass the test. I put my glasses back on and waited for him to return. When he did, he was stroking the hanging black fronds of his beard and had a nervous look on his face, as though he thought I'd be cross.

'Well, one thing to say, your glasses are the wrong prescription. You didn't get them from here, did you?'

I admitted I'd bought them elsewhere.

'Wrong prescription, mate. You been messed with. Thing is though, that only accounts for some of the loss of sight. You're still missing a fair bit of vision from the right side and new glasses won't alter that. You might need to go and talk to your GP.'

'Are you eating enough vitamin D?' my GP said. He looked over his spectacles, as though he were scouring me for traces of the stuff. While he spoke, he scribbled into a squared school exercise book.

I told him I didn't know how much vitamin D I ate and that I had lost a lot of my sight.

'People in this country, they don't get enough vitamin D. Not enough sunlight, everyone sitting at their desks. Right now, we are having a serious push on vitamin D. Lack of it can cause multiple sclerosis, all manner of ailments. Breakfast, is what you need for this. A cooked breakfast, outdoors, with eggs and mushrooms and sunlight. Problem is,' he continued, 'we are talking very great quantities of mushrooms. Enormous volumes of egg. There would be health problems just from eating this many breakfasts in one day. And in this country everyone skips breakfast. They skip breakfast so they can sit at their desks out of the sun.' He shook his head at the folly of our land, our work ethic and aversion to daylight.

'You think I have multiple sclerosis?' This seemed something to worry about.

'No. Did I say you had multiple sclerosis?'

'No. You did not say that.'

'Listen, you say you have gone blind.'

'I do.'

'I'm not an eye specialist. You want to go to an optician.'

'I did go to an optician. They sent me here.'

'You need to go to Moorfields.' He tutted, scribbled extra hard and waved me to the door.

'Mind where you're fucking well going.' The man did not wear dark glasses. His eyes were like a broken doll's, with pupils adrift, off-kilter. He had a mysteriously orderly even-haired beard, so that I wondered how he kept it trim. Perhaps he had someone to do it for him. 'Can't you see I'm blind?'

'I'm very sorry,' I said. 'Only I think I might be a bit blind too. That's why I've come here.' I reached out to put a reassuring hand on his shoulder, but thought better of it. I didn't want to miss and stroke his chin.

'You too?' he said. 'Makes sense I suppose. I'll let you off, this once. Here, do you think they'll sort it out for you?'

'I hope so,' I said. 'It's all a bit new and upsetting.'

'I'll tell you what,' he said. 'I hope for your sake they do. Because you'll not enjoy it one bit, being blind. I'd go so far as to say being blind is really fucking awful.' He went off, with his stick in front of him, tapping as though he were looking for precious stones. I didn't get the chance to ask him about his beard.

They took me down to a chilly basement and into the MRI room. I had to put my glasses in the sort of plastic tray you get at airport security. They made me lie down and gave me earmuffs. I was shunted into a thick metal tube. It was a bit like being a lipstick.

The earmuffs were supposed to drown out the churning industrial racket an MRI scanner makes and partly succeeded in doing so. It was still incredibly loud.

After a while I started to relish the thud and drone of machinery. It was kind of like listening to krautrock. I became attuned to hidden patterns, oblique rhythms. At the back of the racket, I could make out celestial choirs. Sweet voices lifting in harmony. I wondered if I was dying. The voices were raised up in song to a higher being, ascending in praise while the machines cranked on behind.

The mechanical whirring stopped. The singing continued. 'I used to love TLC when I was a kid,' said one of the doctors. 'I used to try and wear an eyepatch to school. Oh sorry, I shouldn't have said that.' She told me I should go upstairs to the waiting room.

Eighteen

'Marie. It's me, I'm at Moorfields. Yeah, that's right, the eye place. Are you sitting down? You're doing yoga. That doesn't tell me if you're seated. I've something bad to tell you. Yeah, I know. Sorry. It turns out there's a blood clot on my brain. Quite a big one. The size of a golf ball, they said. I always thought of golf balls as small before today. What happened is I had a haemorrhage, a bleed, and they say it's formed this clot. They say if this one goes off it really won't be good. I might die, is what they are saying. I'm apparently at risk of another bleed. They are all being nice. But that is sort of the least I would hope for. Can you come down?' Come down in case I die.

There is always a strange sort of fun in giving bad news. Like schadenfreude, if you could have schadenfreude against yourself. But it wasn't all that much fun knowing my body was trying to kill me.

I'd often enjoyed being alone. Seclusion, *down-time*, it's good for you. Except not like this. Not when your body is your enemy. A clot, swollen like a well-fed leech, sat inside my brain. Bumping with each throb of blood against vital neurons, clusters of myself. The bleed seemed to have squashed a bit of my visual cortex, lessening my sight. What might another bleed do, if they didn't stop it in time? A pop and that could be language gone. A tiny bit more blood, swelling through my veins, and maybe I wouldn't love Marie any more. Maybe I wouldn't love anyone. Which part of the brain dealt with love? I was alone and there was something in my head that wanted me killed. Alone was overrated. I sat on the plastic seat and waited for Marie.

She was with me in an hour, rushing through the waiting room, her face charged with tired elation. She was heavy with overnight things. There was a pause while we worked out whether it was safe for us to hug. I hadn't been given advice on this. As a compromise, I put my arms around her while holding my head at an angle. 'I love you,' I said. 'I love you so much.'

'I love you, Stuart,' she said.

'They want me to go to the brain hospital. In Bloomsbury, Queen Anne Square. They said we could wait for an ambulance.' Everything was out of my hands. It didn't feel too bad. I felt carried, taken care of. 'It's almost funny when they tell you, they put on this sort of bad news face. Impassive.'

'Right. Right. You seem to be enjoying this.'

'I'm not enjoying this.'

We sat and we held on to one another and we waited for the ambulance. As long as we kept on holding, I wasn't about to die. The waiting room emptied. Eventually we realised the ambulance wouldn't arrive and Marie led me out into the street to hail a cab.

'I actually feel okay,' I said, as the cab pushed through the night. Marie's lips tightened. Fending off tears, I think. 'It's all out of my hands now, isn't it? And it explains so much. You remember how difficult I've been this last few months? Maybe even longer.' I'd had them for a while now, sudden losses of temper, animal spasms of rage. It wasn't at all like me. Now I had an explanation.

'Yes,' said Marie. 'Yes I do. I do remember that.'

'Oh god, Marie, I'm sorry I've been difficult. But that was obviously my brain. If you think about it. The pressure that must be in there. It's amazing, really, that something so physical can get translated into all these complicated feelings and thoughts you see as disembodied.'

'Don't get overexcited Stuart, please.'

'This hospital, it's supposed to be really good, isn't it? Like, the very best of its kind? One of the best in the world? I'm definitely not going to die, Marie.' Saying this would make it true. 'And if I do, which I won't, I've had a very full life. I've still not finished a novel. That's a shame. But I've had lots of . . . I've had you. That's important. A full life.'

'Can you drive a little quicker please? No, not as fast as that. You'll jolt him. He really mustn't be jolted.' We travelled on, each bump making me shudder, as I clutched onto her wrist. My thumb against her pulse, touching her life.

They had me in orange pyjamas, the sort they use for Guantanamo inmates, Daesh decapitees, prisoners on death row. For reasons nobody told me I had been placed under a ban on fluids, and my headache had come right back. Every so often a nurse would pop through the curtains and take my pulse. There were groans and snores from the neighbouring beds. Marie had stayed until the nurses told her to leave. Now I was alone. Towards dawn one of the patients started singing, a doleful chain-gang hymn. Someone yelled at him to shut up. There were murmurs of agreement round the room.

Nineteen

I woke up to a clean bright ward with a 1950s atmosphere of spick and span. The platonic ideal of the NHS that we carry inside us, all lipstick and bedpans. While I'd been asleep the water veto had been rescinded and there was a cup and a scratched plastic jug on my bedside table. I poured some and gulped it down. My head had settled into the sort of pain you get when you bruise your knee. It was specific, located at the back of my head, an angry dullness. A nurse came and gave me a paracetamol in another cardboard gourd. I was starting to develop respect for paracetamol.

'You new then?' said the man in the next bed. His voice sounded thickened by expensive booze, the tone of a dissolute prefect addressing a young grub.

'Got a blood clot on my brain,' I said. It was hard not to feel a bit proud.

'At your age too,' said the man. He sounded impressed. 'I'm here because of a stroke.'

'Me too, maybe, I think. I don't really know all the terms.'

'Did yours hurt? Mine didn't hurt. Lucky. I didn't even know I'd had one. Reason I'm here is I started talking in binary opposites.'

'Binary opposites?'

'No, binary opposites. Was doing it for weeks. If the cat got on the sofa, something which is inevitable in a house like mine, I'd try to say to people, the cat is on the sofa, just making conversation. Observational humour, sort of thing. But instead I'd say the dog is on the bed. And no one understood what I was getting at, our dog, Cassandra, having long since passed away.'

I wondered if a sofa was really the binary opposite of a bed.

'Come quick my dear, I'd call out, the dog is on the bed. And this alarmed my wife because, our dog having popped her clogs some years before, the sheets would have been in a right state. And I wouldn't say darling, I'd say Chris, Chris being my brother's name.'

'And he's the opposite of your wife?'

'I suppose she is. Chris is my sister. Did I just do it again?'

I told him that he had. He smiled the self-forgiving smile of a drunk remembering last night's debauch.

'Well I won't be doing it at all soon. Going to have my operation today.'

'You mean tomorrow.'

'No, I mean today. I wasn't doing it then. It comes and goes. Periodically.' He retreated into offended silence. A nurse came and deposited fun-size packs of cereal and slices of cooling toast. The ward filled with the sounds of happy chewing.

'You seem a bright young man,' said my neighbour. 'Assuming we both get through this, I might be able to help you out with a thing or two.'

I asked him what sort of thing.

'Russia!' the man said. He pointed a thick-veined hand at the window, conjuring visions of samovars and Cossacks. 'Tourism therein. Travel guides is my business.

You'd enjoy it, clever lad like you. Sleeper trains and frostbite and women in fur coats.'

'I think I would enjoy that.'

'I'm certain that you would,' said my neighbour. 'Tell you what. I'll give you my card, when I'm back from the op. Tomorrow.'

'You mean today.'

'Ah. Nothing gets past you. Eh?' He punched the air in lieu of punching my face and immediately fell asleep. Before I had time to dream of the icy steppes, I saw Marie hurrying across the ward. My face near split with grinning. It was wonderful to see her, to be reminded there was life outside this place.

'Stu. My god, I'm shattered, I didn't sleep a wink,' she said. 'Well I did, but on the sofa. I was messaging all your friends, telling them the news. Lots of dramatic responses. And after, I just dropped.' I hugged her as hard as I could. 'Malkin doesn't help. He keeps running to the door and scratching, like he thinks you're coming home. I swear he does it on purpose.' Manipulative animals, cats. 'It almost seems not real. You don't even look ill. I probably look more ill than you do. I brought you your laptop and some books.'

'I love you,' I said. It was wonderful having her there. None of the other brain cases had someone beautiful to visit them. It was the one advantage to falling sick at a young age. I thought about my funeral, about the girls in their black dresses, weeping for what was, what might have been. It would be a shame to miss a funeral like that.

Doctors came and went. There were scans and interrogations. I had to push on nurses' hands a lot, to show I had some strength or could follow simple instructions. I was taken, in a wheelchair, for a scan. Marie took a picture. I looked like the last, suppressed photo of Lenin,

91

a confused and stricken otter in a shawl. Later, they told me, in a measured way, exactly what had happened. I was suffering – they did not say suffering – from an arteriovascular malformation in my brain. This meant certain veins in my brain's left hemisphere had become tangled and filled with blood. This had caused a near-fatal stroke or haemorrhage which had impacted on my visual cortex, causing, they said, a sight deficit. The peripheral vision on the right side of both eyes had gone away, with my right eye the more affected. They always used this language of deficits, as though the economic lingo would make my illness sexier. The blood clot was a sign my brain was gearing up for a second haemorrhage, one that might prove fatal. The best that I could hope for was it would leave me entirely blind.

The good news was that I had come to the right place. The bad news, or some of it, was that they would need to operate as soon as possible. An operation would save my life and while it wouldn't restore my sight it would prevent it from getting worse.

Over the days a stream of visitors arrived, while Marie sat, patient, knitting to task her hands. My parents came down from Lancashire, grave and fretful, suddenly aged, pestering the doctors for news about my sight. When I told them it was probably damaged for good, my mum tutted as though I should make more of an effort. My dad had a stern and tired look and asked me a lot about the food and the quality of the pillows. 'I knew something like this would happen with you living in London,' said my mum. How drawn her face was, how the worry creased her flesh.

Various friends of Marie's and mine arrived. A nervous pack of colleagues from Pet Concern, dressed up for that night's office Christmas do, wondering if I'd make it to work next year. I enjoyed it, holding court. I was an emperor so powerful that I needn't get out of bed. Rupa from work came down and told Marie not to make too much of a fuss of me. 'He's got the nurses for that. Make sure you get some rest.' My old university friend Alistair, who Marie had adopted lately, as she tended to do with anyone who seemed a bit lost, came and told us of his marital woes. He was through with Lucy for good this time. He'd been working hard to save things but his patience had run out. What's more she was seeing some bloke.

We said nothing about her recent visit. She hadn't mentioned a bloke. Poor Alistair, he looked exhausted. His eyes seemed to be retreating into his skull and he kept on tapping his knuckles with the fingers of his other hand. His upsets had dislodged him, sent him spinning. He'd always been blessed with a preternatural confidence and it was odd, painful, seeing him stymied like this.

'So what you going to do?'

Alistair pressed his fingers against his scalp, unsure even of his words. 'I don't know,' he said. 'I married her. Divorce seems so enormous. Marriage seemed massive enough.' The Alistair I'd known in halls had been the first public school boy I'd ever met and back then his assurance and ready expectation that life would go to plan had seemed both bizarre and faintly contagious. He wasn't supposed to lose his grip on things, just as I wasn't supposed to be ill, not at this age.

'Don't worry about the noise,' said the man in the next bed. 'Reminds me of the pub.' When Alistair had left us, Rupa rolled her eyes. 'I suppose I should be more forgiving,' she said. 'But honestly what a baby. You can tell why she walked out.' I told her Alistair was all right, that she should show some more compassion. I chuckled as I said it, agreeing with her.

Every time I dozed off a new sightseer would come. Just before the ward's early closing, Marie's parents arrived. I was glad that my own parents had gone back to their hotel. Somehow whenever they interacted with Marie's, they would transform from small-town liberals into nervous stage rustics. Or they'd start describing things as 'common', not realising that snobbery was frowned upon in literary circles. As for the Lansdownes, they'd take on an almost reptilian glamour. So it was best they not interact.

'Stuart, Stuart, oh you've got one of those *tubes*. I hope they know what they're doing here. There's a very nice doctor we spoke to on our way in, he said you were behaving yourself. I said that settles it, he's definitely not well.' This was Judy. I liked Judy a lot. She'd had, back in the eighties, a reputation for fierceness among the smitten novelists ('rather like a swan – all very charming until your arm gets broken' according to one wounded magic realist) but nowadays it didn't show.

'We've both been extremely worried about you, Stuart,' said Frank. As always, he had the look of just having thought of a good but unsayable joke. He tweaked at his scarf, or one of them, for his scarves were legion, but he stayed a step back from the bed, a likeably corrupt pontiff offering his blessings.

'Marie, how are you, dear? You look so tired, darling, are you getting enough sleep?'

'I have to say Stuart, you're lucky you aren't dead. Called up a surgeon friend this afternoon and he said people with your problem normally don't get this far. Small consolation if you die, but at least you've dragged yourself past the post. I'd say that counts as a very real achievement.'

'Don't joke darling, please, this isn't a joking situation.'

94

'He's not going to die, Frank.' I was living with a woman who called her father by his first name. This never failed to excite me.

'You, uh, you knitting there, Marie?'

'Keeps me busy,' she said. 'A scarf.'

'Thought it might be a shroud.' He looked us over, waiting for the laugh to show he hadn't gone too far. I supplied it, to oblige. He handed over a hardback wrapped in brown paper and wandered off for a cigarette in the cold. Not stopping smoking was a part of his mystique. I wondered if he enjoyed it. The book was one of his.

I lay back as I had done for all my visitors and tried hard to think of something wise. Serenity, a wider look at things. It could even be something trite. But there was nothing but worry and soreness and, once they were gone, there was fear. I was alone, once more, and scared and the back of my head was pulsing, pulsing, reminding me it was there. I was ten years old again, lying in bed and the noise from downstairs, the telly, the chatter, had suddenly died out leaving only the loudness of silence, the awful realisation there was nobody there but me. When I ran downstairs they were out in the garden, enjoying a summer night, but there was that moment, just that moment, of frightened solitude.

I think that was the first time I ever felt alone.

Twenty

A doctor came and sat upon my bed. He told us his name was Hilary Edelman. He was middle-aged, thick-haired, with a reddish tinge to his skin as though he'd been lightly dusted with cochineal. He seemed to be very excited about being a doctor. It must be an exciting job. While he explained how he would cure me, he bounced up and down on the mattress with communicative glee. 'What we're going to do first,' he said, bouncing, 'is flush your veins with a sort of dye substance so we can have a good look, see what we're doing. We'll only need a local anaesthetic for that. Then, hopefully today, we can block off the damage with glue, which should isolate it, stop it spreading. That'll be with a full anaesthetic.'

'Excuse me,' I said. 'Would you be able to keep still a bit? When you bounce it hurts my head.'

'I wasn't aware I was bouncing.'

'He wasn't really bouncing, Stuart.'

'You were bouncing a bit.'

'Are you sure? I don't think I was. Now, there's no reason for us to physically enter your skull as we can enter it through a vein in your crotch that's connected right to the brain.' He paused as though expecting one of us to try and say something funny. When neither of us did he coughed and carried on. 'Now obviously there will be forms to sign. The nurses will be able to explain risk and so forth. I should say if you don't agree to the procedure the chances of a second bleed are about 100 per cent.'

'You're still bouncing.'

'Stuart.'

'Ah, a reader I see.' He bounced hard at the sight of the small tower of paperbacks on my bedside table. 'You, ah, a fan of Ian McEwan at all?'

'I like his early weird stuff.'

'Stuart,' said Marie, 'don't lie, you loved *Atonement*.'

'I was the model for the neurologist in *Saturday*,' he said. 'Ian – I call him Ian – followed me around for a few months, watching, taking notes. There's an awful lot of me inside that book.'

'I didn't actually like that one.'

'I thought it was a superlative novel. Professional and personal interest no doubt. I expect I've got it all wrong.' With a last, wounded bounce, he was off along the ward.

'I don't think you should have said that,' said Marie. 'He is doing your operation after all.'

'I don't think he'll get revenge and leave me brain damaged just cos I didn't like *Saturday*.' But I worried that he might. I looked across at the next bed but the binary man had been taken for his operation and wasn't there.

Later I realised that he wasn't coming back.

The room next to the operating theatre was close to freezing cold. I'd waved goodbye to Mum, Dad and Marie as the porters wheeled me down. I tilted my head as much as possible so I could see her as I left. Poor Marie. She looked like she hadn't slept in a week and I was pretty sure I looked worse. But at least it was all happening to me. I wasn't just a bystander. They pushed the bed into a giant, slow-moving lift and we trundled down to the basement. I tried hard not to feel scared. This was only the dye job after all. The gluing would come later. That was when I should be scared. Still, I knew there was a chance, even this time, that my brain would panic at the invasion, that I would pass out and wake up altogether blind or not wake up at all. I lay in the adjunct to the theatre, shivering under the bedclothes, waiting to be seen. After a while, two more porters in green overalls showed up and steered me into the theatre. There were screens and bright lights and a bustle of jovial staff. It was as though I were about to take part in a friendly but quasi-criminal fashion shoot. Everyone seemed to want to be very jaunty. I considered begging them for full anaesthetic. There was no sign of Dr Edelman. Maybe he was directing from somewhere up in the wings. My glasses were taken away. Someone lifted up my gown and started shaving my pubic hair. When they'd created a little rectangle of bare skin they applied a tingly paste to it. Unmanned is the word I'd use.

'I should tell you,' I said, 'I don't like needles. They make me go sort of funny.'

'You'll be fine,' said a blurred shape in front of me. There was a sharp pain in my groin. My head filled up with blackness.

'You fainted,' said the blur. 'Quickly, lower his head.' Somewhere in the wash of mingled colours, a small hand felt for mine. I gripped it far too tight. Whoever it belonged to didn't complain, but told me, in a gentle voice, that I would be okay. 'Lift the legs, get his blood back.' My body was something people did things to. Something sexless, passive. Another needle entered me and I tightened my grip on the hand.

'You're going to have to let go now Stuart,' the voice said. 'I have to go and work the machine.' There was warmness coursing through me, the dye running along my veins.

Back on the ward there were fretful mother sounds and reassuring Marie sounds and my father's burring breaths. I was swaddled in sleepiness. When I'd got back I'd burbled at them about the kind handholding nurse and how she was actually some kind of top level neuroscientist, *pretending to be a nurse*. After this, I slept. When I woke up my parents had gone and I was alone with Marie. And I realised something.

I was going to die. You know it, when it comes. Death knowledge, I had it. If they did the second operation that afternoon, as they planned to, I would die under the anaesthetic. A space outside life had been cleared for me. Marie locked her hand in mine and I had time to try and register the detail of it, its size, the damp pillows of her palms, the feel of her fingers between my own. I rubbed my thumb against her wrist until she raised my hand and squashed it to her lips. I didn't know whether to tell her what I knew, if I ought to be saying goodbye. I was in the ante-room to death.

Around the ward, people snored or moaned or stared at the TV. The bald old black guy in the furthest bed sat up in his orange pyjamas and crooned to himself as though he didn't think we could hear. At the end of the ward near to the nurses' bay was a boy a bit younger than me, his head wrapped up in bandage. He was riddled with catheter wires pumping his body with whatever it needed to keep a semblance of life. When I'd been sleeping, Marie had gone over to chat to the boy's mother, offer some scraps of sympathy. But the boy was still going to die. We were all of us going to, but my death would be soon.

I didn't want to die. I wanted so fiercely to live.

Twenty-One

'Stuart? Stuart?' I opened my eyes to see Dr Edelman again, his rump seconds from my bed. He landed, catapulting me into wakefulness. 'Afraid we've got some rather frustrating news for you.' Rocking the mattress with his buttocks, he explained there would be a delay. The embolisation would have to wait until morning. He apologised a great deal for this. He was obsequious, attentive. He was bouncy. Any huffiness about my not liking his fictional alter ego had vanished. He hoped I would forgive him the inconvenience. Rest assured that if anything happened in the meantime I was very much in the right place. With a final, flamboyant, bounce, he sprang off the bed and away. A nurse came to take my water jug and put up a nil-by-mouth sign. I rested my head on the pillow.

'He isn't the doctor from *Saturday*, you know,' said Marie. 'Frank looked in the acknowledgements. It was another doctor from here. It's actually kind of weird that he would say that, don't you think?'

I laughed. I laughed until a strange sound left me, laughter from a part of me I didn't know existed.

I woke up. I woke up and this meant that the operation was over. Which meant I was alive.

I didn't have my glasses but, as far as I could make out, my eyesight was unchanged.

100

The operation was over. I was alive. I lay there in the recovery room and slowly I came to. The radio was playing Christmas songs. It was the day before Christmas Eve and this fact was so ridiculous, and yet so very good, that I laughed from my parched bruised throat. I was euphoric. I felt life had been gifted. I felt as though I'd been awarded a toddlerish receptivity, an awareness of life's grain. There was a sense, what with coming so close to death before dodging him, racing away, that I was almost getting younger. Getting, at any rate, *further away from death*.

My mum crying, while Marie comforted her. My dad having to go outside for a bit, for tears rather than a fag. I loved them all so much. I had been wrong to be so prickly about my parents in the past. And poor Marie, and all she'd been through. My friends and my family and most of all Marie. I was going nowhere. I was staying here, just for them. I giggled until I hurt. I was alive and I loved them and I knew that I always would.

Later that afternoon, Dr Edelman came back. Things hadn't gone quite to plan. I was totally safe, for now. But there was still a risk, a slight risk, that I would have another bleed. Not immediately. Possibly not at all. But as time went on the likelihood would increase. I would need another op in about a year. They'd be in touch to arrange it. Until then, I was not to worry. I should try my best to live well. Not so very much alcohol. No smoking at all. Try not to undergo anything too stressful. Really, I mustn't worry.

I laughed at the idea of worrying. I was alive. I was alive! It was as though I'd been given a fresh set of antennae to make up for my lack of sight and when I got home they noticed everything. The watery taste of the coldness in the air, the grease that rose in steam from our

101

hissing pans to slick over our kitchen tiles, the faint smell of drying dribble on my pillow after a morning's sleep. I would lie on our bed, chuckling and cooing to myself, while Malkin sat on my chest and I would register the patterned swirls of colour in his fur, the sandy underside of his chin, the terracotta of his nose, the feel of his pink belly warm against me.

I was alive. My head felt as though it were vibrating, a struck gong, but even this didn't feel bad. Marie had put up photos of our second date around the bed, the two of us wary, excited, risking ourselves. She had put on fresh sheets and stuck fairy lights along the wall. When we fucked it was cautious at first, as if any exertion might undo the doctor's work. Afterwards, I lay panting, my mouth against her shoulder, surprised at the sweat coating us both.

I mostly got used to the sight loss. After a few weeks your brain adjusts and you forget what it was you were missing. I found my way around easily enough. They had given me a white stick but I didn't ever use it. It was tiny and made me look like I was carrying a magic wand. Sometimes I would hold one arm slightly in front of me, but mostly I took what my brain saw as the whole, only remembering when I'd nudge into someone or badly negotiate a corner. Mostly I was fine. Mostly life was good. Life was incredible.

I asked Marie to marry me. Because I was alive, because I loved her. We were at London Zoo, one of her favourite places, and she was helping me walk along, hand on my arm. I was still weak, at this stage, and I had to stop and sit on every bench. A gorilla was right in front of me and it kept picking up sand in its leathery mitt and watching it spill on the floor. I looked it in the eye. I was entranced. We were both of us alive. I'd never felt a connection with an animal before, not like that I hadn't. Never felt life to be a miracle. I started blathering to Marie about my gratitude, my love and my delight. 'Marie, my god, Marie,' I said. 'You know what I'm going to do? I'm going to become a vegetarian. I'm going to join you in that.' She smiled at me, eyes widening. The next thing I knew I had asked her, babbled the question out. We went on to a pizza place and I kept laughing and holding her close. 'I love you,' I said. 'I'm so happy to be alive.' I wished I could have pepperoni. The veg pizza wasn't as good.

A couple of weeks later I fainted in the bathroom. My tooth banged so hard against my chin it punctured my flesh. A month after that I woke up and it was as though my antennae had switched off. I felt normal. I felt myself again. I felt glum. The euphoria had passed and everything was flat. The vibrations in my skull were slowing down, rattling, approaching stillness. And somewhere behind this, panic. No one had warned me of this. I would have to go back to work soon, in the new job they had found for me, to 'give you some less stress'. That wasn't great but it wasn't what was worrying me. I didn't know what was. Outside the sun shone just the same. The cat still purred on the end of the duvet, shedding fur, licking his paws. Marie in the next room with a ring on her left finger. And I was on my own, on my own with all this dread.

Twenty-Two

It all seemed a long time ago, the joy of it and the fear. We were heading to a car park by the sports centre, to meet the Badger Patrol. We went down the high street, eyed by smoking groups outside the pubs. It was still light and balmy for autumn and if I tried hard I could think of the night ahead as sporting, an adventure. Marie was raring, quick paced, and I tried hard to keep up. The car park was empty apart from a few vehicles, loitering in one corner. A crowd stood by a camper van, looking more like a guided tour than a militia. These were our comrades then. We headed across the tarmac.

A tall woman, in what I guessed were her early sixties, detached herself from the group and set out towards us with a soldierly strut. 'Margaret Clifton,' she said, offering a dry and bruising handshake. 'You must be Marie. And this is?'

'Stuart,' said Marie. 'My husband. He's decided to come as well.'

'Very good. Very good. We need all the help we can get.' Margaret closed this sentence with an unexpected grin as though she'd become aware of something wicked. Whatever it was, she didn't feel any need to share it. 'All the help we can get.' She sounded like a headmistress talking through a tannoy and was dressed with magnificent sturdiness. Most of her bulk was wrapped in

104

mustard tweeds and bracken-coloured wools finished off with a solid pair of boots.

Margaret introduced us to the others. Irene was Brueghel-ish, moribund and northern. She looked as though she were about to burst into tears and it was only later I realised she always looked like that. Maybe she always was about to burst into tears. Brian was the thinnest, driest looking man I had ever seen, as though he'd been folded and left inside a book. He had an Adam's apple like a snake eating a globe and skin that looked like it would scuff you at the touch. Kerry was around our age or younger and had a look of half-hidden embarrassment I found I could relate to. She had a nose-stud and cropped dyed hair, of a blonde so bright as to be approaching green. I noticed she didn't seem to have been dragged here by anyone else.

'Well,' said Margaret. 'Now that we're all here. Is this everyone? I think it is. Brian, keep quiet now, I know you know what you're doing but we do have some new ones here.'

Brian, who had been telling Kerry about factory farming, information she was presumably familiar with, made a *zip* gesture across his mouth and showed a row of thinning teeth. He had a look of having been gnawed on and spat out by various countercultures. An old punk, an old raver, the point on the old Criminal Justice Bill where the frowned-upon cultures meet. The look, also, of a truly world class bore.

'These are the rules,' Margaret said. 'We stick together. We look for injured badgers. We keep to the path. For those of you who got here from London I should point out this is *not* the same as walking on a pavement so I hope you've all brought sensible shoes.' She glanced down at her own boots, which looked like you could keep your savings in them. 'If we see an injured badger we call the vet. We aren't allowed to trespass.' Here, the unexpected grin returned to her face, so that she looked like a ventriloquist's dummy with a secret. 'And we aren't allowed to disrupt a shoot. On the other hand, they aren't allowed *to* shoot if we're near them, so we aren't entirely hopeless. It may be that—' she grinned especially hard and let out a long hiss of amusement, '—from time to time word gets to the sabs. I don't know how but it does. I like to say it travels through the trees. And, oh, look who it is.' Her skin turned confectionary pink. Something pleasant this way came.

I turned and saw a giant approaching. Only it was a vegan giant, exuding tofu-fed wholesomeness. He was taller than the rest of us by at least a head, and looked as though the god Thor had ditched lightning and discovered sustainable energy. He had a beard like a thatched roof. He must have been pushing forty but seemed absurdly healthy and strong. Next to him was a young man whose shoulders slumped and whose skin was pining for vegetables. I didn't like this young man. I'm not sure I much liked either of them.

'Henry, good to see you,' said Margaret Clifton. 'George.' Her bark had a purr running under it, like the sound of a happy quad bike. I guessed this was for Henry. Her grin looked like it wanted to take off from her face. And when Henry returned it, his own smile made all of our smiles – and, yes, there were a lot of them, answering helpless grins – seem sub-smiles, snag toothed, crooked and defunct. He was a healthy-looking guy, was Henry.

'Sorry, I'm late, I told Bri. We had a kitten in, last minute.'

'Forgot,' said Brian. 'Went right out of my head. He volunteers,' he said. 'At the sanctuary, with me. I know

I said I'd mention it but by the time I'd got home it had gone. My memory. I'm going to start getting stuff tattooed, remind me. What's that on your wrist? Oh, it says Henry's working late.' No one was listening to Brian. Instead attentive faces gazed at Henry while he talked us through the kitten's progress. Apparently it had been touch and go but the little feller had pulled through. Margaret looked like a melting ice cap. It was shocking, seeing her touch her curls and simper. I felt how Catholics must have when they abandoned Latin Mass. Something dependable had gone awry.

'I was there too?' said George, the boy. He could not have been more than twenty. His voice was one of those youthful chewy ones that sound as though they're coming through a sock. When he spoke, he scratched at his blond fringe, as though he resented it for looking so angelic. There was something distressing about him. 'At the sanctuary? That's why I'm late.' He glared. No one had asked him. He moved to stand as close as he could to Henry.

'We ready to save some badgers?' said Henry. His voice was a lulling monotone, as though vocal inflections were for sell-outs. I looked over at Kerry, who was standing near to me. Her pupils looked like frisbees. Fancies him, I thought. Of course she does. I couldn't see Marie's face from where I stood and I wasn't sure I wanted to. Henry seemed a hard man to dislike but I thought I would make the effort. If anyone fell over and hurt their ankle he'd probably know how to fix it. *I* would probably fall over and hurt my ankle and I'd just have to lie there and thank him.

Across the car park a policewoman trotted towards us, and we all involuntarily stiffened our shoulders. Marie looked as though she might spit. Recently she'd got like that with girls who wore fur on the tube.

The policewoman reached us and smiled with

well-meaning unease, a supply teacher who hadn't been told quite how disabled we were.

'Evening,' said Margaret, stealing the policewoman's line. 'Can we be of assistance?' The policewoman seemed quelled by this. She leaned her weight from one foot to another and didn't meet our eyes.

'You here for the badgers?' she said, sounding slightly ashamed.

'We are,' said Margaret, the grin erupting onto her face again. 'As we have every right to be, Officer.' A shower of spittle when she hit a consonant.

'Of course,' said the policewoman. I began to feel rather sorry for her. 'How long do you think you'll be out for?'

'We'll be out as long as it takes, thank you,' said Margaret. The policewoman hid, unsuccessfully, a wince. A speck of saliva had hit her somewhere unwanted.

'Well,' she said, after standing there a few moments more, 'you all have a good night.'

'Thank you Officer, we intend to.' Margaret's grin was now slightly bigger than her head.

The policewoman gave a curt nod, and mooched, if the law can mooch, off in the other direction. As soon as she was far enough away – but not, I should say, out of earshot – we collectively exhaled, unstiffened our buttocks and let off a few phrases of contempt.

'Oink,' said Henry. 'Oink.' He chuckled at himself. 'Well handled Mags.' Mags? I didn't fancy anyone else's chances if they called her that. 'Give the bastards nothing. It'll only go straight back to the cullers.'

Marie tutted with genuine anger. A deep awareness of injustice seemed to have been born in her. She had woken me up the other night in a panic. 'Do you think my parents are Tories?'

I had told her I didn't think so, but that it was possible to be a Tory and still be nice. Her dad had been involved in the whole Czech dissent thing in the seventies and eighties and maybe viewed utopia warily. There was always space for context.

She hadn't seemed convinced.

Twenty-Three

The sky was dusking over as we crocodiled out of the village and onto the lanes. Marie raced ahead next to Margaret and Henry. Face flushed, eyes shining, enjoying her moment of usefulness. Kerry was just behind me, up near the front but holding herself separate. Further back Brian whistled, ambling in zigzags along the lane, hands in the pockets of his threadbare baggy jeans. The kid George slouched along, back arched. Irene lagged, wheezing, at the rear. The garlic and peat smells of a country night blended with Marie's familiar perfume. Or maybe it was Kerry's. I liked it, whoever's it was. There were raised slopes of grass enclosing the lane and over them we sensed cows, lowing (whatever that meant), breathing steam, blissfully unaware they were the prime cause of this cull.

'Stile everyone,' shouted Margaret. I supposed she was probably right. Only it was taller and more Aztec-looking than I usually pictured a stile to be, crowned with barbed wire, positioned on top of the steeper of two grass verges. Henry led the way. He barely had to strain, darting over as though he were running upstairs. The rest of us puffed after him, with me somehow at the back, behind even the more zaftig of the badger folk. My glasses weighed down on my ears. 'I'm not really all that well,' I said, to anyone who might be listening. 'I had a thing, a while

110

ago and now I'm not all that . . .' I dropped over the stile and landed slap on the soles of my feet. Henry patted me on the back in a manly way I tried not to let buck me up.

'Thing is, Steve.'

'Stuart.'

'Stu. Thing is, Stu, we all have our off days. I tell you I broke my leg once? Right before the glorious twelfth. Day they murder all them grouses. Still found my way down there. Sometimes you got to put your own shit aside. Can you do that?' I looked up at him. He had, I had to admit, quite wonderful ice-blue eyes, the same sort of blue as Marie's. So blue they were hard to look into. He gripped me in a hug. It was like being clutched by a musky robot.

'I'll do my best,' I said. He smiled a rich, warm smile. I decided to get my own back by doing slightly worse than my best. Not so anyone would notice but enough to retain self-respect.

We fell silent, stomped on, through hillocky cow-pat strewn fields. The sky was purpling over. A cow lazed across the grass to us, velvet-snouted, mascara-lidded. Justifiably unconcerned by the deeds of perplexing bipeds. Margaret shooed it away as though she held it responsible for the cull. We trudged forward, as it darkened overhead, feet stumbling over tufts of grass, clambering over inhumanly proportioned moss-slimed stiles. I began to notice my sight deficit again, as we wandered in the night. We crossed field after field, starting to light our torches, not seeing any badgers. Margaret and Henry made naturalist noises, throaty acknowledgements of some invisible clue, but I didn't think they'd seen anything. There was a rich dungy smell and the grass was beginning to stiffen with the cold. I popped a mint in my mouth and tried to enjoy myself. It was good to be out in the country, whatever the reasons for being there.

'A fence.' It certainly was. More barbed wire, although thankfully it didn't look electrified. 'Do we stop here?' I whispered to Marie and she laughed as though I were joking. Brian volunteered to crawl under and scout around. His employers knew he had been 'naughty' back in the day and turned a blind eye to his activities now. I wondered what form his naughtiness had taken. Something well short of murder, I expect. Marie was up now too, and at the front, announcing she would go scouting as well. Henry decided he was going over too, followed by Kerry and before long the whole damn crowd of us were scuttling onto our stomachs and scraping across the soil. Henry lifted the bottom cord of wire up so that we could inch our way under it, the barbs just scraping the backs of our coats. The ground was damper than I'd expected. Dew and bird-spit, the soil releasing its secrets. When we had all crawled under, Henry flicked his fringe and leapt right over the fence, a nonchalant smirk on his face and we oohed and aahed him as though he were a firework.

'Well done Henry,' said Marie and he winked at her in a way I wasn't sure about. No one winked in this day and age. He'd be calling her 'Missy' or 'Sugar tits' next.

George, the little blond kid, glared at this, as though it affronted him. He saw that I had seen him and he gave me the strangest smirk, somewhere between a fellow sufferer and a sadist. I stepped back. There was something creepy about George.

The next moment we were off, ducking and stumbling through the fenced-off woods, branches brushing our faces, hands clutching at leaves. We were outlaws, herbivorous Robin Hoods.

My glasses wobbled on my nose, my arm kept colliding with trees. My eyesight wasn't helping.

Brian was alongside me, keeping up a monologue as we clambered on, his tone avuncular and angry at the same time. 'Terrible sight the other day, Stu. We found a load of traps. Humane ones they call 'em. Contradiction in terms if you ask me. Two badgers in there, half starved. And we'd had the bad weather and one trap had been positioned right in the rain so the thing was half drowned as well. Course we got them to the vet but we lost one in the end.' While he prattled on I saw Marie at the front with Henry, lost in conversation, George just behind keeping his eye on them. I tried to make out what they were saying, under Brian's relentless drone. 'We made sure those traps got lost anyway.' Marie laughed so much it echoed and no one bothered to shush her.

'Sett ahead,' coughed Margaret. We all tried to look thrilled. The rest of them probably *were* thrilled. 'Grab yourselves a stick.' A stick? I looked around and every one of them had a branch at the ready, deposited there by some helpful woodland sprite. Henry had a huge one which he graciously snapped, handing a third to Marie. I had nothing. When I thought no one was looking, I yanked a branch from a tree.

'What do we want a stick for?' I said. Marie turned away from Henry and smiled at me, in the way she had when I told her I was no use with chopsticks. A sort of fond amazement.

'For the nuts. The cullers come and leave nuts outside the setts. The badgers stick their heads out and they get them. So we sweep them all away.' It was a practical solution. 'Did you break that off a tree? You really shouldn't have done that.'

'Sett' was the cry from the front. Everyone craned their necks to see a snug looking hole in the ground. It was bigger than I imagined and it had a kind of storybook quality, something homely but unreal. A childhood kind of comfort. Margaret gave the order and we all swept our sticks across the soil, dust shooting to shin height.

'Poor sods'll starve,' whispered Brian. 'Too scared to come out and eat. It's this bloody government, isn't it?' I considered which end of him to shove my stick in, but chose a saintly forbearance.

When we were done strafing the ground and the rest of the gang were on their way, Marie and Henry were still stood by the sett. I came and looked over her shoulders. I couldn't see over his.

'Amazing,' she said. It *was* kind of amazing. I tried my best to feel reverent. I hoped that, eventually, I would.

'Makes you want to say a quick prayer to the badger god, doesn't it?' said Marie.

'Times like this you could almost stop believing in the badger god,' I said.

Marie raced off with Henry after the group.

Twenty-Four

Brian was onto the subject of foxes. Apparently the main grievance of a typical badger, outside of marauding yokels, was the fox. The swisher and more cunning animal has a habit of using nearby badger setts as impromptu motels, diving down to fornicate loudly while the occupants are trying to sleep. For an animal (Brian said) with an essentially small-c conservative nature this is a cause of some distress.

We were out of the woods by now and onto another field. The sky was blue-black, speckled with stars. Margaret had told us all to switch off our torches. She sounded as though this were urgent. I kept close to Marie and Henry, hoping I wouldn't stumble. My sight deficit had become more noticeable in this unfamiliar dark. To our left we could see car headlights buzzing along distant spot-lit roads. We tried not to make any noise. A *phut* sound came from some trees up on the hills to our right, followed by a high-pitched yelp. We all stood still. Except for Marie, who was shaking.

'Red light over there,' whispered Kerry. She made it sound vaguely poetic. She seemed to have that quality.

We all peered until we saw them. Pinpoint crimson will-o'-the-wisps, wobbling through the trees. 'LED lights,' she said. 'From the guns.'

'I wish I could shoot *them*,' said Marie.

'Yeah,' said Henry.

'I don't think they deserve to be shot,' I said. 'From their point of view they're doing the right thing.'

Kerry stifled a laugh.

'Always gets me,' said Henry. His voice was full throated, tear-choked, a soulful oaken barrel. 'That sound. Always makes me ...' He covered his eyes with his hand.

'It might have been a car backfiring,' I said. 'You never know. Or maybe it was a badger, but a badger getting away.'

Henry didn't look convinced. 'Might be time to make a call, Brian.'

Pizza? I wondered. Drugs?

'He's calling the sabs,' said Marie. Brian sloped off with his back to us, speaking in what I guessed was a kind of code.

I was hazy on the legality of sabs. Just so long as I didn't have to meet them, I supposed they were okay. Marie seemed thrilled. She had been swotting up on the hard-core animal activists and had what I felt was a romanti-cised view of them. I found them pretty scary. They would peg me as non-committal. Marie, I expected they'd like.

We wound up on a narrow country road. Snaking forward, torches dim. A bark from Margaret and we flattened ourselves against the verge, in time for a Range Rover to zoom past. The window was down and the driver looking out at us. He was screaming a Viking bellow of hostility, a war whoop. It didn't seem like high spirits: he hated us. He hated us because we were stopping him shooting at badgers. And we weren't even stopping him much. Next to me I could sense Kerry freezing and I automatically reached out to grab her wrist. She gently took it away.

116

'You get used to it,' said Henry. He *was* reassuring. He was far too reassuring.

A few hours later I was sitting in a cold patch of wood with Marie, Brian and Kerry, guarding a badger's sett. I wished I could crawl in there to hide myself from the cold. Brian kept on talking, of unspecified prior naughtiness, his intense affection for animals, his feel for the sacredness of life. Kerry stomped around rubbing her gloves together, taking them off to roll fags, occasionally interrupting Brian with an affectionate bit of sarcasm. I wondered if there was or had ever been something between them, but dismissed this as unlikely. She didn't seem the sort to warm to bores. She was far too lively for that. Although Marie sat listening, rapt. I just squinted at the sett, wondering if anything was inside there and if so what it was like. About two in the morning I realised I'd been sitting for more than an hour and my feet were going dead. I stood up, a little too quickly, and the blackness went right over me, as the torch dropped from my hands.

Twenty-Five

'Did I?' Collapse again? I knew I had. I was in bed and couldn't remember how I got there. I ran an interior check on myself, to see if it was serious. It wasn't, I decided. It was the sort of collapse I had to live with, not to die from. Inevitable faints, which should lessen as I healed.

'Yes.'

'Keeps happening, doesn't it?' We were back at the bed and breakfast. I had nothing on but my boxers. Somebody must have undressed me. Marie was wedged in next to me in a broderie anglaise top. The Sunday paper had been delivered and she was scouring it for reports on the cull. There were print-out PDFs of badger research on the sheets. I picked one up. The probable effects of dispersing sick, scared badgers around the countryside, creating perturbation, a badger-nakba, a diaspora of coughing peaky mammals.

'Did you get me back on your own?'

'No. A few of the others helped.'

'Were they all here when you undressed me?'

'Yes.'

'Even?'

'Yes. Even Kerry. I have to say I didn't warm to her much. I couldn't work her out. She seems very protest-y. Very motivated by being on the right side. But she can be sort of flippant about it. As though it's just one of her things.'

'It possibly is just one of her things. Anyway, I liked her.'

'Obviously *you* liked her.' I wondered why this was obvious. 'I did say we'd keep in touch when we're back in London. I want to keep in touch with them all, it's like a family, isn't it, all on the same side?'

'Doesn't sound like much like a family.'

My head felt as though I'd been drinking. My mouth felt papery and sore. I found a bottle of water and drained it. The doctors had warned me recovery would take a while. And already I felt better, if you ignored the times I didn't. As long as I underwent no sudden and traumatic shocks I would probably be all right. I would probably be fine.

Twenty-Six

To have someone think you the best. To have four years of them telling you, reminding you, that you are their favourite man. And this person, doing the reminding, to be someone so extraordinary. Who was going to be a great actress someday, who had grown up among PEN dinners and BBC interviews and had sat on Melvyn Bragg's knee at the age of four, who could do things on a yoga mat that insulted gravity, who had a face as right as maths. Someone who burned with empathy, someone who could not stand to co-exist with suffering. Losing this was no easy thing.

Before I moved, there were evenings I'd be on the bus from work, see the lights on in our waterlogged flat and think she must have come back. But it had only been me forgetting to switch them off in the morning, half asleep and careless.

In the weeks leading up to her going, we didn't talk about anything that wasn't badgers. 'I met with Kerry today,' she said. 'I said I thought I might go on hunger strike. For the badgers.'

'I hope Kerry told you this was mental.'

'She said she didn't think it would work. Don't ask me if I'm okay.'

'You know I am going to ask you that.'

'Well, don't. I'm sorry I found something I care about

that isn't just sitting at home, reading books and drinking tea. And complaining about everything.'

'I care about a lot of things. I just think going on hunger strike is a bad idea. I can't think of it as a good idea in any way. Do you think the badgers will notice? Do you think the fucking farmers, the government, will notice? I'll tell you who will notice. I will notice is who will notice. I will notice and I will suffer and no one who can do anything about this cull will give the slightest shit what you do.'

'You'd like it if I lost weight anyway.' There wasn't an answer to that. She didn't have much weight to lose.

'Oh god, that dickhead Paterson's on again.'

'Who? Oh, him. Oh yeah.'

'Christ, I hate him so much. You know, I think I'd kill him. I really would.'

'We've got a vote. You don't need to go around killing people.'

Owen Paterson was the minister in charge of the cull. Marie hated him. It was a hatred that had to be fed. A hatred that had to scour news websites for interviews and clips, a hatred that went far enough to attend a debate on fisheries just to bring up the cull. Kerry, who'd gone with her, persuaded her not to lob the two fat tomatoes in her handbag at the fatter ministerial face. I felt this was wise of Kerry.

'You are dwelling on this. You are letting it take over. Why don't we go away for a weekend? Or longer? Paris or somewhere. Berlin.'

'You don't get it, do you? I'm going back to Gloucester on the weekends. You really don't get it at all.'

'I do not want you to spend so much time there. I miss you. I want you back here.' I had stopped attending the camp, pleading bad eyes and the risk of fainting.

'Is this you being a husband? You just put on a Husband voice.'

I went over to the fridge. There was just enough wine in it to carry us through this talk. 'I did not put on a husband voice.'

'You definitely did, you put on a husband voice. It was deeper than your normal one. Like, *Hello, I'm a husband.*' She laughed and for a moment she was mine again, and we were both of us together.

'I just miss you when you go away, that's all.'

'It's not like I don't miss you. It's just this is so much bigger. I have to stop this happening.'

I asked her why now and why badgers. She'd never campaigned on anything before. Her passions had always been arty. It was why we'd fallen in love, this shared need to create.

She was drinking some thick green concoction, whizzed up in the blender. Knocking back lots of these mixes seemed to be a sign you were on the right side of the badger argument. There was a whole culture I didn't get here, of dietary restrictions and crying over animals.

'Look, you know how it is with politics. I mean, my mum has some. But they are very specifically related to being a sixty-something woman who knows a lot about literature and appears on Radio 4. And Frank. Well. He's like you. Everything's funny. The whole point of life is to be funny. To be interesting and clever and to be very embarrassed if anyone says anything sincere. So I never tried. And he's so huge, isn't he? He's large, both of them are. It's difficult working out what you think when you grow up with that loud kind of certainty. Assuredness. And taking art as the only thing that matters when actually there's life. So I ended up acting, partly because they'd be horrified if I didn't want to be *creative*, but also cos it's a chance to try on some different people and see if any of them fit. To work out who I was. You can't put your name to anything if you don't know what you think, don't know what you are. And now I know.'

'So why badgers?'

'Animals. Beginning with badgers.'

'Okay then. Why animals?'

'It's hard to explain. It just seems like the root of it all. The power thing. The way we dominate. And you go right down the ... I don't want to say food chain, but all the way through life people being awful and at the bottom there's an animal being ill-treated. And they haven't got a voice. That's the most important thing. They haven't got a voice.'

'I was thinking,' I said, 'about Morrissey. How very articulate people can't stand inarticulate suffering. Is this something like that? The way anti-abortion people, they're physically disturbed by what happens there.'

'There you go,' she said. 'Turning it into a joke.' I told her it wasn't a joke.

'Is everything all right? With Marie, I mean? Is she okay do you think?' Frank Lansdowne was standing next to me at the urinals at the Swiss Cottage Pizza Express. Making me, for the moment, incapable of pissing.

'You saw her tonight,' I said. 'She looks well enough, doesn't she?'

'She might *look* well,' said Frank. His own stream, triumphant, thrumming against the bowl. 'But all this fuss about badgers. This, ah, sentimental approach. I *agree* with her of course. Seems an awful waste of time trying to shoot the fucking things. But her reaction, it seems disproportionate.'

123

I could have hugged him, under different circumstances. I held back, not just because we were both at a urinal but also from suspicion. Marie's comparing the two of us had made me wonder a bit.

'It's horrible,' I said. Come on Mr Lansdowne. You've won awards. You are regularly accused of wisdom. Solve this.

'It all seems to be terribly, what's that phrase young people use? Binary. People don't just get things wrong, people don't just think differently. They are wicked, they are motivated by bloodlust, they must be fought. It's babyish.' The man was in his seventies. The gold jet arced from him, unceasing. 'I worry,' he said. 'This sudden embrace of simplicity. The natural, the animal, the belief things would all be better if we'd never come out of the caves. It's a retreat, it is. Into childishness. Rather as if getting married was this last leap into adulthood and she's taken a fright and jumped back. You know I wasn't always the most terrific dad at times.'

I was standing at a urinal next to my wife's father, one of my favourite authors. What if I went mad and looked at his penis? What if he only thought I was doing that? What if I screamed and then kissed him? I didn't think I wanted to kiss him.

My attitude to the Lansdownes tended to fluctuate. At first all of my dreams seemed realised in their lives. Coming from the northern suburbs, then spending dull years living in South London, they were my first taste of the intelligentsia, of the world of art I wanted. I'd sit out in their garden, watching chubby bumblebees lazily necking pollen, trying to spot Nicole Kidman, who was supposed to live in the house that backed onto the garden, with Marie stretched out in a bikini and insectoid sunglasses, reading the new Ali Smith, and over on the

124

patio, Frank and Judy, boomer titans, opening another bottle, quoting Larkin at some visiting actor or other. *Fuck Lancashire, I was home.* That itself, a line from an early, chippy, Lansdowne book, when his vowels were still ironed down.

But sometimes, about the second bottle, I'd start to change. The talk would begin to seem pat. The garden would look far too neat. It was all a little glib, wasn't it, the Lansdowne scene? Had they actually read those towering stacks of first editions that hemmed in every room? Didn't Frank sometimes write as if modernism was something that happened to other countries, with all those novels about adultery and divorce in Hampstead that said nothing about real life? His own Northern-ness, that gave salt to his first few books, hadn't it become a little self-made-man, a little snorting? And wasn't it easy for him to dismiss, in most of his essays, any attempts at altering the world, when his own world had so little need of alterations? I'd get tongue-tied and cross but never so cross as to refuse another drink. One time I'd had a little too much and back in our flat I had taken up *Memory, My Mother*, the collection of essays I used to love and I'd scanned it through different eyes. The wisdom that I'd fallen for seemed to come from a smug, high place, untested on everyday life. It *was* easy, wasn't it, to scoldingly tease the hotheads when you were basking in a summer garden, your wife's legs had had their own Spitting Image doll, you spent half your life on holiday and the other half on Radio 4? Well some of us would not be tempted. Some of us would stay true to a spartan literary virtue, would stay hungry, stay fierce. I was never going to finish my book.

I wrote 'silly old fool' and 'complacent sod' in the margins of *Memory*, then felt guilty and hid it. He was a lovely and generous old man and I was an ungrateful young swine.

Marie told me she had been crying on the Tube. I put my arms around her, held on tight. 'This fucking cull. I just thought of the waste of it, the loss of all those lives.' I didn't say that they were only the lives of badgers. I wasn't entirely thick. 'This girl came up to me. Being friendly. Touched my arm. She said what's up? Thinking I'd been dumped or lost a baby or something, you know. And I said it's the badger cull. I'm upset about the cull.'

'What did she say?'

'She laughed. She laughed, right in my face. And then stepped away backwards, like I was going to pull out a weapon or explode. Can you believe that?'

'I can believe that. I can believe that quite easily.'

'It's easy for you. I mean, you don't care about anything. You care about sex.'

'Love.'

'You care about love, then, and books. But there's so much more going on.' I wondered if it was true I only cared about these things. Maybe the illness had closed off my horizons. Maybe there was more to life. I wished I knew what it was.

'Marie, it is freezing. Why is the window open?'

She was frowning down at her Mac, oblivious to the goose pimples on her arms. 'I didn't notice.' She didn't look up from the aquarium glow of her screen. 'I'm trying to get people to sign up to a benefit gig for the badgers. Look at this fucking comedian. You'd think he'd be a shoe-in but ...'

'People choose their causes. Not everyone can care as much about this as you do. I've been thinking about

126

your acting. I've been thinking you need to get back into that.' I knelt on the sofa and slammed the window closed. It was ten on a November night and the room was a mausoleum.

'People should care.'

'There is shit in Malkin's tray. Yes, that is definitely shit. How long has that been there?'

She looked up, took her glasses off, squinted.

'You're doing the husband thing again. I miss Stuart. Not this Husband Guy. Stuart Brock.'

'Block. You said Brock.'

'I didn't. You are gaslighting me. This is insane.'

She'd once shown me a drawing she'd done as a kid. A grotesque with lolling tongue, eyes bulging, thick stubble sprouting from his jowls. Labelled, by her fifteen-year-old self, 'a husband?' Had I turned into him?

'I'm not trying to be a husband. I don't want a nice little wife. I'm worried for you is all.'

'You have this angry look about you sometimes.'

'Do I? I don't feel angry.' She stood up, came over to me, circled my waist.

'I'm angry too. About this cull, for a start. It's okay to get cross. We're only, I don't want to say animals, but we are.'

'I think it's my brain thing,' I said. The next morning she told me she was leaving, packed her bags and went.

Twenty-Seven

One night, before she'd been back to collect her things, I rummaged through them looking for clues. A diary revealed nothing. Appointments were listed, becoming increasingly badger-centred as they progressed. The day I proposed to her she had drawn, with her artist's hand, a ring. There was nothing else to go on, until I found her play.

Except looking at it, it wasn't a play. A dramatic monologue then, although it wasn't too dramatic. She'd been working on it a month – squinting, shoulders forward, green tea cooling on the table next to her – so there must have been more than this scrap. I imagined it performed. It would, of course, star Marie.

The character was called Posie, which no one in real life was as far as I knew, but I sensed autobiography. It would be one of those small theatres, somewhere above a pub, two or three supportive grey-haired local art lovers and a smattering of friends in attendance. Frank and Judy on the front row. The lights would dim until there was only the light on the stage. Marie would stand. Talking in the over-timed thespian way, slathering the words' quiet music with actorly overdubs. No, I loved that she was an actor. I read the script:

I saw it the other day, said Posie-Marie. I saw the truth of Wilbur. (The audience stop coughing and start fidgeting.

128

They worry about the time, about going to the loo. A monologue, then, about relationships, and will she scream at some point and how awkward is that going to be? And who, I think, is Wilbur?) I saw and I can't forget it. (Posie looks around as if wondering whether to confide. Drawing the audience in). You spend so long knowing someone, loving someone, then you find out who they are. And everything changes.

I had the afternoon off, Posie said. Wilbur was at the office. He hates his job, says he's only doing it while he writes. Thing is I'm not so sure he much likes writing either. He certainly likes the idea of it. I had the afternoon off and it was hot and I'd had a doze. And I decided I wanted a snack. A chocolate biscuit, I thought. Wilbur has them, he's a huge snacker. (I touched my stomach, aggrieved). We watch TV, in the evenings, and he'll be next to me on the sofa, grazing away. I had to think where he kept the biscuits. He's a hoarder, he squirrels things. I remembered. They were on the top shelf of one of the kitchen cupboards. I should say, Wilbur is tall.

We'd bought some plastic chairs, she said, from the pound shop on our street. Plastic stools, baby-coloured, pink and blue. I grabbed the nearest one to me, one of the pink ones, it was. I stepped up carefully onto it. Making sure I didn't lose balance. And I reached for the highest shelf. They were in a tin, an old blue box of Cadbury's Roses. My mistake was not jumping down with the tin at once. My mistake was opening the box from on-top of the chair.

I had a KitKat in one hand, the open tin in the other. There was a moment when I heard a splitting sound, the sound of tearing plastic. And then I fell through the chair. One leg had gone right through it. KitKats and Wagon Wheels and blood across the floor. I heard the door opening and I thought thank god, he's here, because I

129

needed someone to cry at, someone to clean my wounds. And he came in and he's standing there and I see this look on his face. Just for a second. But it lasts a lot longer than that. He looks at the KitKats and he looks at my torn leg, with the ruby streaking down it. He looks at my crying face and the sweets and the empty tin in my hand, so that I look like I've been designed to scare children from eating between meals. I feel clumsy and stupid and I need him to support me so much. And instead, I get this look.

Just for a moment. This absolute withering, what should I call it, *anger*. Undeliberate, too. If it was conscious it might not have been so bad. This was from somewhere deeper, this animal sort of sneer. The last time I'd seen him look without controlling it, a look from the back of himself, was when we first got together. Only that was a different sort of look.

I think I stopped loving him then.

The script ended there.

I sat in the cold flat. I know how fiction works. I know this wasn't verbatim. But that didn't stop me raging about how untrue it was. Because I remembered that day. It was a few months after my stroke, in the period of flatness I had. And yes, I'd been confronted by a massacre in a sweetshop and Marie howling in tears. But there had been no anger. There hadn't been any contempt. I was being abandoned because of a misinterpreted facial expression. There was an injustice in this. There wasn't anything lurking back there, hiding inside my psyche. I was a good and supportive man.

Calm down, breathe deep. A cause of exit so flimsy could easily be addressed. I would show her who I really was. I would show her she had me wrong. I would certainly win her back.

Twenty-Eight

My interactions with the badger folk had been limited since Marie left.

There had been a flurry of accusatory emails in the immediate aftermath of her going. *Where the fuck is my wife* sort of thing. *I hate badgers*, sort of thing, *verminous plague beasts*, sort of thing. Lugubrious old Irene, from the patrol, was the only one to respond. She had dropped out of direct badger action on account of her bad leg. Her days were spent in tweeting anti-farming slogans, knitting badger jumpers. She told me Marie was 'a good warrier 4 the badgers' and if I loved her to set her free.

My response had been intemperate.

On the whole, I thought it best if I just turned up in the woods. I knew that they were out there most of the time. I hadn't fainted since I'd moved in with Alistair and Raoul, and my health seemed to be looking up. I was sure I could explain myself well enough, how I'd mulled things over and seen the cause came first, how I knew my duty was to stop the cull, no matter how awkward it was. I was pretty sure I could say all that and, if it wasn't going to be believable, it would sound sincere enough. I didn't even tell George about it, from a vague fear he would be unable to avoid prepping Henry. The boy had added me on Facebook and was forever sending me forlorn messages asking me when I was going to shape up and take back my wife. I felt sorry for him, sorry and repelled. He seemed to take a morbid interest in the possibility of Henry and Marie sleeping together, an event, he warned me, that could take place at any time.

'She's not doing anything yet,' he said. 'It's complicated, she says. We have to stop this happening.' It was odd how much he cared, Oedipus Wretch.

I got to Paddington on Saturday morning after a hard week of taking calls about pets. Pets and, increasingly, badgers. I had to explain we only dealt with household animals and for this I was accused of being corrupt, a shill for big farmer. Rupa would pull faces at me over the desk.

I breakfasted outside the Pret just across from the platforms, a newly purchased mini-tent folded in a similarly spanking rucksack. It would soon be Christmas again. It wasn't how I'd envisaged my first married Christmas. But then, the last one had been spent in hospital. I was getting good at adapting to unfortunate circumstances.

At the next table was a young woman I recognised. Dyed yellow-green hair under an absurd orange tea cosy hat, shiny leggings of oil-slick black and a bell-shaped navy coat. It was Kerry from the badger crew. I lifted my newspaper high. My bluffing was not as I'd hoped. She clocked me in an instant, showed puzzlement, excitement and embarrassment in swift succession, remembered too late that I was a Person to be Sympathised With, stood up and hurried over. We hugged. Half way through doing so I remembered I'd only met her once and all this hugging was probably a bit much. She sat across from me and cocked her head.

'Hello,' she said. 'What gives?' She raised an eyebrow for a second then arranged her face into a neutrality her eyes didn't match.

'We're probably on the same train,' I told her. 'Thought I'd help with the badgers.'

'That's a coincidence. With Marie being out there and all.' She smiled. I was being laughed at by a badger person. 'Don't listen to me, I'm not in charge of good ideas. But I'd say this wasn't your best. Do you mind nipping outside while I smoke? S'freezing out there but we've got an hour to kill.'

I finished my cup and followed her, explaining that really I just cared an awful lot about badgers and that everything else paled into etc. but somehow I couldn't go through with it. She didn't have the sort of face you could lie to.

'God, but that girl loves badgers,' she said. 'I mean I like 'em. A bit. Fair play. But she, she. Well she *really* likes badgers. Here, you know about her and Henry?'

I said I did, but that wasn't the issue. She did something with her eyes that made me guilty.

'Your funeral,' she said, giving the words a horribly specific tone, as if she knew where it would be held and the order of the service. 'Hey, things have really changed there. They've all gone over to the sabs. Well Mags is still stomping with the patrol I guess but Henry and Marie and Brian, they're all camping out most of the time. You might find it all a bit hard core.'

'I don't know why everyone assumes I hate things being hard core,' I said. We stood in the sunless street and I cupped her face while she lit her cigarette. 'I like hard-core things. I nearly died a year ago. I might still actually die. I'm the most hard-core person I know.'

'Yeah, Marie mentioned that! She said it really freaked her out you saying she'd saved you. Like it was this great responsibility.' She chuckled as though she couldn't help herself. 'Though she didn't really take it on as a responsibility, did she? Like, I find looking after my niece a great responsibility but I don't hide upstairs when she visits. Sorry. I'll buy you a coffee if you like, although you're probably jumpy as it is. God, I would be, marching into the woods to get my wife back. It'd take more than a coffee to set me straight. Jesus. Shall I sit next to you on the train?'

As we coursed past hills and fields, Kerry filled me in on the badger brigade. Mine was not the only faltering marriage. Brian had walked out on his wife and kids. And you know (Kerry said) she was the woman who got him off the gear, she'd stood by him all the way and now he only seemed to care about these animals. Irene's husband had given her an ultimatum and they were currently estranged. A middle-aged guy in the camp had asked Kerry to 'go into the woods with him' while his wife was preparing the food. The cull was costing more than just woodland lives.

'Sorry,' she said. 'I get a kick out of romantic disasters. Not yours,' she added. 'Sorry. I'll shut up.' But I didn't think she was sorry. She certainly didn't shut up. 'You have to admit it's kind of funny though. Ending a marriage over badgers. Like disinheriting someone over an otter. Throwing your child on the streets cos he doesn't like hedgehogs.'

I couldn't really grasp why she was part of the protest. She stole my newspaper and tutted over injustice, but when it came to badgers she couldn't help discussing her fellow protestors' zeal with a sort of glee, as though she found tremendous pleasure in human strangeness. I wanted to remind her she wasn't exactly an observer, she had pitched her tent with the rest of them. After a while she fell asleep, her breath making little yelps and whistles like a dog dreaming of green fields.

134

Twenty-Nine

We had the same cab driver as the time before, the time I'd been here with Marie. He didn't seem to recognise me. He asked if Kerry and I were married. I told him we weren't, perhaps a little too loud.

It was odd seeing the half-forgotten hedges and dry-stone walls, unchanged while I was so altered. At least in London the scenery changes at the same rate you do.

'Going to propose myself, soon,' the driver told us, with pride. I wished him success, said I hoped his girlfriend in the village would be pleased. 'Doubt it,' he said. 'It's not her I'm asking. Going for a Pole. Cultural differences, I reckon, they like a man like me. Got it all sorted, she's coming in February to see if we fall in love and if we do I'll pop her the question sometime in March.'

I told him I was married myself but we were temporarily separated. Kerry had covered the bottom half of her face with her hands but subdued snickers kept dodging through her fingers. She was bouncing on the seat, I saw, as if life held too much stimulus.

'Hope it all works out for you,' he said. 'Terrible thing divorce. Mine was fifteen years ago and I only have to smell her perfume on the street and I'm straight back where I was. We split to stop from arguing but it never stops, not really. You just do it in your head. Here good for you?' We stepped out onto a narrow lane enclosed by

135

trees. God knows how Kerry knew it was the right spot, it looked identical to the rest. She bent back a branch and scuttled into the darkness, with me lumbering in pursuit, making twice as much noise as she did. We kept on through the trees until we picked up stewing smells, the sound of a car radio. 'Here we are,' she said and, moving quicker than I could keep up with, she swerved past a bush and onto a path.

At the bottom of this path we reached a glade. Although glade gives it an idyllic quality it didn't really attempt. Glade suggests solitary deer, perhaps a couple of nymphs. This place was more mattress-y. There was a camper van, a cluster of ragged tents, a porta-loo and a makeshift kitchen area with an untended pot of soup. Kerry started putting her tent together, something I hadn't done in years. I'd brought the right instructions but felt that using them in front of her would lower me in her eyes. I would sort the tent out later when it was dark and I was tired. That would be the best time. I asked her if she needed any help, which, thank god, she didn't. I suspected this wasn't even the most awkward I was going to feel all day.

As if to prove I was right about this, the camper van door opened and Marie stepped out followed by an enormous St Bernard, its face folded like a rose. She looked, oh dear, she did look well. She didn't look as though *she'd* spent the last month drinking and crying and having unfortunate entanglements with witches. She looked like a woman who had found her right domain. As though living in a camper van and breakfasting on twigs were exactly what she needed to do.

It would, I thought, almost be a shame to drag her away from all this. I also, for a moment, doubted I could. She looked, for the first time, absolutely herself.

136

The dog galloped around, breathing meaty steam on us.

'Stuart?' Marie said, hurrying over. She was wearing a gypsyish get-up, which oughtn't to have worked on her but sadly worked very well. 'What is he doing here?' She looked at Kerry for explanation as though Kerry was to blame for my turning up.

'We were on the same train,' said Kerry, investing a bland statement of fact with a surprising amount of guilty-sounding bullshit.

'I'm coming to help out,' I said.

'He's coming to help out,' said Kerry and absented herself inside her tent. Her shadow was clearly visible, making her, as absent people go, extremely present throughout.

'You're coming to help out. Because that will definitely help, making everything difficult. I don't get this Stuart. I know you don't care about badgers. You've been pretty upfront about that. And I hate to be cruel but I left you. I left you. You can't just turn up to places and expect things to all be normal.'

'I suppose.' This was going to be harder than I'd imagined. 'I suppose I changed my mind. I believe in what you're doing. I believe the cull was wrong. I do believe that. And I just thought if I could help in any way, I would.'

'You're half blind. You faint an awful lot. You think badgers are jumped up fucking weasels. I'm not sure how much help you'd be. Why don't you go home?'

'I'm more or less used to the sight. And I haven't fainted in months. I'm trying to be supportive. Trying to help.'

'You told Frank I was a drunk. I'm not a drunk at all. I don't know where you got that. Just go home. Please go home.'

I asked her to give me a chance. She narrowed her eyes, like a jeweller faced with an especially shoddy fake. And, unexpectedly, she smiled. Her old smile, the one I'd missed. Before she could follow through with, say, a kind word, some sign of feeling, the van door opened again and Henry was there. He wasn't wearing a shirt. His chest looked like a 1980s cartoon hero's, panelled, segmented, hard, expanses of needless musculature, slabs in improbable places. I had no idea what you had to do to get a chest like that and, having done so, what use you'd have for it. You could waste an hour bouncing rocks off yourself but surely you'd get bored. What did she see in this man? While he had been working out or lifting donkeys over streams to stop their hooves from getting wet, I had been reading books. I had written an unpublishable novel! I was the Master.

I was the Master.

'Noisy out here,' said Henry. 'Trying to do some work.' He looked me up and down, as though he were revaluating his belief in the perfection of all nature. 'Stuart,' he said. He extended his hand to me in a way I was sure was supposed to be magnanimous. I paused for as long as I had courage then offered mine to him. Only a few bones broken in his grasp.

'Listen,' he said, steering me a few steps away so that Marie had to stand there pretending she couldn't hear. 'I know you don't think much of me. But I know you do think a lot of Marie. In your way. We both want the best for her, right? And she's got that now. I think we both have to respect her decision, know what I'm saying.'

Well, it's easy for you to respect her decision, isn't it? Her decision seems to involve adopting your cause as her own and moving into your camper van. Be massively churlish of you not to respect that a little, wouldn't it?

Whereas I, spoilsport that I was, I found it more difficult. I reminded myself they still hadn't yet had sex.

'I agree,' I said. 'The best man won.' I wondered if that was pushing it a bit far, but no, the oaf smiled shyly, as though I'd said what we'd all been thinking.

'By saying that Stuart, you made *yourself* the best man.'

'Just don't ask me to actually be the best man. Ha!'

'Mate, I'm an anarchist, we don't believe in marriage.'

'I can see that. Ha. Ha.'

'Ha.' Before I could jump back, he grabbed me in an embrace. It was like being set upon by a cathedral. I had time to gulp in his odour of bracken and incense, before he released me, gasping and cross. Marie tutted loudly and hopped back into the van.

'Women, eh?' he said. I couldn't bring myself to smile at that one. Because she isn't fucking *women*, Henry. She is Marie, and I see that, even if you, you big lummox, never will. My god, how much I hated him.

He hopped back in the van and from inside I could hear two voices, trying hard not to shout. I might as well try and put my tent up. Kerry had to climb from hers and help me, halfway through.

The soup was good, in a murky, lentil-heavy, spinachey sort of way. It was early evening but it had been dark for a few hours, a whale-black sky. We sat on stools or perched on the frosty ground, warming our hands on our bowls. From Henry's van I could hear the sound of two voices singing, alongside some awful plucked instrument. The song seemed to be about badgers. Brian was explaining, lengthily, about the hidden reasons for the cull. Something to do with developers, something to do with Tesco's. 'Black and white, forever strong,' came the song from Henry's van. When the song finished, or at any

139

rate, stopped, Marie and Henry came out and sauntered to our table, both of them glancing over as if they'd expected me gone. I felt caught out sitting next to Kerry. George, who I hadn't thought was around, slunk out of one of the tents and came to stand on the edge of our group. He wasn't wearing a coat despite the cold, not, I think, because he didn't feel it himself, but because he enjoyed other people's feeling discomfort on his behalf. He greeted me in a familiar way I was sure that everyone noticed. When he smiled, which wasn't often, his teeth were speckled with green. Kerry kept talking too loudly and telling jokes and nobody except for me laughed. They were a mopey bunch right then, the Badger Patrol. Defeat and winter sapping their spirits, Stalingrad all over again.

Marie was livelier than the rest. Her subject was direct action. She was furious, flabbergasted, that the cull had not brought down the government. What was needed was something drastic, something real. 'We should actually go for the farms,' she said. I worried, but said nothing.

Henry started talking about Gandhi in a patient way, as though we might not have heard of him. He always spoke as if we were at a slightly lower reading level. I said violence got people nowhere – I was rewarded with a glare. Marie wasn't adjusting to my presence. Kerry agreed with me, said she thought violence was counterproductive. Henry snorted, as though the word 'counterproductive' were an alienating and fancy bit of jargon. Kerry tore a crust of bread in two, with some force. I wondered if she had a bit of a crush on Henry. I found I disliked this idea.

After we were done, and were rinsing our bowls at the sink, I found myself next to Marie.

'Henry,' I said. 'Why do you like him? He's an arse. He has wristbands for causes. He plays the ukulele.'

'Please leave that alone,' she said. 'Anyway, it's a banjo.'

'I'm here because I love you,' I said. 'I love you more than he's had time to. You understand that, right?'

She flicked her fringe with one hand, looked at the ground. 'It's not that I don't love you,' she said. 'It's just that these things change. We're different, Stu. Different sensibilities. And I've got to fight this cull now. This place, it feels like home.'

'Marry me.'

'I already did, Stuart.'

'I haven't got anything bigger to offer,' I said.

Thirty

I got back late on Sunday. Alistair at the door. Malkin seemed to have taken against him in my absence, swiping his ankles on the stairs, snapping his feeding hands. 'She's being a menace,' Alistair said. I told him she was a he and dropped my bags on the floor.

Raoul was home, in a muumuu, watching the flatscreen through thick scribbles of smoke. He had been in this position on Saturday when I left.

I sat and asked him how he was.

'Meant to get some reading done this weekend. I'd gone and put it aside. I didn't have any volunteering. Church this morning but that would be okay. I'd still have time to read.' There were two books on the table, obscured by Rizla papers and clumps of tobacco. Something about the Wobblies and a book on the Latin American church. 'Must have read about a page. And not a page of each.'

'No way to live,' I said. Raoul agreed, it wasn't. He asked me about my weekend.

'It was okay,' I said. 'We found a trap, in the woods. I was going to touch it but then Kerry, she's one of the badger people, she said they've got paint on them or something, glow in the dark. It was all right. Managed not to bump into much. I've adjusted pretty well.'

'You gonna get your wife back?'

'That's not why I'm doing this.' But I thought, perhaps it was. I thought it wouldn't take much to prove my love.

George started calling me up around once a day, so that I had to run out of the office and take it in the corridor with colleagues passing me by. He mumbled at me in his socky voice. He would pause for great lengths of time, so that I started feeling awkward on his behalf until I realised that *he* didn't feel awkward, he was making me feel awkward and he knew it.

He would make cod philosophical remarks relating to his system of life, the ordered anarchy he believed in. Everyone knowing their place although no place greatly higher than another. Influencing others, flexing your strength against them, was evil without exception. Even the mildest impact on another was coercion, led to motorways and drone warfare, theme parks and modern medicine. He was tedious on this score. He told me he didn't believe in bank accounts. Alternatively, he would revert back to the manners of a boy even younger, blowing raspberries or making spastic sounds, refusing to engage. Mostly though he filled my head with my wife, as if it wasn't already full enough. Rupa came past and winked at me, assuming I was talking to Marie. I wished she had been right.

I went out one night with the Lansdownes. I hadn't seen them since Marie had denied my report about her drinking. I was nervous and to fill the silence I told them I had an agent at last. No thanks to you, Papa Lansdowne. He congratulated me, narrowing his eyes only slightly when I told them the name of the agency, the first I could remember. He thought I'd want to aim a little higher than that.

I stopped myself from lamping him with the chilli oil.

143

Write one of your famously irascible reviews of that, old man.

We were in an Italian place in Primrose Hill. Busty serving-girls and waiters in skin-tight keks, happy to flirt with the ageing female diners. Posters of Fellini films on the walls, pepper mills out of a fertility cult, fatty foods and skinny customers. Frank and Judy across from me, still with all their lustre, looking well. Next to me an empty table mat, as though my wife were the Prophet and we'd saved her a seat just in case.

'So everything is going well. Very well. Except.' One wife, absent, saving badgers.

Frank put down the menu, scratched his famous fringe. 'She won't talk to us about anything except badgers. We try and ask her what she's doing and all we get is facts about badgers, snippets of badger lore. Anything else, it's a blank. We ask her about you two, she says nothing, she hangs up. Stuart, are you quite all right? You're drinking rather fast.'

I hadn't really noticed but yes, it seems I had been draining my glass a bit. There was a blubbery lip stain on its rim. 'I'm fine,' I said. 'I'm fine because I know we can get through it. I know we'll be all right. I'm not angry and I'm working on this. The signs are very encouraging.'

'I did speak to her, Stuart,' said Judy. 'This morning. Her mind seemed very made up.'

I took a long sip then wiped my mouth with the back of my hand, leaving a cold kiss on my wrist.

'She's spoiling him, you see,' said George. He pronounced the word 'him' as though it ought to be capitalised. 'You should see how he's changed.' He was still part of the camp but George could tell the things that drove Him now were different. It used to be the animals and now it was all for her. Which was the wrong reason to do

144

anything. You had to protect for the sake of it, not to impress anyone else.

And the violence! Not that there'd actually been any. Not that George would mind too much if there were. He thought that Owen Paterson, for example, probably wanted to die. Otherwise why invite attack? But it went against George's system. Shooting someone, even Owen Paterson, was definitely coercive.

'Are they really talking about shooting him?' I said. I could hear his breath down the line and knew I was in for a pause and a half. Rustling and breathing and picking at his spots.

I didn't like those breaths. They sometimes made me wonder.

'That was an example,' he said. 'But the way they talk now. It's always those bastards, those fuckers, they need to be taught a lesson. I mean, they probably can't help being fuckers? It's probably how they came out?'

'If she says anything about hurting anyone, you tell me straight away.'

He made no promises. I thought I heard him chuckle. Behind him I could hear the wood sounds, twigs and birds and wind.

'The problem is this Henry Ralph. You should never have left him in your house. We get rid of Henry, then Marie will be back to normal.'

The Lansdownes looked at one another, a conspiratorial glance. A glance to say oh gosh, this is what we feared. I could sense myself starting to sweat. I had begun to dwell a lot on Henry. The mystery of his power. 'He's a terrible human being. But her feelings are still with me.'

'Henry is not the brightest and the best,' said Frank. 'But she does seem very keen on him.'

'They're shacked up half the time in his van. They've got this enormous dog. But I'm making sure she's okay. I'm going there every weekend.'

I was hoping for the tears to enter Frank Lansdowne's eyes, for the self-reproach to begin. Rightly so, I felt. Too many soft toys and treats had got Marie acquainted early with anthropomorphism and the inevitability of her will. They should be beating themselves up. They should stand in Benito's and scourge themselves, begging for forgiveness.

Only, this time both of them just looked at me with vulture-ish concern.

'We're rather worried about you, Stuart. Marie said all that stuff about her being in a mess was absolutely untrue. Looked me in the eye. I have to say, she sounded very convincing. She explained her feelings about this cull and asked us to trust her, you know. She didn't sound insane. Misguided, perhaps, but she seems to know what she's about. All this hanging round the camp, I'm not sure where it will get you.'

'You're shaking, Stuart,' said Judy. 'Your hands are shaking.'

I held the end of my fork vertically against the surface of the table and tried to steady myself. I was furious, was the truth.

'You aren't taking too much time off?' said Frank. 'We'd hate for this to become some sort of awful downward spiral. I mean, you haven't got a lot to fall back on if you lose your job.'

No, I thought, no I haven't. And I had called in sick that morning.

'She talks about you,' said George. One time, in the woods when Henry had gone for supplies, Marie and

146

George went walking through the trees. I could see her in her hat and her thick red gloves.

George had brought me up first. Granted permission to reminisce, she had bored his head off on me. The life we'd had together, the future that we'd shared.

I liked this. I didn't ask him what she'd said; I could fill it in myself. The first date in the Foyles cafe, worrying about whether a drink-free date would work. Her calling Judy to tell her she wouldn't come home that night and my surprise at their first name familiarity. Watching her in rehearsals, her hand tapping the air as she summoned up lines, struggled through her role. The stacks of shoes and books and dresses filling our flat, the first time either of us had lived with a partner before. Walks through Hackney Marshes on an autumn Sunday morn. I was sure she had mentioned all that. But I wasn't about to check.

'You have to stop it happening,' he said. 'You have to get her back.'

I wondered why he cared. Actually, I didn't. I knew love when I saw it. I knew it and knew there was hope. I told him I would try.

'We have to pull together,' I said, my voice rising across the table. I lobbed a smile at the Lansdownes but the smile went unreturned. 'She's your daughter, you should do something.'

'I do think your focus should be on yourself, Stuart.'

I picked up the glass and spilt wine over my plate. I told them I was fine.

'This is derogation,' I said. 'You have a duty to put her straight. Listen, I'm scared she's going to do something crazy. Hurt someone. I've seen how angry this makes her. Farmers and girls who wear fur. I would hate for her to

147

do something, to suddenly explode. How do you think terrorists start?'

'They don't start with badgers, Stuart. You've gone awfully pale and you aren't making much sense.'

'I'll sink without her,' I said. 'What if she blows something up? For the badgers? What if she shoots Owen Paterson?'

'I'm sure the prime minister will be very grateful,' said Frank. I searched him for signs of paternal guilt. There was nothing but urbanity there, urbanity and this awful misapplied concern.

'It's her you should be worried about, not me.' I swallowed a wine-drowned tube of pasta, creased my face in disgust.

'All we're saying is, slow down, Stuart,' he said. 'Judy and I, we care for you a lot. You're our son-in-law. At least, you are for now. We don't want you doing anything foolish. Hanging around the badger camp like a lovestruck shepherd, trying to woo her back – it's unhelpful. You don't seem altogether well. And what about your health, your eyesight?'

'My health is doing all right. I get around okay. There's this girl Kerry in the camp, she walks on the right side of me, making sure I don't trip up.'

I looked at all the diners, in their colourful scarves and off-duty pastels. Frank started on about his new book. I would resist it, this lurch into normality. They thought they could just carry on without me but they couldn't. I was going to get her back. My name is Stuart Block, I wanted to shout, and I will not be denied.

All this time the camp was growing colder, people were dropping out. Someone had painted a giant cross-eyed badger on an old white sheet and strung it on a pole.

148

It wobbled in the breeze and we took pride in it, our amateurishness, our defiant lack of skill. We started the habit of saluting it as we passed. Henry used to sit under it, with his eyes glazed, communing with its spirit.

I was proving myself. Every weekend, of soaked boots and dripping branches, I was showing her my love.

'It's good that you are coming here,' said George. 'But you really need to do more. She's still here. Every night she's in his van. He isn't acting the same. She's still sleeping on his floor but it's only a matter of time.'

'You forget he is not my concern.' I was trying my best not to think of him.

'He's *her* concern. She was your wife a few months ago,' he said. 'Doesn't that bother you?'

'You're, what, twelve? What do you fucking know? I'm being patient. Understanding. I'm trying to be there when she needs me.'

'You think I'm *funny* for him, don't you?' I told him I didn't much care. 'It isn't like that at all. It's more, I know how he can be. And he isn't like that right now. Following her around. It just isn't how he's supposed to be.'

I didn't want to hear about Henry. I didn't want to hear how he should be.

I decided to purchase a badger. I could smuggle the animal in with me, produce it at a fortuitous moment and claim full responsibility for its rescue. A baby one would be fine. Sedated to stop it escaping. But the more I looked into the matter, the more I saw a world of men with bad jackets and stubby heads, gathering in rooms. Cockfighters, poachers, baiters. The anti-sabs, the paramilitary wing of species dominance. Dogging without the sex. Posing

149

in car parks, their boots full of bloodied fur. Brutalise a brute, then home to hunch over the video footage, swap files of your favourite cruelty, drink over your kills. I didn't want to meet any of these men. Besides, badgers were pricey. The guy that I was talking to wanted £1,000 upfront, before I'd even met the badger. I didn't want to go bankrupt and get a skunk.

She called me on Boxing Day. Asked me how Christmas had been. I told her I'd gone home, escaping Alistair's cooking, feeling guilty for dragging my parents through this gloom. I pictured her lying on the bed in her childhood room, legs up in the air as she pulled off her socks.

Marie's Christmas hadn't been much better than mine. 'I told them, I don't want to see meat, I don't want to smell it. Frank's glugging sherry from early on, popping out to smoke. I have to sit there with this poor dead bird on the table, dripping grease in front of my nose. Sausages strung all over it, them licking their lips. I took some of the veg but I couldn't swallow it, not with that poor creature lying there. Then the presents came and you won't believe what he bought Judy?'

'Some ham. A herd of cows.'

'A fur coat! Of all the things. I can just about laugh at it now. Now I can. Just about. But then, I was just ... He says the coat is vintage, nothing has been harmed in your lifetime to make this coat. She isn't even embarrassed. Hops up and tries it on! Whirling around the place like she's Zsa Zsa Gabor and Frank making his sort of comments about it, how he does.'

I could imagine. I had been surprised, on an early visit, to see Frank and Judy necking against the fridge. They were proud to reject all notions of the appropriate.

'You know,' she said, 'I shouldn't say this but it made

me wish you were there. Could have done with someone finding it funny, to stop me finding it awful.'

'Thanks,' I said. 'Hey, at least we saved money on presents this year.'

She laughed like I hadn't heard her laughing in a while. 'You can be funny,' she said.

'Do you think we'll ever...? You know. Will we ever?'

'Let's deal with the cull first,' she said. Later on she texted me saying she felt she'd given me the wrong idea.

'You know, you don't seem that angry,' said Alistair. 'When Lucy left me I was furious for months.'

I thought about that. He was right. I wasn't an angry man. This was one reason Marie's stupid 'play' had upset me: it wasn't the truth of who I was. Frustrated, perhaps. A little stressed. A smidgeon of terror, of suffering. But anger? It seemed so aggressive, so thwarted. I was learning, perhaps, from the anarchists.

Another thing about anger: it seemed such a male response, an animal response. You could say that about all of divorce, in fact. It was something angry men with kids went through. They'd tussle over who was the better parent, be envious of anything like new love. They'd live in Guildford. Bury themselves in work after the split. Make fools of themselves on feral and manly forums, cultivate peeves. Hug one another in the woods. Write lachrymose blogs about mental illness and fatherhood. Kick about on a Sunday morning. Or they'd meet someone new and she would be called Sheila and she would not love them but would be glad they were good with the kids and didn't lose their temper like Gary had. Most of all though, they'd be angry.

Of course, there were also Americans. American authors of the unreconstructed school, with their five marriages

151

and their alimony and highballs. They got divorced with a certain style. But they were male and angry too.

Herzog, I said, the book I was reading in hospital? He nearly kills someone at the end and all over a divorce. This is where anger gets you. I wasn't going to be like that. No, I wasn't going to get angry. I wasn't going to get divorced. I was going to retreat from this humiliating maleness. And win back Marie, if I could. *Fuck* this maleness, this animal anger. I was a good, an unsexist man. There was no delight in it, this maleness, nothing but cramped and furious lives. There was no beauty in it! I had come from a house with potpourri! Would anyone in this house, I asked him, even think about potpourri?

Over on the patch of grass, a cat stalked, a rat drooped between its jaws.

The next day, there was a bowl of potpourri on the table next to the filter papers and the Red Stripe can Alistair used for an ashtray.

Thirty-One

One Saturday, at two in the morning, we came across the police. I'd never had as many interactions with the constabulary as this year. There were four of them this time, with a van parked a little way off. They were not, they told us, about to let us through. Marie and Henry and Kerry and George and I. We stood and faced them, trying to appear both peaceable and scary. I was struggling to remember the legal tips we'd all been given. Could you refuse to give them your name? Were you allowed to take photographs? Not that I wanted to. I had a feeling the scene would stick without photography.

Henry knew what to do. He stood tall – taller than usual – and said they couldn't deny us entry to the path. We were citizens exercising our rights and they had no reason to obstruct us. One of the policemen smirked. He was young, I thought, maybe Kerry's age. A zitty face with feline cheeks. It was possible the smirk was power, strutting, showing its stuff. I am sure that's what Marie saw in it. But it could have been something else. Awkwardness, embarrassment. The feeling of having a beautiful woman across from you, vocally hating your guts.

Marie caught it, his shamefaced snicker, and she hissed.

'You have to let us through,' she said. 'We are here to peacefully protest.'

'Shoot going on,' said another policeman. Older than

the other, saggy, with the look of a man who would rather be in bed. 'We can't let you through.'

George tittered. I can only assume at the prospect of trouble. He was a palaver junky, a bother-connoisseur. Although it could have just been nerves. Marie started trying to appeal to the officers' consciences. I didn't think that would work. She told them innocent animals were being murdered back there. That they were standing watch, while evil was performed.

'Wouldn't know about that,' said the older policeman. A few of them chuckled. This might well have been arrogance, I suppose. Marie stood before them and she trembled. If any of those police had been able to picture the curses she silently rained on them they'd have had nightmares for years. The youngest one looked down at his size twelves.

We were interrupted by the sound of a nearby shot. A muffled phut, a whizz and then, almost at the same time – almost, it felt, before it – the yelp as bullet met flesh. Something between a bark and a human cry. After that, a genuine human cry, as Marie let out her horror at it all. From somewhere in the woods there came an answering cheer. Marie was crying. I wanted to rush, to put my arms around her, but Henry got there first. He whispered and she shook her head, before pressing it to his chest. Oh Christ, he was being a comfort. If this badger getting shot resulted in them fucking I was definitely against it.

'Oi,' came a voice from the woods. A torchlight hit our eyes, approaching at a canter. Behind it stood a man. He didn't look very evil. He wasn't especially bloated, his mouth wasn't what you'd call cruel. Neither sybarite nor sadist. He looked, instead, like a harried antiques dealer, powdery and flustered. 'You the protestors?'

Henry told him we were. He seemed to be our

spokesman. Marie was in tears and nobody would have listened to me or George. Henry was, I hate to say, plausible. He had an aura and I didn't. Of course, I was only pretending to be a protestor. That might have been why.

'Bloody sick of the lot of you,' said the man who carried the torch. He didn't look to have a gun. His tone was apologetic, as if his need to have a pop at us went against his inclinations. 'You think you understand all this.'

'We understand, Sir,' said Henry, 'that killing defenceless creatures is wrong. We also understand that this cull doesn't make sense. You're spreading the badgers around.' He gestured as though he were spreading peanut butter. He was the worst person in the world, I thought.

'You think that you love animals?' said the man. 'You think you're the only ones? I tell you what I love – my cows. You think they're just big lumps of money to me? You ever seen a cow with TB? You think that's a pretty sight? Phlegm rattling away and the ribs poking through? It's a horrible thing, that is. And that's my living as well. That's a whole herd gone, that is. I have a bad year, it doesn't just impact on me. That's my workers, the shops. That's the whole community buggered. I don't see you crying about that. I don't see you raising a fuss about my family, because we aren't covered in fur and you couldn't stick us on a bloody tea towel. My wife's nearing a breakdown. Someone scratched her car the other day, right into it with a key. *Murderer* across the paintwork. She's never murdered a thing. Cries her heart out when the herd reaches their time. Closes her eyes in the cop shows. All of a sudden, *murderer*. While you lot, you don't mind watching a whole way of life get murdered, so long as your bloody badgers don't get disturbed. I'm talking to you. You think I enjoy it? Think I do this for fun? You think I got nothing better to do in the middle

155

of the night? I'm here cos there's no other option.' He stopped and glared sheepishly at us, as though expecting a round of applause. The police there to protect him looked more embarrassed than before. 'I'm sick of it,' he added, in a bleat. Tears pouring down his face. 'Sick of it.' His shoulders shook. He looked obscene, as though he'd started undressing or doing something filthy to one of his cows. Even Henry had nothing to say.

Part of me wanted to hop past the police and give the old guy a hug, were it not for our Official Enemy status and something grotesque in his vulnerability. I looked at Marie's face and saw anger and deep contempt for this man, who could go from killing a badger to this excess of self-pity, who could weep for the cows he breeds for the abattoir. I looked at Marie carefully and I knew what I had to do.

'You're a fucking disgrace,' I said. 'You make me sick. I hope your whole farm goes under.' A policeman told me *less of that*, the farmer swore and sloped off, my conscience called me a million awful things. But Marie smiled up at me and I saw I'd got it right. She'd be sleeping on the floor after all.

'God I hate those police,' she said.

'Fucking pigs,' said Henry. 'Did you see the way they looked at the ladies?' I hadn't. 'Must kill them that the best ones are on our side of the fence.'

'Yeah,' I said. I caught Kerry looking at us and I blushed and looked away.

Kerry sat on a well-polished log, scrubbing her boots, knocking off bricks of solid mud from their leather sides. She called me over. 'How's it going, mister?' I told her very well. 'Don't know whether you deserve a medal or a slap,' she said.

'I'm here for the badgers,' I said.

'Yeah and I'm here for the food and the company.' She flicked her towel in my direction. A lump of mud spun off and hit me on the shin. Kerry's pessimism annoyed me. That afternoon I'd been talking to Marie for an hour, about her new passion for this cause. I'd told her I could see it, I really could. She had even squeezed my hand.

'Some of the company here is okay,' I said. Kerry smiled in a way I couldn't decipher.

'Henry though,' she said.

'I don't fucking get it,' I said. 'I mean okay, he's not bad looking if you like that sort of thing. But he's dull. He really is. And that measured calm voice he does.'

'I'm not his biggest fan,' she said. 'I think he's a bit of a twit. But obviously he's not bad looking.' There was wistfulness in her tone I didn't like.

'You're all wrong about him,' I said. It irked me she saw him that way. 'His fucking voice, that monotone. I don't get it, I really don't.'

'Best not to obsess,' she said. I told her I wasn't obsessing. She grinned in a way I didn't care for. 'Hope you're on the right track,' she said. 'Have you thought about how it would be if you and Marie get sorted? Have you thought how much you'd both have to pretend never happened?'

I'm afraid that I flared up. I told her she had no idea about forgiveness. I told her that once Marie was back then we would find our rhythm again. I asked her what it had got to do with her. She shrugged, muttered something about having hit a nerve and focused on her boots.

Marie was right about Kerry, I thought. At least I had a reason for hanging around this place. Her being there didn't make sense. I went back to my tent and sat inside, in a huff. Rain came, tapping the canvas, preventing sleep. Henry, outside his van, started chanting to show how spiritual he was. 'Om,' he said over and over, the rain dripping down his chest.

Thirty-Two

One evening, to our surprise, Alistair told us he was thinking of marrying again. 'Her name is Su,' he said. His voice was husky and reverent. 'I met her last night. She's Korean.' I had sometimes heard Alistair refer to all women from Dover onwards as 'exotics', gifted with hereditary sexual skills. 'She's twenty-one, studying here. She's astonishing. Not like any other girl I've met.' I tried to picture how someone could be unlike every other girl he'd met, and what this said about her or all the others. 'She's into—' he leaned forward '—the occult.'

Raoul made a feeble squeak, the subdued ghost of centuries of inquisitions.

'Forgotten wisdom. Cabbalism. Paganism. Arcana. Freaky business. Astral goings on.'

'What do you mean, dude? What does any of this mean? She's a Wiccan or something, is that it?'

'She charts horoscopes.'

'Wait, this is your wisdom of Atlantis, here? Horoscopes? She reads the star signs? Talks about being a Libra at parties? You made her sound like Crowley, man.'

Alistair beamed at Raoul, glad to have annoyed. He told us how he'd seen her in the smokers' garden of a nearby pub. She had tattoos on her wrists and skin the colour of a half-sucked toffee. Her hair was thick and black, it plunged out from her skull. Eyes that spoke of potential violence, her belly button bare before a yellow winter moon. It was very clear to Alistair that he had met his match. He had fixed his gaze in hers, like a man trying to tame an emu, and stridden across the stub-scattered AstroTurf to meet his destiny. He told her, as an introduction, that he planned to make her his wife. Her lips had parted, in excitement and in shock. He had bought her a lime and soda. He told her he was a poet. But also a man who can chop wood, make fires, handy with a fishing rod, useful with a spanner. He was, he said, a *maker*. He undid the top three buttons of his shirt. She stroked her hair with one hand, the rim of her glass with the other. He allowed her mind to linger on the details of their love. He would write and that would always come first. She would be his muse. They would make, or probably buy, a gypsy caravan and paint it in the gayest of colours. Blue and red and green. Perhaps some other colours. She would be pregnant or else becoming so. The children would run wild but also become poets and painters themselves. She said that he was funny and asked him for his star sign. He said he was Sagittarius, stopping himself, as he did so, from quoting the old advert for Creme Eggs.

'They've changed the recipe,' I said.

'Capitalism, man,' said Raoul.

Alistair told Su he was not like the other men in the bar. He looked at them, the lumberjack narcissi, and congratulated himself on this difference. They had tattoos, as she did, and beards, as did he, but they were aspiring to be what he and she had already become. Complete people. Makers. The free, the authentic ones. He said he would like to have sex with her but only when she had agreed to be his second wife. She said she had to go and talk to her friends but it had been fun listening to him and that he should maybe go on the telly or something. He did a magic trick involving her cigarette but told her that when they were married she would really have to stop smoking. She said she had to go now. He said he understood but that he knew they would meet again. He would not take her number, even if she tried to give it him. The fates would make them meet. It was supposed to happen and so it would. She said okay and went off.

'You didn't get her number?' said Raoul. He seemed to be quite relieved.

'Asked one of her mates for her name. She's on Facebook, I'll message her today.'

Thirty-Three

My dislike for Henry grew larger. It captured my mental space. Swaggering around camp, explaining animal rights in the tone of a patient Sat Nav, eyeing me with, admittedly justified, mistrust. His habits were appalling. He would tell us that his dog was wiser than most people. He would habitually strip to the waist. He referred to the women on camp as 'chica' or 'my good lady'. He cried at baby animals. He mended things with his hands. He would exercise, right in front of us, or start chanting mid conversation. Sometimes he wore eyeshadow.

There was no excuse for Henry. Was my Marie falling for this man? I tried, on the whole, not to think of their closeness. Whenever I accidentally did – at five in the morning, with my work alarm two hours away, and images of his hands on her body rampaging through my skull – I'd palpitate and reel, the world would spin slightly faster. It was not to be considered. There were all the flashes of hope she had given me, the moments when our marriage had still seemed a living thing. There'd been vows. I had written them. Vows ought to hold some meaning. George certainly seemed to think so.

I was wary about putting trust in George but I needed someone to tell me I was doing okay. Alistair laughed at me for wasting my time, Rupa flat-out called me a stalker and Kerry could barely hide her giggles.

Only George had faith. He told me, if anything, that I needed to try harder. 'She still hasn't slept with him,' he'd say. 'Until she does there's hope.' I still had a lot of it, hope. It kept me buying tickets to Gloucester every weekend until we got to March. Everything went wrong one day in March.

Thirty-Four

It might have been Kerry's fault, now I look back on it. Yes, some of the blame lies with her. A quality of mischief she had. Recently, in the camp, whenever Henry got sententious, which was often, Kerry had started grimacing. Subtly, just for me. I enjoyed it, having an ally who wasn't George. It was late on a warm Saturday morning and we were eating our hash browns and beans. Henry was there and Marie. Brian must have been elsewhere, as he wasn't talking. It was Henry's turn to talk.

'Okay guys,' he said. 'I've been thinking.' Something frisky crossed Kerry's face. Something that egged me on. 'What we need, right, is a propaganda blitz.' Marie nodded in a grave way. I wondered if the idea came from her. 'Like obviously the media don't want to know. But ordinary people, the ordinary people, they need to know how simple it is. Because the arguments are all ...'

'The arguments are all on our side,' said Marie.

'Right. So we need to spread the message. We need to tell them that this is a black and white issue.'

Kerry had her fingers over her mouth, shaking.

I couldn't stop myself. 'Sorry, a what is it?'

'Black and white. Issue.'

'A black and white issue. Badgers.'

Kerry let out a sort of yelp. She was shaking and twitching with glee. I was laughing now too.

Henry stood up very fast, knocking over his chair. I worried for a moment he was going to hit me. 'Fuck off, the pair of you,' he said before stomping away.

Kerry and I were left chuckling. I laughed more than I had in a very long time. Until Marie cleared her throat, I had forgotten she was there.

She said we should go into the village for a coffee.

Thirty-Five

It was odd, being out together again. Hard to get the walk right when you can't put your arm over a shoulder, crane your neck for a kiss. You can't walk with someone in an angry way, not that I was angry. So we ambled around Newent, neither enemies nor a pair. She'd been in Gloucester long enough not to have to stop and look in shop windows, point out things of interest. Maybe there was nothing that interested her any more, nothing outside badgers. We'd got a cab into the village. It was our old driver again. He asked us if we were married and we'd muttered, staring at our feet. Things were going to be said. She was going to say things and they would be unpredictable and have the power to alter my life.

Our lives. The essential unit, us.

'There's a tea room just down here,' she said, looking up at me. I tried to read her eyes but they gave nothing away except nervousness. We trotted down a little path and I remembered our first visit to Newent, both of us looking like weekenders, for all our trying to be anarchists. Now we looked like anarchists trying to go straight. She'd brushed her hair and I'd changed into a less muddy pair of jeans, but the outdoors had got to our skins in the last few months, our hands were roughed and chapped and both of us seemed to be looking at other humans as potential enemies. I pushed open the tea room door, ringing a bell, and a few eyes darted to us. Querulous, aged glances, wondering at these scruffy campers. A radio played lulling music, post Elvis, pre-Beatles pop. Tea rooms being amiable places, I felt that we were safe. I wouldn't, in my current get up, have wanted to risk the pub.

I ordered a frothy coffee and a slice of chocolate cake, and waited for Marie while she asked if they had anything vegan. They hadn't, despite her having previously requested almond milk. I had hoped they'd think we were hikers – a hiker couple, say, a married hiker couple – and she wasn't playing along. In the end she ordered a black coffee. There wasn't any food there she could eat.

'So,' she said.

'So,' I said back at her. Her eyes luminous, unreal.

'Sorry about. You know.'

'That man has a real problem,' I said. 'He's wild, a wild man, he is. I know I'm biased but I don't get it, I really don't. This power he has, I don't get it.'

'He has his preoccupations. I don't always get to know what they are, of course.' Was that frustration I heard? Maybe they were in trouble. I could see Henry not wanting to burden her with his problems, and Marie feeling shut out. Given a good few months I could nurture this situation into something really *huge*. I'd given up hoping for the cull to be called off and for her to come back to her senses. The cull could run and run for all I cared, the longer it took the better. Or maybe she'd latch onto hunting or animal testing and I could tag along with that. The process could take months, it might never reach an end. I could go on like this forever, not knowing if I was with her or apart. Schrödinger's marriage. Let it go on forever, I thought. Let it not reach the crisis now.

'I'm going to have to make a decision,' she said. I raced through the available options and settled, quickly, for tears. But when I tried to cry I couldn't. 'It's absurd us being married in this way, me living in a camper van with someone else. The thing is I do love you both.'

'You love him?'

'I'm sorry, but yes, I do.'

'You love me?'

'Maybe, in a different way.'

'The Bloomsbury lot, the bohemians. They'd have taken this in their stride. I don't *own* you and jealousy, jealousy, is a kind of a caveman emotion. I don't see why you shouldn't go and live in the woods with someone but still come back when you're done and be my wife. I don't see why we can't do that.'

'Oh, I can't keep on like that, can I? And even when the cull is off – if the cull is ever off – this is what I do now. I protect animals. That's a lifetime's work.'

'I could join you,' I said. But the thought of another factory farm to picket, all those lorries of geese to obstruct ... No, she would have to come back. She would have to be normal and mine again. Henry, Henry, Henry would have to go.

'You don't really want to join me. I'm different now. Protecting animals, it's my life. It's funny, I should have been a nurse. Or a vet I mean, maybe. Wasting my time trying to act when there's all this work needs doing with actual life. I enjoyed my time looking after you. I felt very close to you after, you know, what happened. I mean, you nearly died. And when you didn't you had this attitude, this sort of reverence. Everything magical. It was infectious. But then you turned your back on that, really quick, and after you just seemed anxious. Anxious and obsessed with your book when there were real things to

168

care about. And I started to drift away. I was still full of that enthusiasm and you seemed to abandon it.'

'I was ill. I was really ill. My brain was just reacting. You learn that, after what I had, how so much we think of as natural is just a chemical response. That's what it was, I think so.'

'I don't think that's how people function. I like how you've been nice about this though. I like how you haven't been jealous. I would have been.'

'I am madly jealous. I am blind with jealousy. The thought of you without me makes me sick. Who would you have been jealous of?'

'I don't know. Kerry.' Her eyelids down, avoiding.

'I wish you'd eat,' I said. I wasn't sure why or where it came from.

'You have to drop all this food stuff. You don't get to control that any more.'

'I don't think it is controlling.'

'Is this why you come here? To check on what I eat?'

'I come here to try and get you back. Come on, it's not for the badgers, is it? I'd cheerfully kill a whole family of badgers if I thought it would win you round.'

She took the smallest of sips of her coffee before placing it down on the table. 'How,' she said, 'would killing a family of badgers win me round?' I'm not saying there was definitely a smile there. But there might have been a smile. I thought I could win her over. It would only take one more push.

'I know you and Henry aren't fucking,' I said. She looked at me as though this were somehow not my business.

'How the hell do you know that?'

'I'm . . . it's obvious,' I said. 'If you're a physical person, like me, it is easy to tell these things. And all I'm saying is don't. Take some time to make sure. Think it all through. If you love him and don't love me, if that's truly the way it is, then fine. But until then, please, for me.'

'Oh Stuart, this is terrible. This is really terrible, Stuart.'

'I don't know how you can love him. He isn't a nice man, I would say.'

'Do you actually want me,' she said, 'or do you just want to prove me wrong?'

We finished our coffees and I bolted down my cake and we wandered along the high street. I asked her if she ever missed acting. She said no, that it was a relief not to have someone constantly telling her to act.

'I didn't really do that.'

'You did. It was really important to you that I become an actress. Not enough to have my family at it, oh darling, you must be creative, it's such a *marvellous life* on the stage. You were like that too. The weird thing was you never thought I was any good. You'd sit there when I was in anything and the look you had, this sort of rictus of embarrassment, you really should have seen yourself.' She did an impression of me, a gargoyle of aesthetic unease.

'I don't remember that. I remember being encouraging.'

'Oh, you were encouraging. You were encouraging because you wanted to be with an actress. So you could exhibit me while still feeling modern and supportive.'

'I remember feeling very proud of you.'

'Do you remember when we'd make love and you'd squeeze onto my waist? I always felt you were trying to squeeze me into someone else. Not the person I was.'

'That's just fucking weird. It's fucking weird and not true.'

'I keep coming back to that moment with the chair. That look on your face, of impatience. I don't know if

170

that will change. And I know that's not the whole of you. It's just. I used to cry all the time, remember?'

'I don't remember that.'

'Call you at work and I'd be crying. I was lost, I think, really lost. Looking for somewhere to be and then I met, I got into animals and now I don't cry any more. I'm sorry, Stuart.'

The driver picked us up at the war memorial. Magic FM on the radio, Fisherman's Friends in the glove-box. This time he knew not to interrupt the silence.

We sat in the back and watched the trees and hills go by. I hoped that we weren't coming to the close of love. Although, as always happens, one person had got there first, was sitting, patiently waiting for the other to arrive.

No. For as long as she'd not made her mind up there was hope.

When we got back one of the campers told us that Henry had gone off into the woods to meditate with the dog, this being his usual practice after losing his temper. Typical of Henry that he couldn't just turn to drink, but had to make his fits of sex-starved grumpiness into something pseudo-spiritual. I had often stumbled across him meditating, bare-chested, his hands upturned to catch the rain or cradle a passing bird. I ventured a grin at Marie and found it half-returned. Smiling at the knowledge I found this funny, but not finding it funny herself.

At one point she put her hand on mine and let me enjoy it, the luxury of her touch. 'I feel like I'm always messing you around.'

'You can do that,' I said. 'Just so long as we get somewhere. I think we will.' I think I did think that. All around us half the camp were still in their tents, although I could hear a few murmurs and rustles, the sounds of

171

them starting to wake. We stood outside her camper van and hugged. She still fit snug in my arms.

'It's good spending time with you,' I said.

'And you,' she said.

'I reckon we'll be friends, whatever you decide,' I said. 'We can hang out as much as you like. I'd be a good ex, I think. I can see us when we're old, sitting in a garden and making each other laugh.'

'I'd like us to be friends. It would help if you stopped coming to camp. If you let me make my decision.'

'Can you promise me you won't sleep with Henry, if I go away? Because I really don't think that you should.'

'Stuart. Don't grab me like that.'

I leant forward and kissed her. Hard to say how she responded. An answering twine of the tongue but her hands pushed soft on my chest. 'No,' she said. And, 'Henry.'

'Fuck Henry. I'm your husband.' The words sounded unconvincing.

She opened the door to the van and I followed her inside. There was a mattress on the floor next to the narrow bed, bare but for two greasy pillows and a tangle of tartan sheets. There were dog hairs everywhere, so that the smell of dog hit your nose on arrival and stayed to scratch at your skin. The plates they brought out for meals were part of a large and dirty collection, lining the sides of the van, giving off a rank sweet smell. But the worst thing was the animal pictures. Dolorous baby donkeys, seals as fluffy as dandelion clocks, meerkats stood to attention. There were soft toys in there too, far too many soft toys, with a look of jumble sales and damp about them, other people's child-hoods. An awful cuteness papering over the mess. I needed to get out. I couldn't breathe and she was standing there, looking self-conscious as if I'd burst in on her, uninvited.

'What's that face for?' she said. She clasped her hands in front of her, shifted from foot to foot.

'It's nothing. It's nothing at all.' I wasn't sure what it was.

'It isn't this bad,' she said. 'Usually, I mean. You've caught me on a bad day.'

'Come home with me,' I said. 'Leave now. Please. Come home with me.'

She shook her head, eyes wide. I found I didn't want to touch anything. I looked at her skin and how miraculously clean it seemed in the midst of all this dirt.

'Oh Stuart, I don't know what's wrong with me.' Panic in her voice, her eyes.

'Marie, you have to come home. This place is, it's horrible, it's really horrible. You have to come back with me.'

She composed herself in a second. Smiling and brittle, ignoring the mess of the place. 'Go away now,' she said. 'Go away now and thanks. I'll give you an answer soon.'

'I'll go tomorrow,' I said. 'But don't keep me waiting too long.'

She turned her back on me and went in there, among the litter and the print-outs of kittens, the dirty pans and the toys.

'I love you,' I said, to the door. But I couldn't shake off the mess of the place and how far life had thrown her from me.

Thirty-Six

Darkness dropped mid-afternoon, and with it came a cold that snuck under our gloves and through the gaps in our buttons, wrapping itself round our bones. I was assigned to Brian and Kerry's group, along with a saucer-eyed, silent couple, both with corn-coloured dreads, and a PA from Nottingham who had taken a sabbatical for the duration of the cull and whose friends thought she was mental. Before we left we saw some old comrades, Margaret Clifton and Irene from our first badger weekend. Irene seemed downcast and bloated, her eyes sunk as though she were trying to look inside herself, her skin pale, gelatinous. I'd read her late-night Twitter conversations with Marie, the two of them working each other into deeper aggravations as they thumbed out the cruelty the badgers faced, the panic in the setts, the mothers missing their cubs. I couldn't understand it, their hunger for further outrage, the depth of their identification, the pornography of animal pain. Margaret seemed as indomitable, as sturdy as ever, solid as an old town hall. She marched through our camp in her mud-scuffed boots, barking out breezy encouragement, spittle flying. It did us all good to see her. The two of them were all that was left of the legal end of the badger army, the part that plodded obediently along the pathways and claimed not to know any sabs. We were the illegals, the paramilitaries. And beyond us the real ultras, the hard-core sabs.

We clutched at our torches and traipsed. Brian was subdued, muttering. I was quiet too, trying to make sense of that moment inside the van. It felt so far from any kind of life we'd had together, the chaos, the jumble of animal crap. I had backed away, for the first time. But if I quit, I would have to get divorced. I would have to live with Alistair and Raoul. I would be a divorced man in his early thirties. A divorced man with a cat. Always the cats who suffer the worst of it. Maybe I should get rid of the cat. He was freighted with significance, the cat of my marriage. I wouldn't see Marie as much in future. Eventually I wouldn't see her at all.

No, I still wanted Marie. There was a chance, and I must fight for it. But then my mind went back to the van, and something frightened me. I noticed Kerry looking at me with what I was sure was pity. Maybe she would scoop me up and marry me instead. Maybe she'd solve it all. I tried not to entertain this. She touched my arm, warning me of a branch coming on my right.

It was best not to talk. To trudge on, mouth tucked behind my collar, down lanes and paths I'd started to recognise, to know. Ducking under stray branches, glumly guarding setts. I was used to walking at night now, my eyesight had adjusted. The first couple of weeks I'd had my share of stumbles. And I still hadn't seen any badgers. All of this fuss for the animals and not one of them had the guts to show its face. You would think, it being my last night, that a badger might pop up. Sorry about the marriage mate and cheers for all your help. But no. There wasn't even a decent moon for me to sulk under. A shy yellow sliver of a thing, lurking behind clouds. A poor fucking show all round. I thought of a walk with Alistair, weeks before, how enthused he was by nature. 'Look at the ducks, there, look at the reeds. The moon there,'

175

pointing it out, a curl of orange peel, 'looking sexy. Less is more.' I lived with a man capable of being turned on by the moon.

It was two in the morning when I saw them. Unless I was starting to hallucinate, my tired brain jazzing up a dull night in the woods. The other four had stopped to roll up cigarettes. I went to stand at a distance, to avoid the temptation to smoke. Cigarettes were forbidden, even on a night like this, but since that moment in the van an old yearning had come back. We were on a soil bank leading up to a gate, just a little off the road. It had been a long time since we had seen any traffic. Even the hired guns were probably in bed by now, sleeping off their kills. I'd gone close to the gate, peering into the field, stroking the torchlight along the grassy bumps and curves. There were cows in there, I think, squatting hotly in companionable rest. I steered the light onto the nearest bush and saw human eyes looking back. A hand raised to a mouth. There were four of them. Sabs, standing tight-knit, clutching each other for balance. The moon's sickly light glancing off them. Self-cut hair and the musty smell of clothes worn far too long. They vanished as fast as I saw them, blending soundless into the shadows. I ran back to tell the others but they shrugged and said there were always a few of the sabs about and they were surprised I hadn't seen them before.

'You couldn't make me a rollie could you now?' It was a few hours down the line and we'd been sitting in a small and twiggy clearing, drinking Red Stripe. Drinking quite a lot of Red Stripe. I hadn't seen any more sabs, although for all I know we were surrounded by them. We hadn't seen any marksmen either. We certainly hadn't seen any badgers. I had decided to allow myself a couple of cans of lager and now I wanted to smoke. One cigarette wouldn't kill me, unless it did. My comrades had filled up the time, and the air around us, with the rolling and smoking of countless cigarettes. The hippy couple had produced an against-the-rules (we were eager not to give the authorities any excuse) pre-made spliff and I had sucked, without relish, on its throat-scratching dog-end, moistened by four pairs of lips. I had lain back and watched the segment of sky overhead, feeling the satisfaction you get when you're good and lost and you give up trying to be found. I had no idea what was going to happen next and there was something okay about this. Brian tried to tell us a story about a squat he used to live in with a man who never pooed. Or rather, he did but only once a week, at a set time. A high happy sound filled the woods, the sound of Brian laughing. It sounded close to tears. Kerry went over and put her arm around him and I felt a stab of envy. Brian wasn't the only hopeless case out here. Her head on his bony shoulder. The hippy couple nuzzled against a tree. 'Kerry?' I said, succumbing. 'Roll us a fag?'

'Sure,' she said, leaping away from Brian. 'Hold on. Are you all right with this? With your health, I mean?' I told her I'd be fine although now she was standing up ready to make one, the cravings seemed to have gone. 'Your funeral,' she said. She set about it, dextrous, while I worried what effect it would have on me. I probably wouldn't immediately drop dead. I would probably survive a few drags. Oh god, I better not have a second stroke. 'You've been gloomy all night,' she sang, 'so I am going to roll you a fag.'

'Thinking about it, don't,' I said.

'I'm doing it now!' she said. 'If it'll put a bloody smile on.' We seemed to be at war. Well she couldn't make me smoke it. Although actually maybe she could. She scampered over and was holding the thing in front of me. 'Come on,' she said. She was on top of me, pushing the filter end into my mouth. 'Time for you to light up,' she said. 'Lighten up.' I spluttered and tried to spit it out but she kept hold of my jaws, with this gleeful look on her face. I wriggled as my mouth filled up with tar. 'You scared I'm going to tell teacher?'

'Fuck off,' I managed, pushing her from me. 'It could kill me, it could fucking kill me.' She shrunk back as though I'd slapped her.

'You didn't say. You never said.' I got up, as the moment seemed to call for a matey sort of wrestle, but she had put herself in a hostile stance, arms around her knees. I said sorry, although I wasn't sure why, and I passed the fag to her.

'I don't think I'll come here again,' I said. 'I think I need to give Marie some space.' I tried explaining about the state of Henry's van but it didn't make sense as words.

'Good,' she said. There was quite a pause. 'I mean, you've been torturing yourself. Haven't you?'

'None of us enjoy it,' said Brian. Kerry went back to him. There was a hooting sound from a while away, a sarcastic owl watching us. I would definitely not return.

'So, go on,' she said. An hour had gone by and we were walking a little ahead of the rest, passing the last of our cans from mouth to mouth. By now I was pleasantly drunk. 'Face like you killed a puppy on you. What's got your goat?' Far too many animals. She was marching on, quicker than suited me, so that I kept spilling beer keeping up.

'I'm good,' I said. 'More or less. Had a chat with Marie today.'

'Well, she is your wife.' She stopped walking, waited for me, and took the can from my hands.

'I told her I'm leaving her be,' I said. 'It's scary though. Today has been the first day I've not been sure we'll make it.' She swigged, stifled a burp. Lives I'd thought would go on together had bifurcated, sprung separate. There would be a lot of evenings apart. More than we'd had together, in the end. Empty evenings, where if you speak it leaves a fingerprint on the silence, silence that shifts around the words before swallowing them, a silence louder than sound.

'Mate, I have to say this, it was over when she moved into someone else's van. That's the end of the chapter as far as I see, although I'm maybe a little old fashioned. Once half of your relationship lives in a van with someone else, it might not be built to last. Some serious incompatibilities there, in this van-based lifestyle.' I grabbed the can back and swallowed. 'Oh, Stu, are you all right? You look like shite, if I'm honest. Oh look, come here a sec. Come here.' She stroked my hair, murmuring meaningless words. She smelt much better than she had any right to. 'That's right. That's right. That's nice, isn't it? You been in the wars, you daft sod. All for a bunch of badgers. Hey. Come on now, let go. Let me look at you? Yeah, you'll be fine. It'll take a while but you will. You know what, I do like you Stu. Hanging round this place like Don Quixote, you mad old sod. I like you more than is clever.'

Behind us we could hear Brian and the hippy couple approaching, boots crunching the leaves. When they reached us they pulled faces as if something was afoot. There was really nothing afoot, I wanted to say. We carried on back to the camp together, as the sun sneaked over the branches, the can warming in my hand. Kerry's arm kept brushing against mine.

179

Thirty-Seven

There was a light on in the camper van, telling us we were last to return. Brian said good night with a prepared sort of cheeriness I found troubling. The hippy couple snuck placidly into their tent, to make respectful, tender and hirsute love. There was birdsong over the hills, actual birdsong, not the ringtone mimicry you get in London. I was left with Kerry in the clearing.

'You'll be wanting somewhere to sleep,' she said. I must have showed something with my face, fear or excitement or both, because she grinned and punched me on the arm. 'It's not the hugest tent but I'm sure we'll cope.'

'I should probably ask Brian. Although Brian has gone, hasn't he?'

'I'm not going to attack you, you'll be fine.' She slapped my wrist.

'Could you please stop hitting me, I've had a lot of bad stuff happen and I'm scared it will make me cry.'

'We better clean our teeth,' she said. We rummaged for our brushes and a bottle of water and went over to the basin at the side of the camp. She shuffled the brush along her mouth, avoiding eye contact with me. Rabies foam on her lips. Did she want to have sex? Would she want to do normal sex, nice sex, with clean limbs and eye contact, or would she want me to tie her up and hit her with a brick? I didn't feel ready for bricks. I didn't feel ready for anything. Only, for god's sake, if I was going to have sex with anyone it really ought to be with someone like her. I wasn't going to have sex. I remembered that witch at the party, the one that I didn't kiss, saying nothing bad had ever happened to her. Something to be said for Kerry, she seemed ready to risk bad things. She'd been out in the woods most of winter and she wasn't even doing it for love.

'You'll make your gums bleed,' she said. I told her I was getting rid of the taste of that cigarette. She looked about to hit me, checked herself and trotted back to her tent. I followed her, watching her walk. As I made my way through the camp I passed by Brian's tent and heard him talking in a soft, choked voice, about a bear having a picnic. I decided he had finally gone mad until I realised he was calling his children, giving them a bedtime story, first thing in the morning.

I picked up the sleeping bag from under my ruined tent and went over to Kerry's. 'Knock knock,' I whispered. She flapped the tent door open and I clambered inside. It was hot, it smelt of canvas and sweaty perfume. Kerry was wrapped in a sleeping bag, taking up the bulk of the space. One shoulder was exposed. It was the nakedest shoulder I could ever remember seeing. There was still time to run away.

'Going to be a bit of a squeeze,' she said. I managed to arrange myself inside my bag, so that I was bent into foetal position. Far more of me seemed to be touching her than was usually allowed. She asked if I was comfortable. I told her that I was.

'Tired,' she said. I agreed, at a high volume. She turned to me in a way I couldn't decipher. I struggled out of my jeans inside my bag, something she seemed to find funny. 'Night Stu,' she said. We were going to sleep then. Thank

God, we were going to sleep. I took off my glasses, put them in their case next to my head, and closed my eyes. Within a few seconds she was making strange whistling sounds, faint murmurs, dreaming without quite sleeping. It was unbearably hot. I wasn't going to sleep at all.

'Hot,' she said and unzipped her bag. I thanked the badger god in his sett in the sky that I couldn't see much of anything. She turned, so that our faces were almost touching and threw one bare leg across mine. This was going to be difficult. Her eyes were shut, her breathing regular. My mouth was very near hers. She started murmuring again, indecipherable half-sentences.

My cock was far too close to her, like that game where you run a metal rod along a wire without it touching. She was breathing loud, her face right next to mine. Her eyelids were like clamshells, streaked with blue. What the hell was I going to do now? She was moving a little, in her sleep, faintly back and forth. A millimetre nearer and she would definitely notice me. There were laws against this sort of thing. She would wake up, scream for rescue and I'd be mobbed by the rest of the camp.

I would have to get out of the tent. She made a whimpering sound and put her hand next to my chest. I would have to somehow get out from under her leg without waking her up. Her leg had the unexpected heaviness slim legs always seem to have. The sounds that she was making weren't a help.

Things were becoming sore. I tried to physically remove myself, in infinitesimal steps. She was moaning, actually moaning. I was in danger of having an accident. I stretched out my free hand and put on my glasses. She was fast asleep, uncovered, dreaming of something she looked to be enjoying. She rolled a little to one side. Now was my chance. I leapt up in what I hoped was a graceful way, slipped out of the tent and into my shoes, I jumped a couple of steps and there was Henry.

He was standing right across from us, peeing against a tree, the evidence of his animal superiority in his hands. In both his hands. He didn't break from pissing but grinned over at me and nodded. When he heard Kerry asking me what was up, a broad smile of victory lit his face. Shaking, he strode over, not bothering to put himself away.

'Aw mate,' he said. 'Aw mate. You've gone and done it now.' He strode back to his camper van, wiping his hands on his shirt. Once he was inside I ran over across the dewy grass and waited at the door. I heard voices from inside, Henry's patient drone without the words.

I raised my hand to knock but didn't do it. There was nothing to be said. I made my way, avoiding guy ropes, back to Kerry. To be fair to her, she apologised a lot. She apologised through her giggles, while I moaned into my hands.

'Henry,' came the voice. 'Please.' Great. The man got everywhere. It must have been ten in the morning and Kerry was calling his name. 'Henry, please man.' She was fast asleep. What was the bastard doing to her? She knocked off a little more of her sleeping bag and I tried my best not to look. 'You. Met. Henry. Please.' She sounded distressed. 'Henry please,' she said. The man had some dreadful power over women. He was even invading their dreams. I put my hand on her shoulder, touched her skin.

'You were having a nightmare,' I said. 'You kept saying Henry's name.' She frowned and rubbed her eyes.

'What makes you so sure it was a nightmare?' she said. And, seeing my crestfallen face, 'Kidding. I think he's a berk.'

We tried to go back to sleep, as far apart as possible.

Thirty-Eight

Breakfast around the camp fire. Brian lolloped over, looking as though sleep had made him even more haggard and tired. He took a bowl of beans, had a forkful, then smoked a cigarette instead, as if it was the last before his execution.

Henry hopped from the van, all a-swagger, and made his way towards us. You would think a forest would be good for hiding in but no place presented itself. He arrived, raised one slab of a hand in a Tonto gesture and sat himself down on a stump, making it look more comfortable than it surely could have been.

'Marie not joining us,' he said. He gave a performative yawn. 'She's still in bed. Might go back myself in a bit.' Drummed out a tribal rhythm on one be-denimed thigh. His smile was that of a happily deflowered teenage boy, itching to brag.

He was bluffing, I thought, he was bluffing.

'Tell you what, Stu,' he said. 'She's definitely worth the wait.'

I could feel the blood crowding my cheeks, a whirring in my ears. I kept quiet.

'I don't mind admitting, I thought she might go back to you,' he went on. 'But last night, it seemed to make her mind up. It's nice that you've accepted it, moved on, you know. And Kerry, she's a nice girl.'

'I really don't want to talk about it.'

'Not saying she's not had her problems. Has her peculiarities. You gotta take good care of her, Stu.'

I stood up, enjoying the temporary advantage this gave me. I hoped he wouldn't stand up too, and ruin it.

'Thank you for the warning,' I said. 'I shall certainly bear it in mind.' It didn't sound as sardonic as I wanted.

I went back to the tent to get my rucksack and call the cab. Kerry was still asleep. I called up the taxi and asked him to meet me on the path.

As I left, I thought about knocking on the camper van, begging one last time. But something held me back. As long as I didn't knock on the door then reality could be delayed, just for a while. I looked over at the badger pole, as it wafted in the cold. Back at the table Henry was laughing at something. I think for a moment he actually beat his chest.

I would have to think very hard. Perhaps try again with the Lansdownes, see if they might help. I raised my fist to knock but once again I didn't. It was time to go home.

Raoul was in the front room watching MTV with a guilty look on his face. Alistair was barging around announcing plans and future glories. The place was filthy but it was home, my only home. I went up to my room and lay on the bed. I was alone.

My marriage was over. I wasn't sure how I felt. I felt horrible. I felt loosed. I put my finger under Malkin's chin, feeling the cotton-soft biscuit-coloured fur of his throat. I gulped up the smell of the basil plant on the window sill. It had grown to a size where it cast a leafy shadow over my narrow book-stuffed room.

I was going to be alone.

The phone rang. It was Frank Lansdowne. I told him my marriage was over.

'Pedantic old fool,' he said. 'Pompous middle-class nonsense. Smug complacency.'

I had no idea what he was talking about, until I had every idea. I knew where my defaced copy of *Memory, My Mother* had gone. The one he had signed and given me himself. Marie had taken it with her and now it had been found.

'We've been nothing but good and supportive,' he said. 'We've done nothing for you but kindness, nothing but good. And yet you write these awful things. Lazy caricatures, jibes. Accepting our generosity then going home to deface my work. A signed first edition, too. I always knew she'd made a mistake with you.' He hung up.

I wondered if this was justice. I decided it probably was.

Thirty-Nine

I spent the first month crying, facing up to facts. I lost weight. At work I struggled not to sound short with the pet moaners who called in, bewailing their missing cats, their cancerous dogs. I had lost my love and was destabilised. I'd come back from the office and hide out in my room, away from Alistair's awful confidence, Raoul's solicitous care. Until the sun arrived and something unwound in me. The past few months I had been walking like a robot butler. A coward approaching the scaffold, shuffling, arms pinned to his sides in self-protection.

Malkin lay flat on the picnic table out on the balcony, basking in the sun. I looked at the unsmudged sky. Marie had emailed a few weeks earlier, telling me to apply for the divorce papers. She told me she had examined her feelings and that she was in love with Henry and the cause of animal liberation. She was sorry but that was it. The cull was on hiatus and the protestors had gone on to other wildlife campaigns. There had been serious flooding in Gloucestershire. I heard Frank Lansdowne on Radio 4. He said the government would have saved themselves a lot of trouble if they'd waited for the badgers to drown.

Rupa and I had gone out for a drink the night before. 'Things aren't really that bad, Stuart. I mean, for goodness' sake, there are other problems out there. At least Marie is looking outward, trying to improve things. This

187

is navel gazing, Stuart. You need to get involved in the world. Come to yoga with me.'

'I'm not convinced that yoga is the model of engagement I need.' I didn't know how she squared yoga with her antipathy to bullshit. She had finally split with the philoprogenitive librarian after he bought a romper suit for her birthday. A child's one, I should stress. I had offered my support but she had laughed and told me I wouldn't be much use and to save my efforts for myself. Raoul, meanwhile, was deep into volunteering. His evenings were spent in homeless shelters, weekends helping at food banks. It all seemed tied in with god or maybe he needed god to justify his natural kindness, stop himself from taking the credit.

Alistair was mostly in the front room, curtains drawn. He had a deep hostility towards daylight. Most days he would watch imported box sets, smoking and dozing off. At night he would cook his awful meals, open a bottle of wine and tell us about himself. Things were going well with Su. 'I expect we'll leave London once it's started. Maybe even share a place. Personally though, I'm all for separate flats. I expect I'll have sold my first book by then. Or the consultancy will have taken off. I wonder if she'll want kids. I reckon we'll adopt some. When I'm fifty.' I asked him when he was next seeing her. 'Oh we don't have these sorts of calendric arrangements that other couples have,' he said. 'We don't need to be tied to meetings, we're not business partners. We have an understanding.' He refilled his glass, hid behind it.

I went to work and managed to do as little as possible without getting sacked. If it was still bright after five I went to the lido and tried to enjoy the heat and coolness on my skin, the sight of the women bathers, lips pursed in involuntary scowls from the glare of the afternoon sun. I cooked meals I hadn't cooked for Marie. I scoured dating apps until I realised I only wanted to talk about what had happened.

Alistair was scornful. 'You can't fall in love with a pixel,' he said. 'You can't download someone's smell.' I said you didn't actually go on the date with the app.

One night I went to the pub alone and ordered a symbolic mixed grill. I was fed up of pretending to care about animals. It only felt symbolic until it arrived. Then it felt all too real. Bacon and liver, sausages and steak. I struggled through each greasy forkful and woke up that night covered in sweat.

I was starting to get better. Some days I felt mostly fine. There would be an election the next year with every chance of a more badger-friendly administration being formed. I thought a lot about Henry. I couldn't help myself. That idiot and my wife. The curious power he had.

Most days I called up the hospital and hassled them about the date of my final op. They always reacted with surprise, as though I had breached some hidden point of etiquette. I had to insist that they dealt with me. It had been a long while since I'd fainted but this shouldn't let them off.

Then, one afternoon, Kerry added me on Facebook.

Forty

I looked at a few of her pictures before saying hello. An embarrassment of marches, banners held high, her fingertips whiting from the strain. Animals and the dispossessed, feminism and pickets. I had to go pretty far to find any beach ones. Just as I'd managed to find some decent poolside snaps, she messaged me herself. She felt bad about that night inside her tent. The other badger people had been weird about it. Marie hadn't spoken to her since and they had always got on pretty well. I probably didn't want to hear about Marie, she said. I said she was probably right. She wanted to meet up. She wanted to talk to me. I spent a while messing with my hair in front of the mirror.

She lived around the corner from a high street in East London that was enjoying its moment of glory. It wasn't far from where Marie and I had lived. I sat outside a delicatessen slash cafe, sipping lemonade from a foil-capped can. Gay couples sauntered in luminous white tee shirts and creaseless pastel shorts. Women with suntans and denim cut-offs. Young men with the beards of Victorian evangelists, sweating in too many layers or wearing tee shirts cut down low to expose chests thick with eddies of black hair. Kerry arrived wearing a navy-blue dress. She wore no make-up or wore make-up that made it look like she wore no make-up. Her hair had grown out since the camp. She sat down, elbow on the table, puckish grin on her face. 'Stu,' she said.

'Hello again.'

'Thought we should probably chat.' She started rolling a cigarette, the shreds wedging under her nails.

'We might as well.' A waitress came out and took our orders. I ordered something with meat, checking first if that was okay.

'I do eat meat, you know,' she said, when the waitress had gone. 'I mean, I know I probably shouldn't. Environment and all. Only when I tried going vegan I was weary as hell, must have looked like somebody's ghost. So I thought, I'll eat meat for the energy and use some of that energy to campaign against eating meat. I also—' she smiled again, this time in a conspiratorial way, as though she sought indulgence '—really fucking love meat.'

'Nothing wrong with hypocrisy,' I said. 'I don't trust people who are consistent.'

'Hmm,' she said. 'That's interesting.' I knew that when clever people said something was 'interesting' that could also mean *stupid* or *racist*. 'So you're basically just saying that goodness makes you uncomfortable. If someone, some person, isn't a complex kind of a muddle, you don't trust them, because they've won, there's nothing you can use on them.'

We sat and ate in silence, chased balsamic around our plates with curls of lettuce, tried not to look at each other. Kerry ate fast, head down, like someone rushing through an exam. When she'd finished, she frowned at her plate as though it had let her down. I spent a good time tearing the foil from the lemonade.

'So you sort of helped end my marriage.' She avoided meeting my eyes.

'Hoo.' She tapped the table. 'I think it was probably

191

over already, wasn't it? I am sorry, though. I deliberately didn't want anything to happen. I was trying to go to sleep. I did, I do sort of like you. I'd started to. You seemed so lost. Sucker for the thwarted, really, I am. But I didn't want any of that to happen.'

'It's done,' I said. She looked relieved and I smiled. I wasn't very good at looking stern.

'So I thought we could maybe hang out. Properly, I mean. To be honest, I don't really have time for anyone at the moment. Anyone. Anything. I've got, like, four or five different meetings to go to every week. Still I thought that we probably should. I got the impression you wanted to, in the tent.'

I thought for a time about this. A new thing. An opportunity for joy in life. I had sort of stopped hoping for this.

'I think so,' I said. 'You're very beautiful.' She nodded. I hadn't known that before this point but now I was sure that she was.

'Well, you are quite handsome. I should probably say that now.'

'Thanks,' I said. I hadn't felt so for a while.

'I nearly said you were beautiful. I should have said that. Would that have sounded weird? Like, you might have been insulted.'

'I wouldn't have been insulted,' I said. The meat would smell, I realised, garlicky and nauseating. I swigged at my lemonade. She bounced on her chair a bit, not, I thought, from nerves, but from her usual excess of spirits.

'I've been single about a year,' she said. I told her I had been alone a while myself.

'Well yeah,' she said. 'I spend my time getting involved with things. I feel kind of useless if I don't.' She grinned, apologetic. 'Devote myself to public works. I thought it might be nice to get to know someone.'

'I'm fine with that.'

'I am taking quite a long time to suggest a simple thing,' she said.

'Yes,' I said. 'You are.'

We went into a school playground that at weekends was a car boot sale, that was, in turn, slowly becoming an organic market. Wholesome young women sold bank-breaking homemade jams next to an avuncular old man selling David Icke pamphlets and anti-bankster flotsam. Kerry stopped to look at this, frowning when she spotted the Icke. This was good. We moved on until we came to a rolling patch of parkland with a pathway winding through. 'It's weird this, getting to know someone. Doing couple stuff. God, I expect it's weirder for you. I mean, you're married and everything. You're married! This is adultery for you. And I'm a mistress.' She laughed for a long time at this as though marriage were automatically funny. I was starting to think this myself.

By a tree, we stopped and kissed. It had been a very long time. Actually, since the witch. This was different from that. She tasted of something other than not-Marie.

'Slow down there, mister. You get this look on your face when you're kissing,' she said. 'Like a starving wolf. Avid, is the word I'm looking for.'

She lived in an apartment block, across the road from a church. There were books everywhere. Polemics, theory, reportage. No novels that I could see. A poster above the bed demanded 'Full Communism Now', next to a picture of One Direction. The bed was a fat blue mattress on the floor, thick with needless cushions and pillows. 'My flatmate's away a few months. Singapore. He works in the city.' She mimed vomiting. 'Is something funny?'

'I didn't say anything.' I lifted a tin money box in the

shape of a Brechtian capitalist, rubbed a coat of dust off its top hat.

'Okay.' She sat on the bed, her knees under her chin. 'I bet you think I'm being a right bitch there? Well, look, I spent ages saying *just cos he works in the city, doesn't mean he's a dick*. Like, any evidence he was all right, I was jumping at it. I really wanted to have my prejudice smashed, you know. But he's *such* a knob.'

She popped out to the bathroom. I opened a note book and saw neat and curvy writing on every page. I had time to see the underlined name 'Henry' before she came back. She didn't seem to notice I'd seen the book.

'You're really into being an activist, then?' I asked. She stood in the doorway and shrugged. As though everyone worth talking to was.

When she undressed her body was solid, moon coloured. I took my clothes off, trying not to feel self-conscious. She asked me to go down on her and I bowed like a dog at its water, my knees scraping on the carpet, cock bobbing against the edge of the mattress. There was an awkward fuss about condoms. I kept pressing my mouth to parts of her, registering each incident of her body. I was sweating, bruised. She kept laughing in a way I couldn't get used to. She said she could tell I was excited. We lay next to each other, panting, sweat rising over us.

'Fuck, but I needed that,' she said. 'We should probably do it again.'

We watched a film on her sofa, unsure whether to hug. She said I should probably go home. She smiled, unconvincing, and waved goodbye.

When I got back, Alistair ushered me onto the balcony and quizzed me about my day. He was enthused. I slept well. Life felt to be improving. The smell of the basil plant soothed me through my dreams.

Forty-One

I got to know Kerry. We talked most of the day on Facebook Messenger, the *ping* as her words hit my phone providing a painkiller release, a second's happy calm. The possibility of happiness presented itself, unplanned for, unconsidered. It would mean giving up on my goal and I thought about whether I could do this, embrace the unexpected, let go of Marie. I thought I should give it a shot.

Kerry's nights and spare days were spent on protests, at meetings, rallies or sit-ins. She worked for the Feminist Library in Waterloo, and this seemed virtuous enough, but she didn't let up after hours. She would be out trying to stop a Sure Start in Enfield from being closed down or waving a placard outside a detention centre. She would get back late, sweaty and optimistic. It went well, she would say. Public opinion was changing. Or some nights she would be cynical, question her own motives, scorning the idea that things would ever change. 'Do I even want them to, deep down? I mean, my life is pretty awesome. Might be bored if I had nothing to protest about.' If I echoed her despondency she would snap at me in an instant. Cynicism had to be earned. Other times she would come home at night in an even darker mood. She was wasting her time, the status quo was far too powerful. People were selfish or racist or thick. I didn't disagree. I said some of this was true but most people were all right.

'Ah, you should teach me to care a bit less,' she said. 'You seem to have it down.' It wasn't that I didn't care and for a moment or two I sulked. I was trying to get back into writing and work out who I was. It wasn't a case of not caring.

She didn't know how to measure out her energy, to keep some in reserve. She would run through the whole lot of it, at the same frenetic pace, until she would flop, wilting, onto the sofa and not come off for a week. After the necessary recovery, she would be up and running again, getting herself kettled, dodging truncheons.

'It's like you want to be a saint,' I said. 'A funny sort of saint but still a saint.' I nuzzled at her throat. I pressed my lips against the ridge of her ear.

'Not an urge you seem to have. I'm going to grab a drink,' she said. 'Do you want one?' I said yes, watched her walk to the fridge. Her windows were open onto the hot dark street below. High heels clicked on the pavement, in tottering return. Snatches of wine song, the rattle of a van.

'Don't you want to do anything with yourself? Except read and write and fuck me?'

'I quite like cooking you meals. I'm adjusting, I told you. I'm deciding what I care about.'

'Maybe *I* should have a stroke.' She led me into her room. 'Stop me running around all day trying to do stuff.'

'Yes,' I said.

'Is it Marie that scares you?' she said. 'Do you think anyone who actually believes in stuff is liable to be a loony? Let it take over their lives?'

'I don't know.'

'Undo this zip, will you?'

'Sure.'

She wriggled away from her dress. 'Must have made you cross though.' Her back to me, buttocks raised. 'Made you really angry.'

'I'm not really an angry person. I never get angry at all.'

'Who does she think she is? Three months into marriage and she's running around like that.'

'I really wasn't.'

'Shh,' she said. 'I'm doing a thing. Does it make you cross that I'm always off at meetings? When I should be at home tending to you?' She raised her buttocks a little bit more, inched her legs apart. 'Make you want to lay down the law?'

'I'm not.'

'You must have so much anger stored up there. Waiting to explode.' Her feet shifted further. I understood, stepped up to her. 'God but you must be cross. God but you must be furious. You must really want to ... Could you shift your elbow a bit? Cheers. Oh. Yeah, you must be angry. You must be so fucking cross.'

The ward was noisy and ill lit. The man in the next bed was moaning. There were banks of wire-strewn medical equipment at odd angles in the corridors. It took a long time for anyone to come and see me. Kerry sat by the bed, looking alternately at her phone and over at me. I had collapsed for the first time in ages. She'd been at my place, meeting Alistair and Raoul. He had cooked one of his special dinners, which she'd eaten with seeming relish.

'It scares me that you will die,' she said. 'It scares me how much I don't want that.'

'I'm not too keen on it either,' I said. She put a hand on mine. Eventually the doctor came and told me it was only another faint. My first one in a while.

We rode in a cab back home. I didn't ask her about the fear and what she meant.

I said I was sorry about Alistair. He could be a little full-on but was actually sweet. She said she didn't know about that, that she had liked him straight away, had even enjoyed his food. I wasn't sure I welcomed this. It had been strange, seeing her in the divorce flat. Raoul had stared and told her she was the first woman he had seen there in a year. He looked at her like he was in the sort of film where live-action people interact with cartoons. Back in my room it was hot and airless. I shut Malkin outside and he wailed and scratched at the door. I was glad I'd put away the picture of Marie.

'I was worried about you,' said Kerry.

'I am incredibly brave,' I said.

We began to undress. I was slow, my movements cautious. I gulped down a bottle of Evian which had been resting on my bedside too long, the plastic turning it stale.

Together on the narrow bed. 'We have to be pretty gentle,' I said. I was inside her and it was like swimming, it felt frictionless, different and familiar both at once. Something was altered. She threw her arms back and knocked the basil plant off the windowsill. There was a crash of it shattering on the balcony below.

'For fuck's sake,' I said. It was hopeless to go on. I pulled back and clambered up so that my head leant out of the window. It was too dark to see the plant. I sat back on the bed, rubbing my eyes. Kerry had her knees up, shielding herself.

I patted her, trying to reassure. My head began to throb. The next day I had to go out and put all the soil in a bag.

Forty-Two

The picture showed Marie outside Selfridges, placard in her hand. I had been looking at it for some time. 'Fur is murder' said the placard. She was looking tired, I thought. Frown lines on her forehead. There was no sign of Henry and this pleased me for a bit until I decided he probably took the picture. Her eyes were shining. I tried to read them. Passion, I supposed.

I thought she'd have suited fur. I thought that in another life she'd have been on Flask Walk in a stole, comfortable, not caring. I didn't know this person, yelling into a megaphone. I didn't know why she cared so much. I couldn't stop looking at her.

'Wotcher doing?' said Kerry and I slammed my laptop shut. 'Are you looking at porn?'

I didn't know what to say. I wasn't sure if porn was one of those things that had become okay over time. 'Yes, I am,' I said.

'Gissa look,' said Kerry. Porn was obviously okay.

'You wouldn't want to,' I said. 'This is really disgusting porn.'

'Okay,' said Kerry.

'I mean it's really horrible,' I said.

She went into the other room.

Kerry soon had me marching myself. Not against fur – I had my limits – but against austerity, neoliberalism, cuts in services, Tories. Non-specific discontent. *Bad things*. I could question the march's efficacy, but I had no reason not to join in.

'Do you really think sitting at home and writing is enough?' she said. 'Don't you want to be, I don't know, engaged with life? Fat lot of good it does us, but at least you'll be doing something.'

'I really do need to write,' I said.

'You disagree with everything this march is against,' she said. 'So why not join it? Why not be *for* something?' I said I'd come but only because she wanted me to. She said that wasn't the point.

We joined the march near Embankment station. There were discarded placards on the pavements. I picked one up that said 'if you can read this, thank a teacher'. I felt extremely radical. I felt spasms of engagement.

'I might even join the Labour Party,' I said.

'Labour Party,' said Kerry, with a snort.

Alistair and Raoul had come along, Raoul bringing corned beef sandwiches. Alistair said he didn't believe in this sort of thing. He was an artist, that was enough. What we needed was to change ourselves. I didn't think he planned on doing so. Recently his talk had been full of his bride-to-be. Their relationship would threaten the status quo. We would quake, he said, if we could only understand it. He was writing a lot of erotica.

Old men waved unread papers. There were teenage girls, faces covered in crayoned slogans. Trade union banners that looked like they should be draped over barrel organs. A few signs blamed austerity on Israel. I worried about this for a while. 'You can't wait for everyone to be perfect before you join in,' said Kerry. 'There'll always be some nutters.'

'Don't your legs get tired?' I said.

200

Raoul told us how he had not been on a march for years. 'I was a protest baby,' he said. 'Red diaper, almost. Inner city stuff. Then my mom got into pyramids and crystals. Took the steam out of her. She still gets on it, past a certain hour. Man, she hates Obama. Takes it personally from him. Like he should know better.' Alistair kept quiet. Kerry said she'd been thrilled when Obama got in. She'd stayed up all night watching the results at her student union. There'd been an American guy there who had guiltily told her he was a Republican. He said he was scared to admit it over here. She'd drunk too much and kissed him, for a bet. And when the new president was announced she'd been so giddy and out of nowhere this old black American woman had appeared, she seemed too old to be a student and Kerry had hugged her and the woman had whispered 'we won, my god, we won.' Kerry had gone back to halls, with the Republican guy and she'd insisted on opening the window and playing Sam Cooke out of it, at full volume, letting his song roll over the quadrant, in through the sleeping windows, waking a world that had changed.

'Sounds stupid now,' she said.

'Not so much,' said Raoul.

The crowd began to boo. We were passing Downing Street. There was no sign of anyone except for policemen at the gates. I booed a bit, to keep up. I always felt sorry for the police. 'Bastards,' said Kerry. Alistair didn't mention his future safe seat. He kept his head well down. Raoul tapped me on the shoulder. 'So, Stu, your friend Rupa, she single now?' She had visited the other day. Raoul had told her this increased the number of women he'd seen in there by 200 per cent.

We reached Trafalgar Square. Misty rain and familiar speeches. A mention of Tony Benn. We cheered. Maybe there was something in all this. I couldn't see what we were changing but maybe that wasn't the point. Enthusiasm returning, the sense that life was special. I looked around the crowd and saw the banner.

At first I wasn't sure. But then, who else could it be? Him, still tall as an oak tree, still with his Timotei glister, his life-raft chest. Her, tiny, sheltered by his bulk, yelling into a megaphone. In a badgers-army tee shirt a size too big. And what did they have with them, on this march against austerity? A giant badger banner, a badger dressed as Guy Fawkes, with a 'tache and a Jacobean hat.

'Henry,' said Kerry. Not Marie, I noticed. Her attention was all on him.

'For god's sake, let's move on before they see us.'

'Its fine,' said Alistair but our stares outvoted him and for once he made no fuss. We edged along in caterpillar formation, squeezing past hoarse pensioners and teenage girls in veils, until we were out of the crowd. Crossed the statue of Edith Cavell and went into the Chandos. Inside there were beet-toned boozers and confused tourists eating fatty breakfasts.

'Need a drink,' I said.

'You really aren't over her at all are you?' She wasn't joking. She seemed cross. As though I were malingering.

'I am. I am. I'm absolutely okay. That was just a shock, is all.' I tried to look like a man who is over his wife. Like someone out of a Caspar David Friedrich, cocking an eye to the sublime. Privately though, I bristled. And not just at the sight of Marie holding hands with her eight-foot lover, seeing badgers in everything. My concern was over Kerry. Why on earth had she said 'Henry'? Why had his name this primacy in her mind? Why was it written in her notebook? It even came out in her sleep. Henry, please, man. Please what? The fucking guy got everywhere.

202

I glugged down a gin and tonic, not looking anyone in the eye, thinking murderous thoughts. Henry had obviously preceded me, just as he had followed. Kerry was his cast-off and he was still in her mind. Did she cry for him when I wasn't there, was his face what she saw before opening her eyes? A standard I could never attain. When she clutched at my chubby body she was touching the ghost of his strength. She saw us, surely, as refugees from two better loves, making do with what was left. Survivors, gripping onto one another in the waves, only to speed up their drowning.

I thought I had hated Henry before but it was nothing to how I felt now.

'What are you thinking?' she said. I told her I wasn't thinking at all. She held onto my hand.

'Stuart,' she said. 'I am starting to fall in love with you. You know that? You understand? I know it's probably too soon or whatever the fuck. But I am falling in love with you and I would like this to mean something. I'm offering you the chance to be really fucking happy. So if you're planning on being a dick, for god's sake do it now so I can get rid of you.'

I blinked a lot and smiled. We kissed. Someone had left a mattress at the bottom of the cliff. Someone had broken my fall. But the poison still ran through me.

'Tell me about your ex.' I couldn't help asking. As soon as I knew, I'd be fine with it, as soon as I knew all the facts. As soon as I knew, I'd be able to let go. How Henry had been the greatest lover she'd had, making all her other loves seem like satires on life with him. How she'd done things with Henry, willing and without shame, that she would no more do with me than she'd stand up and do in church. I stared at her, trying to force out the truth.

203

It didn't work. Instead she told me about some bozo called Neal, with an A (the A, I gathered, was important). He'd been one of those intense young men you get around protest movements, explaining the evils of capitalism over a Guinness while pale and shrinking women nod along. I found a picture on her Facebook: he was boxy-headed, buzzcut, like the kind of American soldier he presumably abhorred.

Kerry had come over to England for university, eager to be changed. This little squirt Neal mustn't have believed his luck. Consumerism was bad, the patriarchy was bad, most religions were bad apart from ones that must be respected, war, when fought by men like his father, was evil through and through. He was going to start a magazine; he was going to start a movement. She'd drunk it down and offered her virginity as the first of the many sacrifices she would make for a better world. She had jumped right under him like a suffragette under a horse.

Oh, he was a genius, was Neal, she insisted on this point. A great, a brilliant man. Only, over the years, he'd backed down. She'd kept going to every protest, embracing every cause. But he'd started to make excuses. The world was a bit more complicated than that, he'd said. He'd declined to explain quite how. He'd applied himself at work, given his Marxist set-texts to the local Oxfam shop. One day, out of the blue, he'd told her he was seeing someone else. Someone the same as she'd been when he met her, only this time ready to adopt his new caution, his quietism, as her own.

Kerry wasn't about to do that. She may have started on this path with him but she would continue it alone, while friends gravitated to the media or marketing, even financial services. She would carry on.

I listened, proud of her. She was unafraid of bad things happening, unafraid of life.

There had been no Henry in this story. I guessed that asking her now would get me nowhere.

'You still aren't over Marie, are you?' she said, after minutes of cloudy silence. 'Don't worry, you don't have to be. I mean, seriously, how could you? The time you spent together. You stood up there and married her. You went and made a speech. You signed the papers. You stood and said your vows. You were trying to win her back a couple of months ago. How can you be over her? I'm trying to remember the last time I made a speech. It was about the environment, I think. If I did that and then the environment swanned off I reckon I'd feel sore.'

'I am. I really am.' I meant it as I said it. Even if it wasn't entirely true, it seemed the right state to reach. An aspiration that became a fact by pretending it already was.

Kerry sat up on the bed, her hands wrapped round her cup of tea. 'It's okay, it's just sort of sad.'

'Honestly I wouldn't go back now even if I could. I am starting to love you too.' It was true, I really was. I still wanted to know about Henry though. I wanted to know what he'd done.

Forty-Three

'We should go out,' said Kerry.

I didn't take this proposal especially seriously. She was wearing pyjama bottoms and one of my tee shirts. From the street below came the sounds of early night, overlapping conversations and car stereo sub-bass. The air of it got through her windows, turned the room into the street.

'Got this book to read,' I said.

'That looks a lot like a phone you're looking at. Rather than a book.'

'The book is ready and waiting.'

She stood up and went over to the window, drinking in the night. 'We should get dressed,' she said. 'I should put on something fancy. I'm not sure you've ever seen me in anything fancy.'

'You always look fancy,' I said.

'We should go to a bar. We should pay a lot of money for lager that we could get from downstairs for a few quid. We'll shout over the music and I'll try and make you dance. We should do this.'

'Alternatively, there is bed. The upside of bed is that I'm already on it so it would take a bit less planning.'

Kerry started to dance to the music from outside. I had never seen her dance. I couldn't tell if she was good at it or if this mattered. I sat up and I watched her. There was a clumsy exhilaration to her movements. But also an embarrassed sexiness, as though the dance was a comment on sexiness. I looked, for a second, at my phone and saw a message from George appear.

'You need to come to Bristol,' the message said. 'We're living there now, with Irene.' He sent me the address.

'Come and dance,' said Kerry. 'Or shall I come over to you?'

'Decisions, decisions,' I said. I typed out a refusal: there was no way I was schlepping over to Bristol.

'She misses you though,' wrote George. 'I can tell she really does. She goes on about you all the time. Henry's all in a wobble. There's something really bad about them.' I asked him what he meant.

'You should carry me to bed,' said Kerry. 'Or carry me outside. Either works for me. God these nights are fine.' I looked up at her and made a sound I hoped was loving and enthusiastic.

'Just wrong,' George typed. 'I can explain it if you come. She said the other day. She said she just hopes you stay friends. She was crying, in the kitchen. She tried to hide it but she was. She does that a lot.'

'Hope I'm not interrupting anything,' said Kerry. I put the phone down.

'Nothing at all,' I said, patting the bed. When I next looked at my phone there was a scroll of messages from George, getting less and less coherent, more fevered. A blue papyrus of entreaties and bribes. Marie missed me, Marie needed my friendship, Marie was at a loss.

A few days later I set off for Bristol.

Forty-Four

They lived in what looked like an ordinary suburb without the broth-y whiff of hard-core activism. Staid, conventional. I'd expected weed fumes, and slogan stickers in every window but the only signs I saw were for estate agents or the local neighbourhood watch. Then I remembered this was Irene's turf. An odd person, but no bohemian. She'd only contracted politics when the badger cull began, spending decades up to that as a dinner lady or on a checkout, I guessed. I wondered what the neighbours thought of the peculiar trio she'd invited into her home, this striking feral couple and their lurking boy hanger-on. Not to mention the dog.

I'd decided to make my visit a surprise. I didn't want to risk a refusal. I would tell them I'd come on an impulse, just wanting to say hello.

Mostly I was curious about Kerry and Henry. If I could get the sod alone for a couple of minutes, I could ask him what had happened between them. He surely wouldn't resist a chance to boast. Kerry? Yeah, we had a little thing. Don't think she ever got over it, poor bitch. It would be one more point of triumph, something to revel in.

I'd be lying if I said there wasn't, also, some curiosity about Marie. What had George meant, there was something bad about them? Did she really need a friend? I would be a good friend. I would help her if I could.

I was at the right house, 95. As soon as I arrived there a lot of my confidence vanished. The house was, so clearly, the street's concession to carnival. In the overgrown grass were several garden gnomes, leering and concupiscent. I counted at least twelve of them. There was a 'Stop the Cull' poster in the front room window. From the grass came a strong smell of dog shit. Nothing reasonable could come from a house like this.

Bracing myself, I rang the bell. Musical, of course, a bar or two of 'God Save the Queen'. Before it had played out, the dog was up at the door, barking, rattling the panes. A woman's voice – not Marie's – yelled at the beast to shut up. Irene was indoors. She took her time in answering, and I pictured her trudging, in carpet slippers, wheezing as she trod. For some reason I assumed she'd be in a dressing gown. But when she did get to the door she was wearing an unsuitable Mickey Mouse tee shirt and grey jogging bottoms. She looked at me with incomprehension.

'Stuart,' I said. 'You remember. I used to be married to Marie. Still am if you want to be strict about it.' She blinked and glowered at me.

'You were rude,' she said. 'I didn't like it.' I had no idea what she meant. Then I remembered our angry exchange on Facebook, which had ended in my suggesting a dictionary. She had replied that she was dyslexic. I tried hard to make the rigid smile on my face into a charming grin of apology.

'Stress,' I said. 'I was stressed. Can I come in?' Before she could refuse I had my foot in the hall, edging past her and the St Bernard. Irene made protesting noises but followed me into the front room.

So then, this front room. I had to stand for a moment and get my breath back. The place was brim-full of tat.

There was a large-scale collection of monarchist para-phernalia: doilies and commemorative Royal Doulton plates, tea towels of Princess Di, union jack mugs and a Kate Middleton calendar. To match this, there was a slightly smaller display of animal mementos: stuffed toy cows and plaster otters, a hedgehog clock and, inevitably, badgers. Badger toys, badger cross stitches, a badger poster and, worst of all, a toddler-sized badger manne-quin wearing shades and a leather jacket with the words 'Setts Appeal' studded on the side.

It was, I should say, spotless. Irene, at least, didn't suffer from her lodgers' aversion to dusting.

'They're not here,' said Irene. 'Don't know why you are.'

'Just dropping by,' I said, with what I hoped was bonhomie. She opened her mouth for a few seconds then grabbed a yellow cloth and started scrubbing the ornaments.

'You should get off and go,' she said. 'You're only causing bother.'

'Cup of tea would be nice,' I said. I sat down on a badger cushion and tried to look at home. I soon realised that this tactic would only work if Marie and Henry had, say, walked in at that moment. As they didn't, I was left sitting there, the amiable mask I'd adopted turning quickly into something else. Irene dusted and hoovered around me, tutting and glowering and refusing to bring me tea. The St Bernard sat opposite, his mouth all folds and slaver, cords of drool hanging from his jaws. I began to wonder if I had done the right thing. My phone was out of data, thanks to an archaic package I had never got around to changing. A shame.

A message from Kerry might have dragged me onto my feet. Onto my feet and back home.

After what might have been an hour, but felt like several more, a car pulled up outside. Irene took a ponderous glance in my direction, shaking her head as though I were a lost cause. There was the sound of keys in the door and the dog bounced from the room. I could hear Marie cooing and fussing him. Touching him.

I tried to sit like I was only passing through.

Finally, Marie came through the door, laden with carrier bags and smiling ear to ear. She stopped dead and gawped at me as though I'd been buried a week. I had time to notice how much older she looked and to hate myself for doing so. 'Stuart,' she said. So she remembered my name at least.

Henry came in after her and stood in the doorway. George, I thought, was onto something. This wasn't the Henry I remembered. As though he had been cowed somehow, his swagger been constrained. A lot of the colour gone from his face, which still left him russet hewed by everyday standards, but for him was pallid and grey.

'Hey Stu,' he drawled. He didn't even confront me. 'What brings you here?'

'Yes *Stu*,' said Marie in a much less amiable way. 'What are you doing?'

'I was in the area,' I said. I realised I had no plausible reason for this. 'Meeting an agent about the book. They weren't interested. Story of my life, haha. And I thought that I'd come by. I thought it was silly, us avoiding one another. We're all adults after all. We have a lot in common.'

'We've got one thing, at least,' said Henry with a sneer. 'Badgers I mean.'

'Badgers,' I said. 'Exactly.'

'Did George suggest this?' said Marie. She opened the

211

door and yelled his name. There was no reply, the boy having presumably snuck off. 'Did he put you up to this?'

'Yeah,' I said, seeing no reason to lie about it. 'He said you'd welcome a visit. I can head back if you'd prefer?'

'That boy is a nightmare,' said Marie. 'Henry, we have to do something.' She spoke to him, not like a lover, which I'd feared, but like one half of a couple, which was worse.

I reminded myself about Kerry, about all the promise she offered.

'He's only a kid, Marie,' said Henry. Irene, who had been dusting especially hard just then, dropped her cloth and let out a high keening sound.

'Oh Irene, Irene,' said Marie, rushing towards her howling landlady and stretching her arms around as much of her as she could. The whole scene was becoming morbidly emotive.

'Stay for dinner Stu?' said Henry.

I looked him in the eye. There was none of his old challenge there. The man was exhausted, right through. That look on his face was defeat.

I told him I'd love to stay.

Marie did most of the cooking. Tossed spices and vegetables together, like she'd done in the days of our marriage. All four months of them. I'd missed the way she cooked. I'd missed her. Kerry was fun, of course, but she could be a little self-righteous. No, I didn't think this. I went into the kitchen and saw Henry near Marie, standing by the stove with a bottle of wine and I had the strange sense of seeing my own life from outside, as though someone much more handsome were playing me in a film.

I went back and sat in the dining room. There was a framed colour photograph of a Yorkshire terrier on the wall, professionally done. I asked Irene about it and she brightened, telling me at great length about the animal's puppyhood, maturity and final struggle with illness. I could hear the wok sizzling from the other room. The St Bernard huffed at my lap.

We were just getting to the terrier's extended deathbed scene when Marie and Henry came through with the food and the wine.

'Is she telling you about Jack? Poor little Jack. I wish I'd met him.'

'Feel as though I have,' I said. Henry caught my eye in a way that made me uncomfortable. It was the look, I thought, of a fellow-sufferer, a sufferer *of women*. I didn't quite have the courage to glare at him but I tried my best to look blank.

George chose this moment to stomp down the stairs and join us. He had his hoodie on, obscuring most of his face. Underneath the top he seemed to be wearing pyjamas. He said nothing to any of us. Marie sighed. As long as George was around there was someone at the table less welcome than myself.

'You have a guest, George,' she said, in the tone of a determinedly civilising mother. George shrugged even more than usual, went into the kitchen and came back with a bag of white sliced bread. Pulling slices from it, he tore them as if he were soon to be feeding ducks, piling the downy tearings on his plate. His commitment to unsettling those around him was getting to be impressive.

'It is nice to see you all again,' I said. I wondered how long before I could politely take my leave. Already this journey felt pointless, a failing. My phone buzzed. A text from Kerry. She hoped I was having a great day with my friend, the fictional friend I'd told her about. I wondered if she guessed, suspected that something was up.

213

I must have been looking guilty because Marie chose this moment to speak.

'How's Kerry?' she said. 'It's nice that we've both met new people. Means we can hopefully be friends.'

'Exactly what I want,' I said. 'It's important to stay friends.'

'She asked me if I minded,' said Marie. 'Kerry did. Before she contacted you. I've not heard from her since. She's very *active* for someone like you. Who likes a quiet life.'

'I don't know why everyone thinks I want a quiet life. You always made me feel like you were Liz Taylor and you'd accidentally married Philip Larkin. Anyway, me and Kerry are just cheering each other up.'

'I told her I didn't mind at all. It's weird though. I don't think I want to hear about it. Sorry.'

'I propose a toast,' I said. It was vital to keep the subject back on our new friendship. 'We've all been through a lot. A year ago – less than a year ago – we were getting married. Making those solemn vows. But it's the modern world and nobody takes those seriously anymore. No. What matters is that we can be friends. After all, love passes. It may seem exciting at first but sooner or later the first traces of apathy and inertia come in, don't they? Followed, eventually, by disgust.'

'This is a very long toast,' said Henry.

'I'm getting to the point,' I said. 'And that point is. That friendship. Amity. Knowing you can rely on one another. These things are stronger, truer than love. So my toast is to friendship. To friendship.'

I waggled my glass. Marie sighed. I hoped that this sigh was a sign she was deeply moved.

'You can't rely on anyone,' said George.

'Love is stronger than friendship,' said Henry.

'Dogs are good friends,' said Irene.

Marie said nothing.

'What do you think of Kerry, Henry?' If we were going to be awkward we might as well do it properly.

Henry put down his fork. If he was hiding something he did it well. There was nothing to read in his face. Too much nothing, I thought. You'd have to make an effort to communicate quite so little. 'Horses for courses, isn't it?' he said.

Irene started talking about badgers. I refilled my glass of wine and found I was missing Kerry a lot. I looked across at Marie. She had barely started her food. Looking up, she gave a half-smile.

'It's sweet that you want to be friends,' she said. 'I think it would be nice. Sometime.' I grinned into my drink. I didn't want to catch Henry's eye. I didn't want him to see I knew I'd won.

I was waiting at the bus stop. The melancholy of parting had been bearable this time. Friendship seemed quite feasible. I would work hard at it. I would appreciate Kerry too. A healthy accommodation was possible. Love would become friendship and thus endure. Things would be okay.

My thoughts were full of charity. George might have invited me over to cause some trouble but the result had been a pleasant meal. Even Henry, well, he was a clodhopper but Marie would see that soon enough. He wasn't actually a bad man. You didn't devote yourself to badgers without some level of misplaced empathy.

Footsteps broke this reverie. It was Henry running towards me. He stopped, tossed his hair and stood next to me, a little too close. Being Henry, he was barely out of breath.

'It was so good to see you,' he said. I hadn't expected that.

'Same to you,' I said.

He grabbed me in a hug. 'Feel like me and you are due one of these,' he said. It was warm in the middle of this hug. It was stifling and moist. His stubble rubbed against me. It was taking much too long. 'Let it all out,' he said.

'I don't want to let it all out,' I said. I tried to wriggle free.

'You know, I respect you,' he said. 'You've always been so good. You basically gave me your happiness. You saw I wanted it and you gave it all to me.' He finally let go. I stood, panting, and felt myself for injuries. 'I always think of it. I wake up in the morning and I drink my coffee and I look at Marie lying there and I always think of you. Back in London. How you gave this to me.'

'Yes, well.'

'It's an amazing thing you did.' He hit me on the shoulder in a matey, crippling way. 'To just bow out like that. Sometimes when I'm holding her I wonder if I could do it and you know, I don't think I could.'

'No.'

'I won't deny there's been troubles,' he said. 'It's tough, taking someone on. You might have noticed I'm quiet.' Oh god was he ... was he going to *confide* in me? 'I can't stand suffering, you see. Same with those badgers. When I see it I just fill up, you know. With what do you call it, empathy.'

'Suffering is tough,' I said. He moved to crush me in another hug.

'It's hard,' he said. 'So hard.' I was swallowed up by his embrace, unable to move. It was like being trapped in a flesh sleeping bag. 'You're a good man Stuart,' he said. I could feel the words forming inside him, rumbling

216

against my face. His enormous body was shaking against me. Maybe I would be trapped in this hug forever. I could be a parasite, feeding on scraps of his tee shirt and flakes of dead skin. Eventually we'd be fused, inseparable. But no, I could see the sky above me, feel the air enter my lungs. He freed me.

'I try my best,' I said.

'You take care of Kerry now,' he said. 'I know her pretty well and she's ... I'll shut up.' He opened his arms again but I jumped back off the pavement. 'Gotta take care of those ladies,' he said. He ambled off down the road, without the usual peculiar lightness of hefty people. His step now matched his size, carrying himself as though he were carrying heavy boxes.

I felt less satisfied than I'd hoped for from this visit. I felt perturbed in ways I hadn't planned for.

Forty-Five

I went to see Kerry the next day. I had woken thinking about her, with renewed excitement. I wanted to race and tell her how great she was. I wanted to tell her how exciting the walk from the station to her flat was, the delirium that comes as you approach your lover's house, knowing you'll soon be there and in their arms. I wanted to say I'd seen Marie and it hadn't made a difference, tell her I was ready. Except this would involve admitting I'd been to Marie. Plus there were Henry's repeated allusions – his concerned words-to-the-wise – to Kerry being unwell. I thought of these as territorial, faux-friendly attempts to do the dirty on a good thing, knock some of the shine off it. But what if they weren't? At three in the morning they sometimes seemed genuine. My body believing it, keeping me awake, even as my mind argued otherwise. It all had to be considered. So we spent time in her room, our conversation circling topics, approaching closer and closer, before leaping back like kids playing Mr Wolf.

One day, badger activists picketed my office, after our press team refused to give a comment on the cull. There was a suggestion we were in cahoots with the farming industry and no amount of insisting we specialised in pets could dispel this common belief. I'd started emphasising the first word of Pet Concern whenever I answered the phone, until Rupa advised me to stop. And then they were on the doorstep, cardboard placards with red-inked numbers of the badger dead, photos of heaped badger corpses. I looked for anyone I recognised. (I looked for Marie, for my wife.) But there was no one, although at least half of the protesters were wearing badger masks.

Someone threw a toy badger at me as I left. It looked exactly like the one I'd bought Marie when she'd started paying attention to the cull. I looked to see who'd thrown it but so many of them were wearing badger masks. And badger toys were all very similar.

There was one protester, face hidden behind a paper badger mask, who might have been Marie. I waved at this protester but she didn't wave back and the crowd was too thick to get through.

My Family Court forms were returned to me. I'd missed out some vital sections. I told Kerry about this and she looked sad and troubled as though I were getting them wrong on purpose. Then she said there was no rush, that she understood it was hard for me. I told her it was a genuine mistake.

'You still love her, don't you? I can tell you're still kind of angry.'

I held onto her, told her this was crazy. I kissed her nose, avoiding the stud.

In the evenings I tried writing a new book, going to the local Idea Store, trying to ignore the name and the smell from the cafe, sitting amid the Language Students and the noisy kids, the women-less men killing time. But life was starting to feel more important than work. I saw Kerry as often as I could, tried to forget about Henry and her. I called the hospital regularly, badgering them for my next op. My local NHS had decided not to pay for it. This did not make me feel all too valued. The man on the end of the phone line assured me this was a technicality. That eventually someone would pay. I reminded them that I could technically drop dead, but I worried they were hoping for that.

An email arrived from Marie. I'd been mostly not thinking about her although her acting career had restarted in my dreams, the no-nudity clause gone from her contract. I was trying to get used to how little I saw of her. The email said she wasn't feeling too wonderful, that the first set of divorce forms had made it all seem so real. More, she said, than our getting married itself. Otherwise she was good. She'd been on another protest, outside a store, Kooples, who still used real fur in their hoods. She'd joined her local vegan society. She didn't mention Kerry or Henry at all. She did mention her parents. Judy had managed to cope with the end of her daughter's marriage by deleting it from the historical record, barely ever discussing it. Frank was working on a new poetry collection. As for the badger brigade, she told me Brian was taking the end of the protests badly, had started drinking again. Only Margaret Clifton remained the same, stomping over the grass in her stoutest boots, unchangeable as the hills. Marie ended the message by asking if I could recommend some good books.

I thought about not responding but eventually I sent her some recommendations. I sent her the list and then another message saying, 'You ruined my life.'

She didn't respond to either.

Forty-Six

It was a bright spring day and I'd booked some time off work, so I decided to brave the church. The old church, no longer sacred ground, where we'd been married the year before. I didn't tell anyone I was going. I walked over to Canonbury, enjoying the sun, philosophically determined to be unphased by what I saw. I hoped no one else was getting married that day. I hoped that the place wasn't cursed.

It was empty when I arrived but the door was left unlocked. I stepped in, awaiting epiphany. Some rush of sorrow or joy. Only nothing seemed to come. I went and stood on the spot where I'd waited for her, closed my eyes and pictured her appearing. She looked scared, the way I remembered, overwhelmed with the solemnity. Led to the sacrifice. No, this was rubbish. I'd looked at the photos, more than once. There were no clues at all on her face. I sat and scraped the dusty wooden floorboards with one shoe. There didn't seem much point in hanging around.

After loitering round the church, I went on a cemetery walk. I was feeling a little bleak and wanted to surround myself with comforting gloom. I went down to Upper Street and bought a London guidebook. I would visit as many graveyards as I could. I might, I reasoned, stop in the odd pub too. I could see myself enjoying a day like this. I couldn't trust someone who didn't like old graveyards. The worn inscriptions, the youthful ends of the dead, the ground firm, ballasted. A sweet and secret day. Only in the last graveyard I went to, a regimented expanse in East London, I saw someone I didn't expect: I saw Kerry.

I couldn't swear it was her at this distance. What's more, I'd just been thinking about her, which can lead to this sort of confusion. How I hadn't heard from her all day and how this was unusual. How things had got better lately, how the strange mistrust I'd had for her was a leftover from Marie, how there was no need to transfer it. How appealing the thought of a new life with her had become, to shrug off the past and start anew. And just as I had thought this, I'd spotted her, on the far end of the plot.

I had to stop and squint, missing my eyesight. How could I be sure? She was only a shape in the distance after all, but it was her shape, her outline, the form I was starting to love. Her walk, her trotting pace, eager to explore. She was wearing something I was sure I'd seen her in, a dark blue dress with a lighter blue pinafore shape on the front. So was she visiting her dead? Or was she like me, a grief tourist, enjoying the melancholia? I wanted to call her name but I didn't want to shout, this being a place of rest, but also from the fear I was intruding on a private rite. We were far from either of our homes. I felt, as well, that my excursion was naturally a part of my earlier visit to the old church, that I couldn't explain the one without the other. She was standing before a grave and lifting her phone. Was she photographing the headstone? It couldn't be her. But it certainly looked like it was.

There was a way to settle this. I pulled out my own phone and found her in my recent calls. I pressed my thumb on her name. The woman in the distance glanced at the blue wafer in her hand, put it in her pocket and started to head off. My call went through to answer-phone. It was definitely her.

I followed, hurrying as much as seemed compatible with respect. I reached the aisle down the middle of the row of headstones but by then she was almost at the old black gate that led out onto the street. I rushed forward, getting tsk-ed at by a kneeling man in a suit, clutching one limp flower in soily hands. I smiled an apology, tried to measure my steps. Cursing in a whisper. When I got to the gate I looked down the high street at the chicken shops and nail bars and I couldn't see Kerry at all.

All I could do was go back, hoping to at least investigate the row of graves, find the one she'd been to. It was prob-ably a relative, some old uncle she'd never mentioned. A private grief she'd saved for someone else. Listen to me, envying a dead man. Having got to roughly the spot I found I wasn't sure on the row. I walked up and down a couple, angrily reading the stones, but I couldn't see any that matched hers. And who even knew it was a relative of hers, or, if it was, if they shared her name?

I tried calling again but got no answer. I didn't know what I'd say if I got through to her. So instead I found a bus back to Hackney.

That night an old fear kept me from sleeping. It was Henry, who had taken one love from me and could easily take another. Ridiculous when spoken, but then night fears always are.

Forty-Seven

I worried, a bit, about Alistair. He didn't seem to be eating. Or, sleeping much, for that. He was parked in our front room, typewriter on the sticky table in front of him, working on his epic Rage poem. He'd booked a room to perform it, a basement under a Vietnamese restaurant. He talked about this event as though it would surely mark his triumph. Except now when he said it, I'd see panic in his eyes. I asked him about Su. This didn't seem to placate him. He babbled. 'She'll be there,' he said. 'At the reading. She'll definitely be there. It's going well.'

'You seen her at all recently?' I knew he hadn't; I asked him for the fun of being cruel. He gave me a look suggestive of deep patience.

'I don't need to see her,' he said. 'We have an understanding.' He scratched some words hard on a scrap of paper, the tip of his tongue poking out. I said nothing. 'We don't need to be in each other's pockets like you and Kerry. We're like ...' He scribbled out the words, whatever they'd been. 'We're like twin fucking stars or planets is what we're like. Separate but in orbit. We don't need fucking *face time*.' He lit a cigarette.

'You smoking regular cigs now?' I said.

'Only now and again.'

I padded upstairs to Raoul's room. He was in there, sat at his desk, taking notes from a book by Karl Polanyi.

There was a cross on the wall and a picture of Taylor Swift, but otherwise only a single bed and a small shelf of theological texts. A musty smell, but somehow cleaner than the rest of the house. I sat down on the bed.

'Thinking of becoming a priest,' said Raoul. He was writing by hand, with a fountain pen, neatly looping.

'Wow,' I said. And, 'Good.'

'Don't know if I actually will. I fall down on the celibacy but it's not like it would change much.'

I liked it in this room. I liked the order, the sense of routine, things folded and put in place in accordance with some system. I briefly thought it would be good to be a priest. Not for me, but for Raoul. But then it seemed such a bleak prospect. 'Thing is with celibacy, it's like suicide. Once you go for it, you've gone for it, haven't you? As though things will never change.'

'I dunno. I'm thirty-four. Don't see things suddenly changing any day soon.' This seemed more morose than I'd hoped for from Raoul. I tended to go in his room in search of uplift, as though he were doing missionary work among us.

'Alistair's event soon. He seems a bit distracted.' Raoul put down his pen.

'All that stuff he tells us. 'Bout how he's going to be this great figure. And his fiancée. He works hard to believe in all that. Really hard. Takes some effort that stuff. Faith always does.'

I left him to his note-taking. I'd hoped he'd have been perkier.

Forty-Eight

It was a Saturday. I hooked out my earplugs with a fore-finger, stretched out on the bed and savoured the morning sun upon my sheets. I swigged at my water, soothing my night-dry throat. I had it back again, just for a second. The feeling I'd gained and lost after the stroke. Lying there in bed, I had it again, the sense that everything in the room, the books leaning on my wall, the sunlight dancing on the papers scattered round, the posters of 1930s films and Malkin rumbling in joy next to my face, were *right*, were meant to be happening. Everything was good. I found that I was laughing. I found that things were right with me once more.

My door opened and George stepped in.

'What are you doing here?' He looked peaky even by his standards: his eyes set deep in his cupid's face giving him a disturbing wizened look, a prematurely knowledgeable child; his summer uniform of sweat-smelling winter coat, jeans baggy to the point of being harem pants, a jumper and a woolly hat; scabs across his fingers as though he'd spent the last few days in punching walls. I saw what I should have seen earlier – the kid wasn't well, not at all.

'Your flatmate let me in,' he said. 'The bald one. He was going just as I arrived. I told him you'd asked me over.' He dropped onto the bed, putting as much force into his narrow buttocks as he could.

'Kind of you,' I said.

'He gave me a flyer for tonight.' Alistair's big reading, the public debut of his poem. 'Don't worry, I'll be back in Bristol by then,' said George. 'I'm not really into that stuff? It's *dirty*, showing yourself like that.'

'It's not going to work,' I said. George did a decent job of looking perplexedly innocent. 'Whatever it is you're planning.'

'S'making a social call,' he said.

'It's never just a social call.' He made a sound like two balloons rubbing together. 'Well, you're honestly wasting your time. You got me on the wrong day. I'm happy. I'm really happy.'

George straightened himself as well as he could and tried his best to look innocent. He was very bad at it.

'I've given up on Marie,' I said. 'It was never going to work. As far as I can tell she's doing okay now, doing her bit for wildlife. You're just going to have to accept it. I did.' He wriggled like hooked bait. I could almost feel sorry for him.

'You're just giving up,' he said. His voice started to crack. 'You're all ... none of you believe in it, none of you keep it going.'

'You're right,' I said. 'I'll show you.' Covering myself with the duvet I crawled over the bed to the chest of drawers, riffling through my papers until I found the forms. 'See this?' I said. 'Divorce papers. I've kept on putting them off. But they only need a signature.' I looked over the forms, checking, as carefully as I could, that I'd put everything in place. My elbow up in the air in case George should grab and snatch them. He was twitching, knuckling his eyes. I had filled it all except for the bottom, where a space awaited my name. I grabbed and shook a pen, scribbled it down.

'Come on,' I said, pulling on jogging bottoms. 'We're going for a walk.'

Outside it was glaring and hot, an August day. I rushed down the concrete concourse across our block, heading towards the street. George raced, huffing, behind me, slowed down by his stupid get-up, yelling at me to wait. The post box was just at the corner. I reached it and held off for him, the envelope in my hand. He was panting now, not bothering to hide his anger. His face had turned the colour of sunburn.

'Wait for it,' I said, holding the forms to the slot. George stood, asthma-breathed, the sun hurting his eyes.

'Don't fucking post that! You won't be able to go back to her. Henry.'

'I'm going to post it. Soz.'

'You could still make it all work out,' he said, clutching at his side. I tickled the envelope against the slot, teasing.

'And ... Sent.' The letter gone, landing soft onto the others. I was going to be divorced. As bureaucratic exercises went it was on the significant side.

'You shouldn't have done that,' he said.

I'm sorry to say that I laughed. I should have known better how it felt to lose your hopes.

'Why not, George? You should do it yourself, you know. Get a mental divorce from the both of them. Go and do your own thing. No point waiting for other people. I'm going back to the flat.'

'You're a bastard,' said George.

I started walking away from him, hoping he wouldn't follow. He didn't move at all at first, as though my posting the forms had stunned him. Then his tread started behind me, quickening in pace. I flinched as he got nearer, as though he might jump up and hit me.

228

'I'm not going to yours,' he said. 'I give up. I'm giving up on all of you.'

'Fine,' I said. I wondered what on earth would happen to him, this jobless intense little person. It was hard to imagine any kind of development for his life.

'Wait,' he shouted. 'Wait. Why don't you just ask her? Ask your girlfriend what's going on? Ask her about Henry. Cos she knows *all* about it.' He turned and ran away from me, faster than you'd think.

Forty-Nine

The flat was empty. Only it wasn't the leisurely emptiness of a happy day indoors. It was the emptiness of
anticipation.

It must be nonsense. George was a stirrer, the sort of
person who can't walk past a pond without lobbing in
a stone. His words might mean nothing at all. Against
this though, there was all I knew about Henry. Who'd
had no qualms about sleeping with my wife. Maybe
Kerry wasn't his past. Maybe she was his future? I could
see him picking Kerry as a post-Marie refreshment, an
after-dinner mint when he'd had enough of the main
course. And what about all the evidence on her side?
She'd spoken his name in her sleep. Henry, please man.
She'd jumped at the sight of him at that protest. Even her
skulking around graveyards began to seem suspect. What
was the fucking girl up to?

I tried to stop myself thinking. Paced the floor, stroked
the cat, poured out a glass of wine. I considered writing
but my brain wouldn't shift from accusation. Was there
not, it asked me, something quite weird about Kerry?
Who, it reasoned, is really that fucking selfless? Every
evening, every day, a cause to further, an underdog to
defend. Who in the world has the time? Apart from
Raoul. But then, he's bribing his god, reserving the best
seats in heaven for himself.

No, Kerry was too good to be true. There was something self-involved about her trying to be a saint. I worked in the charity sector. I'd seen how it went. Convince yourself – convince others – that what you do is good. Before too long the definition of good becomes whatever it is you do. You give yourself a multitude of breaks. See: Marie with her devotion to fluffy creatures, not caring at all about the damage she'd left behind. If you want to meet a bastard, scratch a saint.

This was definitely nonsense. I poured myself another glass of wine, enjoying it. I hadn't drunk this much in a while. Certainly not alone.

Kerry was not a bad person. A victim, then. Of Henry and his ways. Who could resist a man like that? Strapping, dedicated, a healer of wounded birds. Hands you could fit an otter on. The man was irresistible. My head hurt from thinking. He had probably sweet talked her into it, whatever it was she'd done. Let's not obfuscate – he had lured her into his bed, just as he'd done with Marie. *Shut up, Stu. Shut up.* He'd be good, you could count on it. Good enough for Marie. The orgasms he'd given her. His fingertips over her skin. Oh this was really too much. And another glass of wine. I had posted off my papers. Things were definitely going to change. The collar would soon be off. As soon as the postman came, as soon as the forms were processed. Until then my head was full of Henry and all he was doing with them, with Kerry and Marie. And another half a glass.

I stopped thinking. My mind too tired and slow for any more. My thoughts were foolish and I was going to stamp them down. I stumbled up to bed and lay in the afternoon light, sleeping it off.

Dreaming. Dreaming that Marie was there. She was there and I could hear her, detect the patterns of her speech, the rise and fall of communication, but I couldn't make out the words. Then I could smell her, her sweat, her perfume, her breath, touch the slight static shining on her hair, the coolness of her mouth. She was here, she was in the room with me, I was with her and still married, waking up.

'Is everything okay? You've gone quiet. Alarming. Oh god, I probably sound mental, I'm sure you're fine. Call me when you can. xxx'

I smiled at this evidence of love. I'd obviously got things wrong. To dismiss my suspicions was to bring them racing back. It was a poison, running through me. Dismiss, dismiss, dismiss. My mouth was dry and my head thumped. I stood up and reeled, clutching at my bookcase. Drinking, I had to remind myself, was not a good idea. I was an invalid, and must learn to live like one.

It was not quite dark, not quite day outside and I still had time to get to Alistair's R-Age. I showered, tottering, hoping the water would help. It did, a bit. I looked more or less presentable. Thank god, the event was nearby.

I messaged Kerry, telling her I'd been asleep. I blasted myself with deodorant. I put on a new tee shirt she had chosen. I looked, I thought, okay. I looked like I was holding myself together very well. I fed Malkin, had a glass of water and left the flat.

The restaurant had one poster in the window, advertising the night. It was free entry, at least. I wondered if they'd pull a decent crowd. Alistair had pestered me to take part but I'd pleaded my work wasn't ready. The truth being, the work was, I wasn't.

My friends were sitting at a table upstairs, wolfing

down a shared banquet. Raoul was there and Alistair, holding court in what looked like pancake make-up. For reasons unknown to me, he had drawn an extra eye in the middle of his forehead. Rupa had showed up and Kerry, at the end next to an empty seat. I sat down, kissed her and said hello to them all. There was another free seat, I noticed, next to Alistair. Free, apart from a giant teddy bear wearing a sash.

'This your girlfriend?' I said.

'S'a present,' said Alistair. His voice a parody of gusto. 'For when she arrives. Ahoy there. Glad you could join us.'

Kerry asked me if I was okay. I tried saying I was, but I must have sounded about as convincing as Alistair: 'We're still waiting on Su,' he said. 'Did I tell you about Su?'

'You might have mentioned Su,' said Rupa.

'This will be quite a day for her,' said Alistair, daring us to laugh. 'Seeing me in action.' Raoul muttered something which sounded like 'first time for everything', but I'm sure Raoul was too nice. 'Tonight should seal the deal. Yeah, we're going to be fine.'

Kerry caught my eye. I tried returning her glance but somehow found I couldn't. I felt there was something sneaky about it, this private language of mocking. I was going to be better than that.

'Guys, I've got an announcement to make,' said Raoul. 'I've signed up to work overseas. I'm off to Colombia, work with poor kids over there. I'm in touch with this network of kind of dissident priests. Felt it was about time.' He glanced around the table as if he were hoping that one of us would ask him not to go.

'Oh that's so exciting,' said Kerry. Kerry the atheist, I thought. I told myself this was probably wine sourness, nothing else, but I couldn't stop from scowling. Rancour about the world. She and Raoul got caught up in a big conversation about the logistics of his trip and from there into Liberation Theology, the Gospel according to Marx, while I picked at some spicy squid.

Rupa filled my glass. 'You look down, Stuart,' she said. An astute woman, Rupa. 'Is everything okay?'

'I'm fine,' I said, possibly a little too loud. She cast a regretful look at my brimming glass. 'Honestly.' I tried to sound genial. 'Could I have some of the rice?'

A woman in fishnets, a long thin coat and a pink fright wig came over and said hello. She was, she said, a confrontational poet. Alistair barely acknowledged her. The poet sat down and smiled in a sweet way that didn't seem too confrontational.

'I know what you're all thinking,' said Alistair. At that moment I was thinking about Kerry and Henry, and, to a lesser extent, whether the poet took her clothes off as part of the act. 'You're thinking Su hasn't turned up.' I was going to say I wasn't but I'd been thinking it minutes before, so I supposed he had a point. 'Well, she'll come. We can all be sure of that.'

Kerry tapped my wrist and whispered something about the situation and whether I could help. I shrugged by way of response. There didn't seem much I could do.

'You know what?' said Alistair. 'I might send her packing. I suppose that I can do that. There have to be some boundaries. It's okay being all free-floating and improvising your way through life—' he shot an evil glance at the confrontational poet as if she were famous for living this way, '—but it's no good if you just don't turn up for meals. If everyone did that then how would places like this keep in business? If no one ever bothered to turn up for their meals.'

'Amen,' said Raoul, heretically.

'I'm going to tell her we're done. I will not tolerate tardiness.' He emphasised each word with a rap on the table, rattling the chicken. 'I bought her a bear, for god's sake.'

'She might still turn up,' said Rupa, who seemed to be on her best behaviour.

'Give me a fucking drink,' said Alistair. Fat beads of sweat started to appear under his make-up.

'You seem to be wearing slap,' I said.

'I'm going on stage, Stuart. You've got to create a bit of fucking distance.' He pronged a shrimp with a chopstick and munched it with every appearance of unease. The door opened and we all looked towards it, like regulars at the saloon when the lonesome stranger walks in.

She was tanned, with a sulky look about her mouth. She wore headphones and not much else. She scanned the room from behind enormous sunglasses and slid across to our table. If we had any doubts as to her identity, Alistair's grin dispelled them. She raised a hand in a gesture that was about a tenth of a wave then looked around the table for an empty seat. Seeing none apart from next to Alistair, she glided towards him and sat down, dislodging the bear without giving it a glance. She started concentrating very hard on her phone. 'Su,' said Alistair. 'You had me worried, there.'

'I said I would come and I came,' said Su.

'Everyone,' said Alistair. 'This is Su. Su's my ...' There was a pause, as if the unreality of their courtship were finally making itself known to him. 'Everybody, Su. Su, everybody.'

'This really isn't what Korean food is like,' said Su.

'It's Vietnamese,' said Alistair.

'Hello Su,' said Kerry. 'Alistair's told us a lot about you.'

'Yes,' said Su.

'You're a student at St Martin's, was it?'

She said nothing. Her shoulders gestured at but didn't quite perform a shrug.

'It's Goldsmiths,' said Alistair. Su frowned and yawned. 'She went to Goldsmiths.'

'And you're studying ...?'

'Yes,' said Su. She lifted her laminated menu over her face. Kerry grinned at me and this time I couldn't help but return her smile. Alistair grabbed his own menu and started to wobble it needlessly.

'So were you okay?' said Kerry. She brushed my fingers. 'I was worried you might feel ill.'

The truth was I had been feeling a bit frazzled. Maybe my suspicions were just a synapse throbbing, creating a whole structure of worries, the way that grit makes pearls. I told Kerry I'd been ill all day. Her concern at this seemed unfeigned. I wished I could forget about Henry.

'Yes,' said Su, this time in what sounded like triumph. 'Nick's coming.'

'Nick,' said Alistair.

'I was thinking with my thing, right,' said the poet, 'I'm going to need a lot of space. I like to really prowl the room, you know? I like to jump around. It's cathartic is how I see it.' She didn't explain if it was cathartic for anyone other than herself. Alistair looked in need of some hasty catharsis.

'Nick?' said Alistair.

'I told you about Nick,' said Su. 'Nick's the funniest, you're going to love him.'

'Funny,' said Alistair. I could tell he was silently pondering if funny was code for 'gay'.

'Gotta love the Nickster,' said Su.

'Have we?' said Alistair.

'I once dated a man called Nick,' said Rupa. 'He was really into getting me pregnant. And not just cos he wanted kids. The shape of a pregnant stomach. He had videos.'

'Are you sure you're okay?' said Kerry.

'N-dog,' said Su. 'N-dog in the area.'

'So yeah is there going to be space for me?' The poet was still talking. 'I don't just read, I *perform*?'

The door opened again. We jerked our heads in unison, checking out the stranger. A hirsute, stocky young man with his hair in a bun and a neckline down to his nipples. He waved at Su, and a bit less at the rest of us, and swooped down to his friend. There was an awful lot of hugging. Alistair mouthed the word 'gay?' at me. I squirmed. Su and Nick started taking photographs of each other.

'Alistair,' said Alistair, holding out his hand.

'Yes,' said Nick.

'Algonquin Round Table this,' said Kerry.

'I might go downstairs, then, and look at the space? It is downstairs then, the space?' said the poet.

'We can get you a chair if you like, Nick,' said Raoul. 'Then Su doesn't have to sit on you.'

'It's boiling in here,' said Alistair. 'Is anyone else boiling? Look, I'm really sweating. Sweating because it's so hot.'

'Let's go for a walk, Stu,' said Kerry. 'This is unbearable. Look at where that boy has got his hands.' I looked. 'You should probably stop looking now,' she said.

'How long have you two been friends, then?' said Alistair. 'How long have you two been mates?'

'Nick,' said Su, slapping him, but not very hard. Nick started kissing her neck.

'Come on,' said Kerry, slipping her hand into mine and

leading me through the restaurant. I turned to see Alistair pushing his chair back and heading down to the basement followed by the poet, still asking about the space.

Outside there was a cool breeze, easing the warmth of the day. Packs of drinkers whooped down the street in primary-coloured tops. There were bars lighting the pavement, with crammed tables out front, the couples chattering, men sat back, their legs spread, women forward, hands encircling their drinks.

'There's a park thing just through here,' said Kerry. The night air was relaxing, away from poor Alistair and the worries of the day. I hoped he'd be all right. Not that I had high hopes for his poem but it would be nice to think he could get through the performance without crumbling.

We were out of the main streets, through old railway arches and lock-ups that now held artisanal makers of cottage cheese, purveyors of imported chillies. We walked on into what looked like, but probably weren't, the poorer streets. Ex-council flats, Asian shops, pubs turned into homes. The green, when we arrived there, was well-lit but deserted. The two of us started wandering, in a silence I hoped was comfortable.

'Are you really okay?' she said.

There was going to be no skating this. I was going to have to be selective.

'I mostly am,' I said. 'Truth is, I sent my final forms off today. For the, you know.' I wondered why I couldn't say the word. 'I'm glad I did it but it definitely stirs things up.'

'I bet it does,' said Kerry. We had reached a bench and she sat on it, patting next to her. I could smell her perfume and a hint of cigarette smoke. She must have been stressed herself. About me, I thought. Or Henry.

'I've been thinking about, well, us,' she said. My blood fizzed in expectation, fearful or thrilled, I don't know. 'There's something I wanted to say.'

Oh Christ, was she dumping me? I didn't want to go through this again. Why were people always doing this? Why could they not just fucking well *keep still*? She lit a cigarette and I asked her for one myself, knowing I wasn't supposed to. I dragged hard, savouring the tar on my palate. It tasted abrasive, like a penance. She sat up, slouched, sat up again, holding herself as though it were a much colder night than it was.

My phone rang. I made an apologetic hand gesture, hopped up and took the call.

It was Rupa. The reading had hit the buffers. Alistair had dashed around the little basement space, insulted the performance poet and vanished for several minutes. 'When we found him,' she said, 'he was calling his ex-wife. Asking her to come back.' She paused after saying this, as though asking me what I thought of *that*? 'He's with Raoul now. Nice boy, Raoul. A good friend. I see you've gone and scarpered. Leave the difficult stuff to the rest of us, eh Stu?'

'Now really isn't a good time, Rupa.'

'Well, just you be back soon is all I'm saying. He's insisting on going ahead and he'll need you there to support him. Don't let everyone down Stuart.' Her tone implied that letting everyone down was a favourite trick of mine.

'I'm busy, I'm really busy. All right? I didn't just … Look, I can't talk.'

I put away my phone and told Kerry about Alistair's antics. We laughed a bit at his problems which made our own ones seem so adult and serious. She stopped laughing first when she realised we were being cruel.

'Sorry, we were talking about?' I said. I could see aloneness, back again, stretching out before me and with it, the awful longeurs of single life: the noisy bars, the forced shows of confidence, the need to be constantly busy. I was going to miss her, I knew it, and I began looking for arguments to keep her near.

She lit another cigarette. 'Well,' she said, smoothing down her dress with her free hand. 'I – before I say this you should know I haven't changed my mind. I love you.' A nervous smile as though I were the one about to walk out on her. It dawned on me that no one was walking anywhere.

I giggled, a little too much, until she started to look insulted. 'I love you too,' I said. 'I love you.' I sat back down on the bench and looped my arms around her. We were kissing and I was stroking her hair. An unfamiliar elation, a victory. Our kissing increased, got hungrier. I tried to concentrate on how pretty and good she was, and how much she loved me. This was a good thing, a great thing.

I closed my eyes and all I could see was Henry's face.

'Stop,' I said. She had already stopped though, as if my suspicion were something she could taste. She had a wounded look, as though I'd told her off. 'You were going to tell me something else.'

'Yes,' she said. 'I was.'

'I think you should tell me now.' She put her hands to her face but shuffled close to me along the bench. 'I'm going to need you to tell me what it was. Especially as I have a feeling that it is linked to me. Especially as I think it's about Henry.'

I held on to her wrist. She looked frightened, I was shocked to see. As though I were someone threatening and strange, not the person she'd just announced she wanted more of.

'It is about Henry,' she said. 'I wanted to set things straight.'

I was right, then. I almost enjoyed the victory. I definitely enjoyed how upset she seemed. It seemed deserved to me. I had been right not to trust her, after all. She had deceived and betrayed me and I had nothing except my triumph to enjoy.

I thought about marching off but then I wasn't sure if she would follow.

'You look insane,' she said. 'You look wild. You look like I've gone and done something wrong.' I asked her what she had done. She said that it was something I could repeat to no one else.

Fifty

Kerry had first met Henry at the Occupy camp near St Paul's. She'd been a few years out of university and had already embarked on the path of virtuous and ineffectual activism she'd kept to ever since. She'd gone with Neal to spend a week there, their equivalent of a holiday.

I told her I'd been there for an hour or so myself. 'Maybe we saw each other,' I said.

She ignored this. She was intent on telling her story.

She'd gone with Neal, then. The communal library of theory and polemic which had put me off on my visit, the pinched radiance of the campers, the banners about the NWO, Bilderberg and the Zeitgeist Movement, everything that had made me want to run, all of this entranced her. 'I've got more cynical since,' she said. She must have been very un-cynical before.

It felt, she said, as though the revolution were close. That it would only take people to listen, honestly listen, to these brave and smart young people and the rest was sure to follow. There'd been a few doubting noises in her head, murmurs of disquiet, but she'd quelled them. The way the boys did so much of the talking. The way so many of the people she met there seemed to be not just unhappy, as she was, not just furious, like her, but actively damaged, stutterers with manky teeth, boys whose rage seemed to spray, untargeted, over the world like so much spit. She'd worried about this, in a protective way. About seeing these people, these good young people, fail and lose their hopes.

Neal though, who back then was better read than her, who could back up all his impulses with a quote from someone dead, Neal was cynical and said so. He voiced all her buried objections in the most annoying way. She was trying so hard to believe in this and all he could do was doubt. 'I'm being a constructive critic,' he said, after hours spent belittling the camp. 'We can't just switch off our brains because we're a part of something.'

For the first time, she hated him. They'd gone to a meeting in a hot tent, smelling of tarpaulin and feet. Everyone in there seemed to agree with everyone else, although some people only wanted to talk about their own particular obsessions. There was a scuffed-looking German guy who kept putting his hand up and talking about his ex-landlord, who he said had contacts in high places. He was obviously unwell but nobody could say that and there was no one to steer the conversation away from him until this other guy spoke up.

She didn't need to describe him. I could see him, his eyes twinkling with compassionate enthusiasm, his gentle mastery. The size of him. He prickled Neal, this guy. (I found myself, for the first time, liking Neal.)

'It was such a challenge to him,' she said. 'He had to criticise, just to show this guy.' Neal was standing, when there was no need to, and he had his hand in his jacket pocket, as though addressing a jury. Telling them they needed a strategy, they needed to be serious. Not as encouragement, even if he thought it was, but to crush them. Sitting next to him she felt herself tainted by his cynicism and the implied agreement of her silence. What was worse, she did agree, at least in part. The problem wasn't what he said so much as his motives for saying it, his need to score off this older, wiser guy.

When Neal was done the newcomer responded and not in the same spirit at all. He understood all Neal's objections. He agreed with most of them. He was reasonable, cajoling him with kindness. He left Neal looking utterly destroyed, she said, and the worst thing was she found herself enjoying it. She could feel herself silently cheering as this guy left her boyfriend speechless.

Outside the tent Neal had raged. 'You enjoyed that,' he kept saying. 'That fucking old hippy.' She'd told him it wasn't okay to *brand* people like that. He told her he was going home and that was when she'd done it. The cruellest act of her life. She'd stayed. Visiting meetings, listening to talks. She'd found herself speaking freely, surprising herself with the things she said, ideas she hadn't been sure of. Not having to check all her opinions by his. She'd made new friends, yarned over the veg stew with a woman from Cardiff who had quit her call centre job to come and live on site and a thin unpublished essayist who kept drunkenly bringing up Gramsci.

She'd started drinking. There was a dangerous hubbub of excitement in her, as if she knew that to stop surfing this enthusiasm would be the start of guilt and regret. She had to keep talking. And towards the end of the night the big guy, the older guy, had approached her once again. Full of concern. Asked after her boyfriend. Could tell he'd maybe trodden on his toes a bit back there. She'd said, 'he's not my boyfriend,' before she'd had time to think.

I didn't ask her what happened in Henry's tent. I mean, I knew, didn't I? And I knew I wasn't angry about it any more. I couldn't quite grasp why I'd been angry at all.

'The thing is,' she said, 'we talked for most of the night.

That's kind of the rule in these places. You chat about capitalism for three hours and then when you're done you can bone. I got the whole history of his involvement in social movements and you know what? He never once mentioned animals. Didn't mention them at all.' She had gone home the next day, back to Neal. They had a lot more relationship left. But every day she thought about the man from the camp.

From guilt, I said. Just guilt. But Kerry, it wasn't your fault. You were drunk, of course, and so young.

'It was guilt,' she said. 'But it wasn't just guilt.'

You liked him, I said. She said yes.

The next time she had seen him was last year. She'd gone onto the badger camp, just as a one-off, the same as she'd go to every climate, poverty, peace meeting she had time for. She knew the arguments about badgers, was convinced that the cull wouldn't work and believed, in a vague way, that cruelty and dominance over animals bled into cruelty and dominance over nature, over women and the poor, over children and weaker lands. She was happy to do her bit. Still, she knew that, as someone who couldn't go a week without red meat, she was not a convincing participant. The issue summoned no song in her. She attended, but out of duty.

She'd gone on the patrol. Margaret was running it and there were a few others who had trickled away from the group by the time I came along. Last to join them, striding across the tarmac, he came. Henry. And all of those feelings, the ones she'd just about accepted as dead, turned out to have been hibernating. There he was, swaggering towards her, with this moonstruck blond *kid* scampering after him. It took him a moment to recognise her. That or his acting was great. God but she wanted him, god but she felt guilty all over, although Neal had long since gone.

The same thrill, the same fear, as all of her restrictions slipped away. He'd approached her, as they patrolled, saying it was good to see her again, sounding her out for another visit. He'd upgraded to a camper van, at least. She wanted so much to say yes. She was sorry but she did. Only this time she said no. Something held her back.

Maybe the way this teenage boy clung after him, nodding along to Henry's every pious observation, as though he were Socrates with just a dash of Buddha. No, it wasn't that. She wasn't going to judge George, she understood their appeal, these adults who hadn't buckled, who kept the strength and certainty of adolescence against every pressure there was. The problem, 'and this sounds mad now but it's true,' the problem was his love of animals. Remember, they'd spent a long night talking. Not just talking, I thought, but didn't say. Capitalism, neoliberalism, imperialism, every bloody -ism, and not a word about animals. Yet now they were his passion. He worked at a sanctuary. He had been part of the sabs movement, had liberated battery hens and mended broken paws. He was something of an amateur naturalist.

It all screamed fake to her. More than that, it screamed 'cop'.

'A cop?' I said. 'Come on.'

'I don't know. There's no proof. I don't have any proof.'

'You cheated and you feel strange about it and now he has to be a cop. He's a sleazy old ratbag. Isn't that enough? He has to be a cop?'

'I don't know. I was reading a lot about it. The guy who infiltrated the climate people. The ones in the eighties, who were sleeping with all these protestors. Lying to them. Maybe it all got blurred. But I couldn't stop thinking about it.' She sighed, long and heavy.

Henry please man. Henry policeman.

She went to George first. Regretted it straight away. Asking leading questions, pestering him. Did he think that it was possible? He was rattled. He was furious. She thought he was going to choke. She'd never warmed to him and maybe she was imagining, but George seemed to get worse after this. He'd never been a sunny presence, but now he seemed to exaggerate himself; the deliberate mumbling, the clothes, the nonsense that he'd spout. She was scared she had broken the boy. She spent a while assuming he'd go straight to Henry, braced herself for a confrontation that never came. Which made her think, well, maybe it *was* true. Maybe George was too scared of it being true to ever risk finding out.

She realised she was spending all her spare time at the badger camp, not because of the badgers but because of her obsession with working it out, as if one day he would let his guard down and say "ello 'ello 'ello' or pull out a truncheon. But he never slipped at all.

Around this time Marie and I showed up.

'A hunch,' I said. 'That's all you've got.'

'Pretty much. But it was like I couldn't get off it. And to watch Marie falling in love with him, see her buying his whole back story, well, I tried to hint he wasn't all that but she wasn't open to arguments. It was why I was rooting for you, at first, until – well, you know how that changed.'

'I don't believe any of this. Just because he was focused more on animals?'

'I spoke to someone at the Met. Technically this stuff isn't supposed to happen at all any more but he reckoned it still does. But he didn't know any Henry.'

'I'm sure there isn't anything to know. Do you still love him?'

247

'Of course not,' she said. 'I was mad at him and hurt and I needed to know the truth. And the reason I'm telling you, I decided it was getting too much. I realised it doesn't matter, not now I have you. So I'm leaving it be. We can both walk away from it, go for something new. I never found anything anyway. Right now, all I've got is the name,' she said.

She told me that undercover policemen worked under stolen names. Dead kids mostly. Born in the same year, didn't make it to puberty, bingo, a resurrection as an anarchist. 'I looked up records, wasted so much time but ...' She thumbed down her phone and I knew what she was going to show me, knew where in East London it was, and despite this it still took me a moment to register, the headstone with 1971–72 as the dates and the beloved passed-on baby: Henry Ralph.

Fifty-One

'I'll fucking kill him,' I said.

I scared myself in saying it. The words were unwilled atavisms, they came from a murky, ancestral place where people owned other people and honour still existed. It wasn't a cosy place or one where I'd last very long. At the same time I felt dizzy, whirling and sea-sick. I was still sitting down but I grabbed the bench. I was very aware of my eyesight. Of how it would stop me fighting.

'You won't kill him,' she said. 'You won't do anything at all. This might all just be rubbish. It was a stupid obsession, something I fixated on. And what good would it do?'

'He's sleeping with my wife,' I said. 'He's sleeping with my wife and lying about who he is.'

'She's not your wife,' said Kerry. 'Any more.'

I agreed with her. I had to.

'We need to forget about this,' she said. 'Even if it is true what can we do?'

What was George's system? Non-interference. I wasn't convinced. We started walking back, holding hands, and all the time I was thinking this was the last time I'd be doing this, the last time spent with Kerry, the last time I'd be walking, guiltless, with her.

We got back to the restaurant, almost without my noticing. I was several steps removed from everything around me, thinking instead of his hands upon my wife, thinking of myself standing over him.

How did you murder people now? I didn't have a weapon.

I wasn't going to murder him. I would have to hurt him though. Was hurting him enough? Was hurting a guy like that even possible?

There were knives back at the flat. It was getting late. We went down into the sweltering basement. A moon-faced young man with an acoustic guitar was trilling and growling wordlessly.

I was surprised at the size of the audience. Alistair was in a corner talking to four women in summer dresses. He had a big, frazzled grin on his face. About half of his make-up had gone, the third eye still staring.

'My god, Stu,' said Rupa, appearing in front of us. 'You missed Alistair's poem.'

'Oh,' I managed to say.

'You never told me he was good. I mean, really really good. He sat in a corner scribbling these last-minute revisions, changing the whole thing around, and then he went to the front and it was just…I've never heard anything like it. He said it all, really he did. It was like watching a birth.'

I tried to work out if she was joking. It didn't seem she was. Normally this would have been the worst news I'd heard all day. Alistair was talented. Only fucking poetry, but still, an actual talent. Rupa knew her stuff, as well. Maybe she fancied him. As if that was any comfort.

It was a good job I was barely there.

'Shall I go the bar?' I said. Kerry looked at me in a nervous way I knew I would see over and over.

'I think I should go,' she said.

'No, let me go. What will you two have?' Kerry said a gin and tonic and Rupa told me she was fine.

Instead of going to the bar, I went upstairs, squeezed through the queuing crowd and left the restaurant. I needed another fag but I also wanted to keep my head as clear as I could. It already seemed to be spinning. It already seemed to be squeezed.

Should I go back to mine and get the knife? I was already pushed for time. And I knew all the knives would be filthy. I wasn't going to turn up and stab him with a knife covered in cake.

I walked to the nearest train station, past bright lit expensive restaurants and bright lit expensive people, people who would never set off to Bristol intent on getting jailed. I went down a cobbled side street to the station. Pop-up bars and diners had sprouted all around, with tables outside them full of friends and couples, clutching buzzers that would rattle to announce their food. They all of them looked so happy.

At the station I patted my pockets till I found my Oyster card. I ran up the stairs to the platform three at a time and stood at the end, in the breeze. I didn't want to be near the group of girls passing a bottle from hand to hand, the vicarly man in glasses trying to read, the boys with their W. G. Grace beards and buttoned up collars. My eyelid was twitching. I looked at my phone and it was already full of missed calls.

Oh Kerry, my darling, goodbye. I supposed I could still go back and join her, pretend that she'd said nothing. If I couldn't get on a train, that was what I'd do. Chance would decide for me, as I didn't seem to have much ability of my own.

No, I had to do this. The train approached and I got in and stayed standing.

I was going to rescue Marie. I could not have her deceived.

251

The train decided to wait for five minutes between stops. I tried hard not to look crazy, not to fidget or swear. Anger was surging through me, righteous anger, anger I could ride. I wanted very much to talk to someone but there was no one that I could. A middle-aged black woman in a heavy purple coat was trying to say something to me. Something concerned, I think. I must have looked unhinged.

Come on, come *on*, you stupid train. Everyone travelling with me was young, horribly so, tanned limbs and statement beards, pack laughter and talk. I was at a great distance from them. Although I could still go back to Kerry and my flatmates, drinking in the restaurant. If they were still there and not hunting for me all around.

We started moving again. I would get the Tube to Paddington. It was now ten fifteen. I could get there in half an hour or so and catch the last train to Bristol. I walked down the escalator, down into the Tube. There was a group of men in shirt sleeves, smelling of a day's drinking, blocking up the route. I shouted 'move' at them at the top of my voice and they peered at me as if they were surprised I could speak at all. The one at the furthest end edged out of my way. I rushed down the rest of the stairs and zigzagged through the crowd to the right platform, elbowing whoever got in my path. 'I'm blind,' I shouted, if anyone complained. I must have bumped into a few.

There was a two-minute wait for the next train. I wondered if I should just dive under it when it came. I could stage it as a trip, a stumble, so that the driver wouldn't feel any guilt. How would it affect my fellow commuters? The ones nearest would be horrified, I supposed, although it would give them a story to tell. The further people got from my squashed remains the crosser they would be. Screams turning into tuts as they travelled along the line. I didn't think I could do it. There'd be comforts even in prison. I could get on with my book. It was best to stay alive as long as possible. There was so much to like about life.

The train rushed in and I could imagine it slamming into me, the crash against my skull like a brain haemorrhage, only coming from outside. I was sweating worse than Alistair had been an hour and a lifetime ago. Maybe I was turning into a genius as well. I crammed myself into the carriage and closed my eyes.

When I got to Paddington station there was a small crowd lazily staring at the changing times-display, with sleepy, beery faces. I hurried over and, shutting my bad eye, I looked along the display. There was a train to Bristol in fifteen minutes. The decision was not mine to make, not any more. Although there was still a chance I might not get a ticket.

I looked at my phone and it was full of texts from Alistair, Rupa and, most of all, from Kerry. It was best I didn't read them. I walked to the ticket office and found myself near the front of the queue, just behind someone with a long list of questions to ask. I stared at the back of their head, imagining my brain problems spreading, transmitting to them, picturing them falling, clutching at their skull, while I smiled, stepped over and got my tickets fast. Eventually the poor customer, not knowing they had a death sentence, went strolling, puzzled, away and I stood before the cashier.

'One way to Bristol please,' I said. 'Actually, make it a return.' It cost a shocking amount. Still, if t'were done and all that.

I would probably go on the lam, rather than turn myself in. Although they were bound to catch me eventually and it wouldn't do me any favours to be evading justice. Maybe the jury would look kindly on me. I needed medical treatment and there was the whole matter of my sight. I wouldn't last long on the run. Oh god, I would miss my books.

Oh god, Kerry, I'd miss her.

I hoped I had time to buy a six pack for the journey. Something to take the edge off my agitation. 'Quiet carriage please,' I said.

I hopped on the train at ten past ten, just before it set off. I would soon be beyond the pale. The pale! I was pleased to find I had a table seat. Just so long as the canteen – the *buffet* – was open, I would be fine for the journey. There was pleasure even in awful train journeys.

That despicable swine was lying with my wife. Lying to my wife. You get used to not really knowing the person you love but there has to be some kind of limit.

I would have to punch him in the face. I had never punched anyone and wasn't really sure I knew how. Those men who aim for the nose, happy to see it burst. Dislocate a jaw. I wasn't one of those, unless I was.

A couple, who had been making a great show of putting their bags in the luggage area came and sat across from me. The man gave a wary nod, somewhere between apology and defiance. The woman didn't look at me at all. They were my age, or he was. I tried not to stare at her.

I would go and get a drink. I went down the corridor, jerked by the carriage's motion, at one point almost falling into someone's lap. People dozed in headphones, self-encased.

There was no one at the buffet except the guy behind the counter. He was about fifty, with wrinkles like a Shar-Pei or W. H. Auden. He had one gold ear stud and leathery hands. I bought three cans of Stella. He put them in a paper bag with the train company logo on them. I staggered back along the rattling aisle to my seat. The boy across from me sneered deniably at my purchase. His girlfriend was reading a thriller, which was disappointing. I did not offer them a can. I opened the first one, getting my fingers wet, and swigged a soapy mouthful.

'Alan though,' said the boy across to the girl.

'My god,' she said. 'He doesn't stop, does he?'

They began a, presumably rote-learned, conversation about the foibles of this Alan, his love of extreme sports and his richly-peopled love life. I spilt some beer, apologised and dabbed the table with a napkin. They stared at me, or he did. She didn't look once. She was gloriously pretty. I wondered if I should tell them about my life. What would be the fucking point of that? I stifled a burp, but not well.

'Are you okay?' said the boyfriend. His bedside manner was unimpressive. There was an unspoken 'fuck off' after the utterance. I went and stood in the corridor and when my legs started to ache, I crouched down.

It was half an hour past midnight when we arrived. Clifton Street was reachable by bus. I felt preternaturally awake, endlessly so, but also as though I hadn't slept in months. People seemed to be opting for taxis. A bus seemed safer. I saw the train couple, with all their cases, their too-cold summer clothes, flagging down a cab. Back to their beautiful home, back to their beautiful bed and their wonderful, restful lives. I wished that I was him. I would have monetisable knowledge and skills, a gorgeous lover, civilised politics that I easily squared with my personal wealth, and the prospect, ahead of me, of more rewards, more bliss.

I looked at my phone to see the new unanswered

messages. I clicked on the most recent one. Kerry asking me 'for the last time' where I was. 'I love you. Come home.'

Well, I thought, I love you too. Only some loves are sonnets and some are sagas: too long, boring in places, but not to be ignored. I decided not to reply.

The only other person at the stop smelt strongly of cannabis and occasionally muttered to himself. I was nervous for a second but the way he shrunk when I turned to him showed me I was now scarier than him. I wasn't sure if I welcomed this. I stood in my tee shirt and shivered, wishing I'd had time to go back home to get a jacket and a knife. The headlights of the bus veered around the corner towards us.

Perhaps Marie and Henry would be out. Or so satisfied from whatever night they'd had together they'd be impossible to wake up. Unlikely, I thought. Between Irene and George and that bastard and my wife there was sure to be someone in.

The bus was fuller than I expected. Five young couples spilled over the back and adjacent seats, passing a bottle of something pungent back and forth, talking over each other in loud excited voices. They'd be off to a party, I imagined. I found myself envying them a great deal. I wondered what would happen if I tried to join them. Introduced myself, extended a paw. The best case would be a night of being treated as a comic interloper who, as they sobered, would become increasingly a person to be rid of. The worst case would be an instant shunning. It was best I stuck to my job.

I focused on the facts. Henry was a cop. Henry had – let's not hide in euphemisms here – raped my wife. Was quite possibly doing so right then. Because she was fair game. He'd encouraged her in this badger mania at the expense of my marriage, my home, my life. I was exactly right to go and tell her. I was morally right to get revenge.

Although I was beginning to have doubts about that. The adrenalin starting to sap. I wasn't sure I was the sort of person who killed with a straight face. I should at least chin the usurping sod. And while my thoughts repeated all of this, again and again and again, another voice said, what if it isn't true? What if Kerry got it wrong? And what, the voice said, is your motivation here exactly? Yeah, she has a right to know, apparently. But what if she's happier being lied to? I'm not convinced you have her best interests at heart right now. Who exactly are you getting your own back on here? Because let's be honest now. All this chasing her around, all this trying to get her back. Saving her from herself. I'm not sure it's all that romantic, after all. It's punishment, is what it is. Punishment and spite.

This snide sort of insinuation was exactly why I needed more beer. I was going to rescue her. I was going out of love.

It was probably too late for beer. The bus was at my stop.

I hopped off, wiping the sweat from my forehead with the back of my hand. An old impulse made me check my phone. Kerry had tried to call again. A text message too, telling me how scared she was. Her anger would start later, once she knew that I was safe.

More missed calls and texts too, and these were from Marie. 'Stuart, Kerry says you ran off in a state and might be coming to me. Worried about you darling. Call me.'

Obviously Kerry was going to call Marie! Why hadn't I thought of that? The two of them had been protest-pals way back. I was amazed she hadn't called her straight away. Probably hoping that I wouldn't do anything as daft as head to Bristol. And now I was at the door.

There was no sign from the message that Kerry had told her what she'd told me. The lights were on in the house. In a state, indeed. Kerry trying to discredit the things I'd come to say, brand me as disturbed. She'd stolen my surprise. The curtains had opened and Marie was standing there. Looking entirely radiant, I saw, fuller, more herself. Was I really going to do this? I pictured Henry touching her. The front door opened.

'Stuart,' she said. 'Are you okay?' Pretending that I was might not convince. I came to her but I brushed past her offered hug and went through to the kitchen. The knife rack was over by the hob. I went and looked at it, sizing it up. I should offer to step outside with him and pick one up on the way out. I pulled the knives in turn out of their slots, trying to choose the right one.

'Stuart. What the hell?'

'It's okay,' I said. 'I'm here to protect you, not hurt you. I'm fine. I just have things I need to say. Kerry didn't tell you about that did she?'

'She said you were unwell. She was frightened.'

I went into the front room. They were all of them in there, waiting. Irene in a thin cotton nightie with her blue veined shins on show, George in a corner smiling as though this were Christmas Eve, the dog lying on the sofa and Henry over by the old fireplace. He was wearing one of the homemade badger tee shirts and jeans that were baggy for a man of his age. A look of kindly patience on his lying face. A reasonable face, a let's-all-be-adults face. I still think if he hadn't had that look on his face, if he'd looked knackered and defeated as he sometimes did, I might not have ever done it.

'Stu mate,' he said. 'You all right? You look rough. Marie's been worried about you.'

258

'Evening all,' I said. George giggled. I told him to fuck off.

'Stuart, what's going on?' said Marie.

''Ello 'ello 'ello,' I said. I tried to stand like a policeman. 'What's all this then?'

'Fuck sake,' said Henry.

'Should we get an ambulance?' said Irene. 'He don't seem right.'

'I'm fine. For god's sake why does everyone keep assuming I'm not fine? I've got news.'

'Sit down Stuart. Have some dignity.'

'Hahaha. Or what?' I held out my wrists to be cuffed.

'Stuart, are you going to explain what the fuck this is all about?'

'This fucker,' I said, pointing, 'is a policeman.'

'Shut the fuck up Stuart.' I looked at Marie's face registering this news and from somewhere inside me came laughter. I laughed until a strange sound left me, laughter from a part of me I didn't know existed. It wasn't a nice kind of laugh. 'Are you really so fucking dumb? You think you can just waltz into the Forest of Arden and everyone can fall in love and change their personalities, but people don't change like that. Or when they do they have a reason. He's a rozzer. A boy in blue. The Sweeney, the fuzz. He's a fucking flatfoot and he knows it.'

I was interrupted by a slam in the side of the face. Henry had decided enough was enough. I reeled, the pain rushing up to my cheek.

'Bastard,' I said. 'Come outside.'

'Don't be ridiculous Stuart, he'll beat the shit out of you.' They were all standing around me, Marie beseeching, Irene hovering in everyone's way at once. Henry pale from anger or guilt or both. Only George was still seated, chewing on the collar of his tee shirt.

'Oink,' I said. 'Oink. Oink.'

'All right. Outside then. I'm a pacifist but I can make an exception.' Henry set off for the back door. I hadn't considered that. There was no way I could grab the knife if we were going that way. 'Can we not go out the front?' I said.

'Come on outside,' he said, standing at the door. 'Take your glasses off.'

'Okay. Okay. I will. Just let me get some water.'

'He's going to run off,' said George.

'I'm getting a glass of water, you twelve-year-old cunt,' I said.

I staggered into the kitchen. There was blood trickling down my face. Hot, growing colder, stiffening the hairs on my cheek. I pulled out the biggest knife. It was pretty grubby. Marie must have put it back without washing it. She used to do that all the time, it made me horribly cross. I had yelled at her about it once until she'd burst into tears and lay on the bed, not speaking to me, until I'd gone to her and apologised. I hadn't always been great. I had the knife.

I hid it behind my back and went through the front door, trying to remember what the thugs in the hospital said. 'It's not proper shanking if you see the blade.' Was I really cut out for shanking? Still, the punch had given me an odd burst of energy. A high it was, almost. Everything seemed distant, spectral, as I marched through the front room, the screams and gasps as they saw the knife seeming to come from miles away, canned horror, easily ignored.

I was there in the night air and I was in front of him with the blade pointing to his hand and homicide in my face. I hoped that he would see how much I hated him and he would learn before he died.

I stepped closer and closer and I stood before him,

unable to do a thing. Henry took the knife from my hands and threw it on the floor. I didn't even resist.

'You ain't a murderer mate,' he said.

I was crying.

'I hate you so much,' I said. 'I hate you and I can't even hurt you, you fucking lying cop. I can't do it because I'm all right. Because I'm not a fucker like you.'

'Someone get him inside and sorted out,' he said.

'You fucking rapist cop,' I said.

'Shut up Stu or I'll hit you again,' he said.

'You stupid lying bastard, stealing a dead kid's name. What's your real name, Henry, you *shit?*'

That got him. He was next to me with his nostrils wide and his breath hot and he was standing back and lifting his elbow and he was going to swerve round and punch me hard in the face, so that I could almost feel it before he did, I could feel the pain coming up to greet his fist and my eyes were sore and I knew then that this was something else, that I was falling and the punch never met my face, that he was above me, looking scared, and Marie was panicking, saying, 'It's okay, it's okay, this happens to him, it probably isn't a stroke,' and before I blacked out once and for all I managed to say, 'It is.'

Fifty-Two

I was on the sofa and Irene's stubby fingers were pressing paracetamol into my mouth. She had laid me out pretty well. Henry was nowhere to be seen. George had vanished too. That said, I couldn't see much – my glasses seemed to have gone. I could hear Marie crying in a corner but I couldn't make her out.

Irene touched my brow lightly and told Marie to go to bed. Her tone was commanding in a way I hadn't expected. 'I was a nurse for thirty-odd years,' she said. I smiled, said there was nothing wrong with me, and passed back out.

The next thing, I was being raised onto a stretcher by firm professional hands, Marie fussing by my side. I realised I was happier, calmer, than I'd been in a long time. I stretched out and felt her answering hand. She said she'd got hold of my specs. Perhaps we were back together now. Yes, I expected we were. Henry seemed to have gone, anyway.

I was in the back of an ambulance juddering along. Marie had tears in her voice and I wondered if they were for me. I was in a hospital and West Country accents were telling me to keep calm and still. I was sleeping and they would have to operate soon.

'I'm sorry,' I said. 'I'm so sorry. Are we getting back together?'

'No,' Marie said. 'Oh god, should I have said yes? What if he dies?' And she started crying again.

I had my share of visitors. Alistair and Rupa came by. Were they a couple now? This was absolutely the sort of thing I didn't want. On the other hand, they looked very happy together. I hadn't spotted before how attractive she was, the freshness of her looks. He looked well too, rejuvenated.

They asked me what happened and I told them as best as I could. Rupa told me I needed to look after myself. Marie had been so upset, she said. She was back home now and recovering. I had been a bastard, they said.

I asked them to tell Kerry she didn't have to visit me, that I didn't think I deserved it. I hoped she would ignore this prohibition but she didn't, and never came.

Most of my time, I spent sleeping. Confused, memory-heavy dreams. The old flat with Marie. Malkin on my chest. The old uncomfortable bed we shared. Alistair intoning, covered in greasepaint and sweat. My parents. Only they were actually there, I realised, ruffling my hair too hard, squeezing my hand till it ached. A doctor's voice telling me I would live. I tried hard to feel grateful.

After this, delirium, frantic dreams. An unexpected amount of sex in these. I hadn't lost that, it seemed, although it would be a long while before I could do anything about it. But sometimes there were badgers all over me. I was Gulliver, pinned down by tough black claws. Wiry fur scratched against my face. I was moaning. This continued for a while before blankness happily came. The dreams stopped playing. Instead there was heavy slumber, dark and comforting. I woke to ring for morphine, then lay back. And one day it was especially bright on the ward and I realised Marie was there, sitting with her arms folded over her stomach, the sun on her face. The sunlight made her younger, so that she looked exactly how she was the day I met her, that first time in Foyles.

'Hey,' I said. 'I suppose I owe you an apology.'

'Probably. I suppose I owe you one too. I'm only flying by – Frank isn't very well.'

I told her I was sorry to hear that. Was there anything I could do?

'Doesn't look like it, now, does it? Concentrate on getting better.'

I wanted her to come across and place her hands on me but she stayed sat at a distance, as if to come closer was dangerous.

'Henry,' I said. She told me to change the subject. 'I went for him. I went for him. I've never been so angry. But I couldn't do it. Could I? That has to show something.'

'I'm not sure that it does,' she said.

I did walking exercises, to prove that I still could. I pressed the hands of nurses, to show I knew how to do that. Hands from Africa and the Caribbean, slender hands from Eastern Europe, older hands from Bristol. I struck up conversations with the others on my ward. Tried to take comfort from being the youngest person there. I listened to my mum as she warned me, again, to give up on Marie. 'Not after all this,' she said. 'Not after what she's done to you.' There was no point explaining that in my mind we were evens. That I had done my worst to her.

One afternoon, the day before I was due to head back home, Irene came to visit. She sat where Marie had been sitting, dressed smartly as though for church. She asked me a lot of questions about my treatment. Funny, I'd had no idea she was a nurse. There were reservoirs of capability in her, after all. Disaster seemed to have given them something to do. She didn't seem befuddled or adrift.

'We haven't heard from *him*. Ran off the night it happened.'

I took this as proof that I was right. He'd be back at Scotland Yard, training up to infiltrate the Women's Institute or Crufts.

'He might be,' Irene conceded. 'But then, he might have just thought that he'd killed you. Wanted to get away if the police turned up. I don't think we'll see him again.' She coughed to herald the introduction of weighty matters. 'She's heart-broken, Marie. She didn't deserve that, she didn't, whatever she did to you.'

I was tired and for the second time in a year I'd almost died. I didn't need to be critiqued again. I sat up, feeling a twinge in my skull as I did. 'It wasn't me that was lying to her. You can't put the blame on me.'

'George had already told her,' she said. 'You don't think he wouldn't have done that? He's back with his mum now, best place for him. He told her the lot a few months back.' Well this was unexpected.

'She didn't believe him?'

'Not at first. Not ever, not entirely. She came to me about it. Always first person they come to. I said *are you happy*? And she was. She loved him. She'd thrown herself into him. I told her, leave it then. There's some things always best left.'

It didn't make any sense. He was betraying the badger cause.

'True,' she said. 'But then he'd do that anyway whether she had him or not. She made her choice and it was him. Plus, soon after, there was the other thing.'

I asked her what about the other thing, and before she'd even told me I had guessed just what it was and why Marie was looking so healthy, so content. I asked Irene to leave me alone, thanked her again for coming and put my eye mask on.

Fifty-Three

They cured me in the end. My eyesight remains the same. I still get tired easily, though they tell me that will pass. I feel pacific, muted, locked in a blissful lull. I wonder if this is permanent. It's nice to be alive. I remember how I laughed at Marie's tears, I remember choosing the knife and it feels another person, a person with claims I've abandoned. Now I wish everyone well. I smile in a bland and tolerant way, and yesterday a dog came to snuffle at me and the owner said they can read character, they can tell I'm a nice man. I feel that they're right: I am nice. But I'm not so sure that I'm me. I'm a blunted, kinder person, a person without claims.

A few months back I caught up with Kerry and was told politely not to bother again. She had a new man, a fellow protester, who she said was very kind. The way she said this sounded like a rebuke. She was considering joining the Labour Party. After coffee we went for a walk but found we had little to say.

One morning I got a letter telling me I had to return to Queen Square. Strange to be there again. I spent a night on the ward, reading, with one eye closed to help me focus. I hadn't told anyone I was going back into hospital. It seemed very important that I have this done alone. They came for me in the morning and they led me down to the cold room where they operate, basement level. One up from the mortuary.

I was wearing one of those backless gowns they make you wear to remind you of your vulnerability, your closeness to death. I took off my specs and lay down while a blurry doctor plunged a needle into my brow. The needle contained anaesthetic which just about covered the pain of having the injection in the first place. Once they'd woken me from the faint I fell into at this invasion, they started hammering a four-sided brass cage into my head. The cage had thick-spaced brass bars. It was heavy around my face. I asked if I could go to the loo. A nurse had to lead me there, a cautious hand on my arm. I stood in the sponge-floored bathroom and put my face close to the mirror. I was a head in a cage. A monster from a circus, a mediaeval torture victim. The sections where it was screwed into my forehead were rimmed with drying moats of blood. I was quite proud not to faint a second time. To do what I was told.

'Ready when you are,' I said. They led me to a chair and nailed the cage to a headrest behind me, trapping me in position. 'This only takes half an hour,' they said. 'You might find yourself with a little bit of a headache.'

'Used to it,' I said. One day soon I would be able to romanticise all this. The illness. The divorce, which had come through the week before. The adventure with the badgers. The look on Marie's face when I told her about Henry. I'd be able to dress it up, cheapen it into anecdote. A hard luck story, but would you look how well he is now? Made the best of it, didn't I, came out softer, gentler? I might miss out the look on Marie's face. Might miss out my laughter and where it came from.

'This across from you, this is the gamma knife. We're going to need you to keep as still as you absolutely can which is why we've strapped you in. We're going to be using the gamma knife lasers to operate on the damaged parts of your brain. It's vital you don't jerk your head. Tell us if you feel a sneeze coming on.'

'You expect me to talk?'

'Haha. We get that quite a lot.'

'Get your hands off me you filthy ape.'

'That isn't really relevant.'

'Sorry. Sorry. I'm scared.'

When they took the box off my head, I felt like how I'd always imagined the bends to feel. The world pressing at my head, trying to squeeze inside it. It felt an awful lot better inside the cage.

Fifty-Four

Three months later, I was back at Marie's, as a visitor, a supporter, a payer of respects. A promise I'd made and wanted to keep.

Mrs Lansdowne opened the door. She greeted me with a perfectly measured frostiness. I sensed my visit was a matter in which her wishes had been ignored. Marie was in the front room. Sitting on the armchair with a rug over herself, one of the family cats upon her lap. Back in the safety of home, she looked both as young as when I met her and impossibly experienced. I'd always felt that for rich people experience can be bought off, transferred onto others. Her appearance didn't confirm this. She stood up and let me kiss her, awkwardly on each cheek. I got her left ear and right eye. 'Shall we go to the garden?' she said.

We sat out in the sunshine, at a white cast iron garden table and drank elderflower cordial and didn't have much to say. I still couldn't look at her stomach.

'You all set then?' I said.

'Yes. I think so. Daunting, but I always wanted it. And you ... if you're honest, you didn't. You didn't want it at all.'

'I wanted you. That was the main thing.' She didn't

seem to hear this. She looked tired but beatific, like a knackered Renaissance Madonna. There was no way of telling her anything. 'I still would like to help.'

'I know you would,' she said. There were butterflies and flowers that I would never know the names of, creeping to the sky. I had thought I would spend a lot more time in this garden.

'I still don't get why you did it,' I said.

'I just hope it never happens to you,' she said. 'I hope you never love like that.'

I wanted to tell her I had but I wasn't sure it was true. It might have been true at that moment though. It might have been true right then.

'I think we should go back inside,' said Marie, frowning at the clouds. We walked through to the house. I could hear Judy and Frank murmuring from his study, talking about us.

'You going to be okay?' I said. As if there was any truthful answer you could give to a question like that.

'I'll be fine,' she said. 'I think it might be good.'

'You know I'll be around, right? You know I'll always be around for when it comes?'

'I know you will,' she said.

We went into the front room where I'd left my bag. There were still pictures up I remembered, of us on our second date. My hair shorter, no bags under my eyes. Her smiling, no lines on her face and her arm stretched out, holding the camera. Both of us grinning.

'I keep meaning to take that down,' she said.

'I'd better be going,' I said.

'Do you know, I couldn't believe how I felt about you back then? I went around telling everyone. I couldn't believe how I felt.'

'Yeah, I suppose you did,' I said. Not much but all I had.

'There is something you could do for me.' She reached out for my hand. 'A favour you can do. Something I can't manage.'

Fifty-Five

I went back to the woods. It seemed the least I could do; after all, she couldn't go herself.

George was also absent. He was still back with his folks. I hoped he was being forced into education or education being forced into him. It was hard to see any other hope for the lad, talent for manipulation notwithstanding.

There had been no sign of Henry, but then I expected that. Marie had received an email from a friend of his telling her Henry was abroad but would contact her on his return, whenever that was. She assumed the 'friend' was Henry himself. She hadn't replied.

Margaret was there and if she knew about all that had happened she did a good job of not showing it. Everything not directly connected to badgers could be safely filed as trivia. Brian was there, too. He loped over, slapped me on the back. 'Stu mate. Good to see you. I didn't expect it what with, well you know.'

'Well, you know,' I said. I had been scared of a hostile reception. I almost wanted to hug him, although there seemed less of him than before. You could hug him just using your hands.

'I know mate,' he said. 'Once you get caught up in this badger thing you can't keep away, believe me.'

'It isn't really that,' I said. He looked at me as if he

understood exactly what I meant. I was pretty sure he didn't.

There were a couple of newbies with us. A woman about my age who worked for Boots as a buyer and had caught animal-politics from the cull the year before. A clerical looking man in his forties who kept rubbing his spectacles and talking about the 'war on wildlife'.

'Kerry not been?' I said.

Brian smiled in a way I was sure was rather wistful. 'Nah, mate,' he said. 'Shame that, would have been nice to see her. Spoke to her the other day. Checking on my sobriety. She's seeing some bloke. One of them climate fellers. Good lads. Sorry, not treading on old feelings there, am I?'

'No,' I said. 'Sure he's a lovely guy.' Sure he was very *kind*.

'Jammy sod I reckon,' said Brian.

We took our torches out, following the familiar route I'd used to traipse with Marie. But it was dark and we walked for miles and soon enough I found myself alone. I kept going, torch in hand until I found a sett. I could be of use right there. I sat down, popped a mint in my mouth and started guard duty. The sett had the wonderful cosiness that badger homes give off. Who would want to hurt them? Splendid creatures, minding their own business.

My buttocks ached. I wanted to lie down but I was worried about the cold. Not that it was very cold. Climate change working its magic. While we worried about badgers the earth was roasting up. Would badgers go first or would we? The country would go before the city, I think I'd read. People would traverse the globe, some would even leave it. Ponds would frazzle into salty patches of muck. A billion unread books would sit on unused computers, quietly humming. Goodbye Frank

Lansdowne, but also goodbye Chaucer, ta-ra Dante. Goodbye Alistair, goodbye Raoul. Goodbye to Kerry, to love, goodbye Marie.

Pale stars acned the sky. The moon peered over the trees. I wasn't sure I was helping much. My lids began to close. The next morning my joints were stiff, my eyes were bleary and the sett that I'd been guarding turned out not to be a sett. It was only a hole in the ground. I needed to get out of the woods. I stood up, brushing the twigs and soil off my jeans. Around the corner I almost stepped on a badger.

I knelt close and looked at it. A red gash in its shoulder, if badgers even have shoulders. The blood had spilled onto its fur, dirtying the white. The wound was open, pulsing. The animal was breathing as though it were fighting off three enemies at once. A war-creature, I thought, built for combat, armoured and sturdy. Its lips were a leathery black. Teeth on display. It would snag my fingers if I touched it. It was also dying.

What was I supposed to do? I didn't have the vet's number or a phone signal if I'd had. I was going to have to kill the fucking thing. With what? My bare hands were no good. I no longer went near knives. A branch would have to do.

I went to the nearest tree. Whispered an apology to the badger and to the woods. Felt the branch's weight, picked one that seemed the right size. If I got a suitable swing on, I could dash out the animal's brains. What would they look like, dashed brains? I had never seen them before. I wasn't a violent man. Still, I knew I had no choice.

I couldn't even get the branch off. A tug and it came, scratching my palm in the breaking.

I walked back to the badger, hoping it had died. The breathing was softer, less laboured, but the animal was grabbing hold of life. Okay, it was time for the dashing. I practiced on a clump of grass, focusing on the patch I wanted (the head, I decided it was) and bringing my stick down. I missed the hoped-for spot and the impact felt feeble, undeadly.

When I tried again I got the right spot and the landing sent soil scattering on both sides. I tried a last time and this hit hard but missed the point. I walked back to the badger.

Its breathing was calm now. Calmer but still there. The blood was clotting and I could see a bit of bone, with the flesh quivering around it.

The animal's eyes were bright, glassy buttons. It was still alive, still beautiful. The eyes probably weren't imploring me. They probably couldn't see me at all. And what were they imploring anyway? To be left to die in peace or to be aided into silence, with dignity and a broken branch? I had it held above my head although this wasn't the angle I'd practiced. I swerved my arms back, bent one leg. I had it raised, raised, and I tried to drop it, bring it down upon the head, and I couldn't do it.

'Stand back,' came a voice. There was a man in a red cagoule standing next to me. He had a gold necklace, cropped gold hair, boozy, bestial handsomeness. Somehow I noticed all this before I noticed his gun. 'You're going to have to stand back mate. If you want me to finish the job. Mate, I can't shoot him if you're standing there. Mate, will you clear the fucking path and let me finish?'

'Sorry,' I said and dropped my branch. I have a horrible feeling it landed on the badger. I saluted the marksman, trying to look like a country squire giving orders rather than an urbanite too weak to euthanise an animal, and set off in the wrong direction. The shot, when it came, made me jump, although I had known it was coming. I started walking off and then ran back to him, saying, 'I couldn't kill it, I couldn't do it, I really don't have it in me. I'm not capable, I'm not.'

'It needed fucking killing,' said the man.

The road from the woods took a long time to get to and when I eventually found it, there was still a long way to go to my bed and breakfast. I skipped the distance, ecstatic, proud of not having hurt. It had been alive and I couldn't have harmed it. I laughed out loud. Life was a wonderful thing.

I thought for a second I saw Kerry, searching for me, in a car, but it was someone else who only looked like her.

When I got back I ate a just-in-time breakfast and sunk into my sheets, asking not to be disturbed for the rest of the day. By the time I left it was dark again and the cullers were setting out, carrying their guns to the woods.

Acknowledgments

Writing books is a much more collective endeavour than writers let on and this book has many parents beside myself. I will try and remember as many as possible below.

Mark Watson acted as midwife of this book, giving advice and support throughout. It is very unlikely this novel would have been finished without his input. Any flaws and errors of taste in the book are of course entirely down to him.

Everyone at Sandstone helped shape my manuscript into the book you have just read. Special thanks must go to Keira for her excellent edit and Ceris for telling the world this book exists. I am also grateful to Catherine Taylor for recommending them to me.

Sophie Buchan did a fantastic early edit and has been a valued source of gossip, advice and stories about bears.

I have been lucky to find some wonderful trusted readers of this book – Emma Townshend, Poppy Toland, Lee Cheshire, Becks Jones, Amber Massy-Blomfie & John Osborne. If I've forgotten any others then I apologise to them. During the writing Helen Underhill gave support that was critical in every sense and for which I am very grateful.

Peter Kirby-Harris gave me a roof over my head and the inspiration for one of the characters.

My parents and sister have been wonderful throughout.

Lastly to the Poets of the Bamboo Grove: Will Buckingham (who also provided a roof and more wisdom than it's fair for one man to have), Hannah Stevens and most of all Sarah McInnes for being the funniest, smartest and most beautiful person in the entire history of the world.